MURDER AT
PEACOCK MANSION

Blue Plate Café Mysteries

Book Three

Judy Alter

For Linda, who says I "get" small towns, and for Jeannie, who gave me the story line years ago

Acknowledgments

With thanks to Fred Erisman, who reads everything I write
and says this may be the best one yet,
to Lourdes Venard, editor superb,
And to Kim Jacobs,
Calliope Designs, for an outstanding cover

Chapter One

I was stewing in my own juices that April evening, as I sliced tomatoes and green onions and diced avocado for a salad. David had said he was coming in for dinner and I'd fixed a *tourtière*, a French-Canadian meat pie I'd been longing to try. It came out of the oven smelling heavenly, and I optimistically poured wine and tossed a salad. Surely David would be along any minute.

But by eight — an hour later than he said he'd be here — David hadn't arrived and hadn't called. I sat on my impatience until eight thirty and called him. No answer; I left a message. He didn't call, and the evening dragged on. I put the now-cold tourtière in the fridge and picked at a bit of the salad, but I had no appetite. By ten, he still hadn't called. It wasn't like David at all. He simply wasn't the kind of guy to stop for a beer and let time go while he swapped stories with someone or to simply forget he'd promised to be here. I began to worry. It stormed that night — a good East Texas thunderstorm with sideways rain, heavy thunder, and frightening bolts of lightning. As long as David wasn't on the road, the storm was not a threat, but it added to my anxiety.

David Clinkscales had been my boss when I was a paralegal in Dallas. It's a long, convoluted story, but when he decided to work from a lakeside cabin, not far from Wheeler, where I once again lived, we went through several crises — and two other men on my part — and finally

1

had been a couple for about six months. Everything suited me fine. I knew I was falling in love, but so far we weren't tripping over each other. David came to my café two or three times a week, and we generally spent weekends together.

So by morning when I hadn't heard from him I was less angry than worried. I could hardly send Chester Grimes, our local police chief, out to check on him. Chester and I go back to one of my previous adventures when he was on the force in Crandall. He rescued me when the brakes on my car failed on a downward slope on the highway. Chester not only got my car fixed but took me to his home, where his wife, Carolyn, fed me a tuna salad sandwich and a glass of wine and suggested I take a nap. After protesting that I'd never sleep, I fell sound asleep. They've been good friends ever since, and when the chief position came up in Wheeler, Chester applied and got it.

I had no proof anything was wrong, although Chester knew me well enough to trust my instincts and would believe me. But David's cabin was out of his jurisdiction. Perhaps David had unexpectedly been called back to Dallas and in his haste forgot to call me. About ten thirty I called his office, casually asking if he was in. No, they hadn't heard from him all morning and had in fact called but gotten no answer. Maybe he'd forgotten to charge his cell phone, but I didn't believe that either.

So I plated salads, trying to get a jump on the lunch rush at the Blue Plate Café, vowing silently that when lunch was over I'd drive to the cabin. Marj came into the kitchen, interrupting my worried thoughts. She was almost breathless with excitement. "Kate, Mrs. Aldridge is asking for you. She's here, in the café. Sittin' at a table like she comes in every day. But she particularly wants you."

I turned toward her, thinking murderous thoughts about whoever this Mrs. Aldridge was. "And who is she?"

Marj scoffed. "Everybody is this county and the next knows about her. She lives up toward Canton, in a big mansion — they say she killed her husband, oh, years ago. But she doesn't ever come out of the house, so you best hurry and find out why she's here today."

I had no idea why her visit was urgent if she'd been holed up in that house for all those years, but I made a deliberate effort not to snap and take my worries out on Marj. Instead, I gave her the salad plate to finish and deliver, wiped my hands, and went into the main room of the café, still wearing my apron. Of course, there was no way I could miss the woman Marj was talking about. She wore a charcoal gray flannel pantsuit, slightly warm for this now-sunny April day in East Texas, with an ecru lace jabot at her neck. (I prided myself on even dredging that term up from memory.) The entire outfit was stylish — or would have been twenty-five years ago. I was suddenly more aware of my apron, clean though it was, and my flyaway hair.

She rose as I approached and held out a hand. "I'm Edith Aldridge, and I appreciate you taking time to talk to me."

"Of course. I'm Kate Chambers, Johnny's granddaughter. Perhaps you knew her? She ran the café for well over thirty years before her death." I gritted my teeth and remembered Gram's lessons about manners and making customers feel welcome. A tiny part of me was still watching for David to come through those doors, but he didn't.

Sitting back down in one of the mismatched wooden chairs, Mrs. Aldridge said, "No. I can't say I've ever been here." She looked slowly around, taking in the battered tables and chairs, the pine-paneled walls, the chalkboard menu with chicken-fried chicken prominently displayed as "Today's Choice." She looked out of place in the café, and I didn't wonder that she'd never been there. She was probably used to dining in upscale restaurants in New York, or at least Dallas. Before she became a recluse.

"I'd be proud to serve you lunch. The chicken-fried chicken is a bit heavy but I recommend the tuna or chicken salad plate."

"Oh, no. No, thank you, dear. I just want to talk. If you'd sit and listen, I'd be grateful." There was none of the imperious tone I'd expected, between her appearance and Marj's obvious awe of the woman.

But I wasn't in a mood to sit and listen to a long story. Worry made me jittery, and I almost jumped every time the door opened. "It's soon lunchtime. I'll be glad to listen until I'm needed. I have to be sure my customers are well taken care of. May I get you coffee or iced tea?" Funny how manners can gloss over the surface of worry.

"Iced tea would be lovely."

I got it, brought myself a glass of water, and joined her.

Her first words were, "Someone's trying to kill me, and I need help."

Oh, wow! I so do not need this kind of thing today. "Someone's trying to kill you?" In spite of myself I was curious. Who would try to kill this elegant, pleasant lady?

"It's a long story, but they get the house when I die . . . and I believe they expect to find a hidden fortune. Of course, they won't. But I couldn't convince them if I tried."

"Who are *they*?"

"My late husband's children. Three of them."

"I'm sorry for your loss." It was almost an automatic condolence.

"No need. He died thirty-three years ago, right in that very house. I was accused of murder but acquitted. Something about circumstantial evidence."

I nearly spit my water across the table at her. "Did you kill your husband?" *Nothing like being blunt, Kate.*

No outward indignation that I'd even thought it necessary to ask. "Of course not, but the idea occasionally surfaces and feeds the children's paranoia. Not that they're children any more, all in their fifties or damn close. Walter provided for them comfortably, but I think they've run out of money. And they rehash the whole thing with each other. The more they talk about it, the angrier they become."

Somewhere in there was a story I needed to hear in more detail . . . but not from the horse's mouth, so to speak, and not now. Yet I couldn't resist asking, "How do you know they're trying to kill you?"

She stared into space, hands calmly resting on the table, no sign of agitation, while I fidgeted and twisted my hands in my lap. "I've been watchful for thirty years. After I was acquitted, the judge ruled I could stay in the house until I died. Then it would revert to Walter's children." She paused a minute, gently twisting the ring on her left hand and thereby calling my attention to the largest diamond I'd ever seen, circled by small emeralds. "I've been watchful ever since.

"I've installed hard-wired smoke alarms, panic buttons throughout the house. I wear a medical alert button" — she waved at a utilitarian wristband with some kind of non-clock face — "and I only eat what I myself or my trusted cook prepares for me. My lawyer is on record as knowing the facts, so I've thought I was safe. But last night, I found a trip wire in the middle of the main staircase. If I hadn't had a flashlight and spotted it, I'd have caught my ankle and cascaded down the stairs to the terrazzo floor. Undoubtedly, I would have broken my neck. I'm sure that was the hoped-for result."

"Did you call the police?" Seemed obvious to me.

"So they'd dismiss me as a foolish old woman? No, I did not. As I said, I don't want those vultures to know I'm on to them. There's one more thing. Also last night someone broke into the safe in the den . . . my late husband's office. They spread papers all around but I'm quite sure they didn't find what they wanted—a treasure map. I have no idea how they bypassed the security alarm, but I've made arrangements today to have it upgraded, the codes changed and all that. It doesn't rely on the telephone but has a separate communication system."

And probably cost a fortune. I was impressed by how businesslike she was.

Marj popped over to the table, curiosity written all over her face, an order pad in her hand. "You ladies doin' all right? Can I get you something?"

I gave her my most subtle threatening look and murmured, "Everything's fine, Marj. Thanks for asking."

When she was gone, Edith Aldridge said, "No doubt she's curious. Most people still believe I killed Walter. Believe me, I did many times but only in my mind. I would ask that you keep our conversation confidential. My life could depend on it. It's not a very exciting life these days, but I'm not ready to lose it."

"Mrs. Aldridge, why are you telling me this story?" The low hum of conversation filled the café, and as people came by they gave me one-armed hugs or patted my shoulder and asked, "How're you doin', Kate?" And then most of them stared with frank curiosity at my guest. I had to get to work running the cash register and after that I was going hunting for David Clinkscales. I could hardly sit quiet as I listened to my strange guest with her bizarre story.

"I want you to find out who really killed Walter. Then I hope I can live in peace, without threats. I've heard that you had some . . . ah, success . . . even with the death of your own grandmother."

Astounded. There's no other word for it. Flat-out astounded. I wanted to tell her that was family, and I didn't go looking for trouble, especially when it was a stranger's trouble. "Mrs. Aldridge, I own a café. I cook for a living. I am not by any stretch of the imagination a detective. If you wish to keep this quiet, speak to your lawyer about a private investigator. Now, if you'll excuse me, I have a business to run." *And a lover to find.*

She rose immediately and extended her hand. "Of course, Kate. It's been thoughtless of me to keep you so long. You'll come see me when you get curious enough. Here's my private phone." She handed me a business card and was gone before I could react.

I pocketed the card and turned toward the cash register. The next hour and a half went by with mind-numbing slowness. Only it didn't numb my mind. Only half of me was present, smiling at people and saying I hoped they'd enjoyed their lunch. I shortchanged one man—he was nice about it—and charged a woman who'd had a salad plate for chicken-fried steak.

Marj finally came up behind me. "Kate, you okay? Need me to take over? Counter's slow, and I can do it."

I was slipping out of my apron as I answered. "I do, Marj. I really do. I have someplace to go. I'll be back in time for dinner. Can you wait for me?"

She nodded, and I slipped out through the kitchen. As I passed through, Gus, the wizened old dishwasher, said, "Miss Kate, that dog of yours is sure upset about something."

Huggles, my huge, loveable doodle dog, was indeed running up and down the fence line, barking furiously, more upset than I'd ever seen him. When I slipped through the side gate, he did not run for loving. Instead, he barked at me, his tone indicating that he had something really important to tell me.

Chapter Two

Huggles simply would not let me get in the car without him. He barked, he tried to body-block me, he ran around the car, and jumped on the passenger seat door.

"All right, silly dog. Have it your way. This is probably a fool's errand anyway." I opened the door for him to hop in and ordered him to the back seat. In truth, I was glad to have him for company. I could talk all the way to the lake, and he would simply whine.

And whine he did as I barreled down curvy, two-lane country roads. My mind was on David, but a part of me was wondering why I'd never heard of Mrs. Aldridge if the whole countryside knew about her and thought she murdered her husband. I'd have been about fifteen when the murder happened—I never did find out how he'd been murdered. After I found out David was all right, I'd do an online search. Probably I'd been wrapped up in teenage concerns and Donna, my twin sister, for sure was wrapped up in her football hero/boyfriend, Tom Bryson, who was now my brother-in-law. I suppose while older folk remembered, talk had died down before we paid any attention. Mrs. Aldridge was right—her story intrigued me enough that I'd be going back to hear more. But not until I found out where David was and why.

An old pickup coming toward me honked and veered, and I realized my mind had strayed off my driving. I was sailing along at too high a speed in the middle of the road. I steered to the side and waved to the driver, a classic gesture of apology.

As I turned into David's rutted, single-lane road I suddenly felt foolish. What would I say? Why was I there? What if he did indeed have someone else with him? Oh, not that I thought it would be another woman . . . except perhaps the ex-wife who despised him. I could hardly say I was just in the neighborhood and thought I'd drop in. As I crept along the road, branches scratching my car—he promised to get them trimmed—I told myself I'd think of something.

When I pulled out of the woods into the clearing that held the cabin, I could think of nothing. David's house had burned. The fireplace stood grotesquely, like a lone survivor, and the walls still smoldered, but the roof had caved in. The porch and the steps up to the house were blackened but still there. I sat and stared for a long while before my brain commanded my body to get out of the car.

Ordering Huggles to stay, I opened a window so he'd have air and cautiously got out of the car, headed for the house. Huggles was about two seconds behind me, ignoring my order and leaping out that open window. I headed for the house, wildly calling David's name, though I was sure nobody could be alive in that wreckage.

I stopped and stared, my voice dying to a whisper on the April breeze. I was heartbroken—for David, who'd enjoyed life so much; for myself, who'd finally found love; for the community and the world, who'd lost a good man. Tears rolled down my cheeks, and it took me a minute to realize that Huggles was again barking frantically, nipping at my hand, pulling me by taking a bit of my pants in his mouth. He wanted to go to David's car, which sat parked some distance from the house.

The dog pawed frantically at the door of the two-seater Mercedes that had been David's lone indulgence since his separation.

Scolding Huggles and telling him to calm down, I opened the door to prove to him nothing was there. Only there was David, sprawled out on the seat, wet, dirty, and shivering with cold in spite of the hot day. Blood had dripped from his nose and the corner of his mouth, and one eye was swollen and turning purple. I was quite sure he was unconscious, but the shivering and the still-dripping blood told me he was alive. I could only scream.

Huggles jumped into the car and began licking David's face, wiping away the blood. David moaned and made no movement. Then, slowly, a weak but familiar voice said, "You could wake the dead, Kate."

I may just have. Truly, a part of me felt that I'd saved David by talking to him. I was never so glad in my life to hear a sound. "David! Are you all right?"

His soft tone was almost ironic. "No, I'm not. Call 9-1-1."

I did, and they kept me on the phone forever. They'd ask what happened, and I'd ask David, and he'd wave his hand weakly as though to say not now. Finally, I settled for saying it looked to me like he'd been beaten and someone had burned his house down. That got an immediate response, though the operator told me to stay on the line. "Can't," I said. "I have to see what I can do for him."

"Water?" His voice was so faint I almost had to ask him to repeat what he said.

There was always a bottle of water in my car, and I ran to get it.

Huggles, meanwhile, had settled down on David's feet.

"Is Huggles bothering you?"

"Keeping me warm."

I went to the other side of the car, opened the door, and gently as I could, raised his head so that he could sip. "Just small sips," I said.

"So thirsty."

I took it away before he could drink much. There were so many questions I wanted to ask, like "Where are you hurt?" From the looks of him, he'd have said, "Everywhere." Or I could have asked what I could do for him. But, what, really could I do? How did he get out of the house and into the car? I'd hear in due time, I supposed.

I called 9-1-1 again and told the emergency operator they might need directions to get to us. I'd now stay on the line. The operator said "Fine" and then the line went blank. I sat, one hand stroking David's face and the other with a death grip on the phone. Slowly, my heart quit pounding, and I took deep breaths to calm myself. I had to be calm for David.

I talked to him in what I hoped were soft, reassuring tones, telling him he'd be fine, help was on the way, I loved him.

At that, he roused enough to ask, "Are you sure?"

I leaned my face over his to give him a sound kiss and said, "Yeah, I'm sure."

He sighed and seemed to fall asleep, which made me frantic. I felt for a pulse, not that I was any expert. But I thought I found it. I didn't know enough to judge whether it was weak or strong, and I was beginning to panic, alone in the woods with a man who could be dying.

Huggles never moved. He just lay on David, staring mournfully at his face. At one point, I saw David raise a hand to place it on the dog's head.

Another time, with some effort and what looked like a wince of pain, he raised a hand to my face and gently stroked my cheek. I grabbed his hand and held it to my face until I could tell by his expression the effort was causing him pain.

All this time I held the phone, waiting for that blasted operator to come back on. How many emergencies could there be in Van Zandt County? The ambulance crew would have come out of Canton . . . or maybe Van. But if I could make it from Wheeler in less than twenty minutes, surely they should be here by now. It had been over thirty minutes since I'd called.

At long last, I heard, "Ma'am?" *What a way to start the conversation!* I bristled. "My guys are on FM 1902 but they don't know what to look for to find the house. They've driven up and down for ten minutes."

Ten minutes when they could have been treating David! "Are they coming from Van or Canton?"

"Van."

"Okay, look for a green mailbox, with the name Clinkscales. It's on the left side of a small, one-lane dirt road. Across the road is nothing but a pasture, and there's thick undergrowth on either side of this lane."

"Okay. Hold on."

I could hear her relaying this information while I bit my nails to the quick. And then, suddenly, marvelously, there was the sound of a vehicle pushing its way through the brush. The emergency vehicle pulled into the clearing and after a moment, when the driver apparently stared at the smoldering ruins of the house, he made an abrupt turn in our direction.

"Help's here," I told David. I eased his head off my lap and then ran to meet the ambulance.

Without words, the two paramedics rushed to the car with its door open and Huggles snuggling on David. "What the hell is that dog doing here?"

"Keeping him warm," I replied tightly. "Huggles, come!" The dog reluctantly crawled out of the car, casting a long look back at David.

"That dog dangerous?" the taller of the two men asked. He was young, skinny, and thoroughly incompetent-looking, as far as I was concerned. Yet when I assured him Huggles was harmless, he moved toward David with a calm efficiency that relieved me. His companion, who said, "Hi, I'm Josh," had the same calm focus. They cared about David, not Huggles and me, and I kept Huggles back.

The two paramedics elicited some responses from David, then got a portable gurney and eased him onto it after putting some kind of collar around his neck. Then they took blood pressure and all those vital signs — whatever they did — and raised the gurney to shove it into their vehicle, which sort of was an ambulance and sort of just a county rescue vehicle.

My mind whirled, remembering the sleek ambulances of Dallas, and the big hospitals. "Where will you take him?"

"County hospital in Canton."

"Can I ride with you?"

Josh's companion, who finally identified himself as Abner, said, "With that dog? No, ma'am."

I was tired of being called "Ma'am."

Josh eased things. "You don't want to leave your car here either. You best take the dog somewhere, and then meet us in Canton."

Sounded reasonable, and I was ready to follow that plan when a pickup drove into the clearing. Huggles and I ran to Chester Grimes, who managed to give us both hugs at the same time. Huggles was standing on his hind legs, with his front paws on Chester's shoulders.

The ambulance driver honked once, sharply, and I turned. Josh stood by the door. "You want to say good-bye to your friend?"

Of course I did, and I rushed to climb into the ambulance, followed by Huggles, whose entrance was blocked by Josh. "Sorry, pal, no dogs."

Chester followed and asked what happened. Josh's reply was simple. "Somebody beat the crap out of him." He jerked his head toward the house. "And burned his house down. I expect they meant to burn him in it. Be interesting to hear what happened that he was in that car. She" — he motioned toward me — "probably saved his life."

"She would," Chester said.

Within seconds, I was on the ground, holding Huggles' collar, while Chester put an arm around me. The ambulance honked twice and headed down the lane.

Chester turned to me, almost on the edge of anger. "And why didn't you call me?"

"It's not your jurisdiction, and I didn't think it was right. Besides, when I got here I was so . . . so frightened. I couldn't think straight." I swore I was not going to break down, but Chester was so comforting I could feel tears running down my cheeks.

He put that loving arm around me again. "You okay to drive?"

"Yeah. I have to be."

"Atta girl. You go to Canton to the hospital. I'll take Huggles home and take care of him. No sense asking what happened. I guess neither of us knows."

I shook my head to say I agreed. "Would you call Marj for me? Tell her what happened. I won't be at the café."

"You darn sure won't," he said heartily. "If she needs help, my Carolyn can pitch in. Best cook in five counties."

I grinned, hugged him, and headed for my car.

15

Huggles was still whining. And I was crying. I never once thought about Mrs. Aldridge and her strange situation.

Chapter Three

The ambulance roared off, as much as it could roar down that skinny road, and I followed, stopping for a minute to look over my shoulder at Chester and Huggles. They both were prowling around the ruins of David's house. Chester would stop, pick something up, and sniff it. Neither man nor dog ventured into the shell of a house — they just searched the perimeter.

A part of me wanted to turn around and ask what Chester found or to prowl with him. I heard Huggles bark to draw Chester's attention to something, and Chester turned to pick up an object I couldn't make out.

I turned my head and drove off with a short honk as a way of saying good-bye. Then I drove more sedately than the ambulance. I figured they saved the flashing lights and sirens for busier roads and didn't need them on country roads. The ambulance was no longer in sight, but every once in a while I heard that blip of the siren they gave to warn someone. They made it to the hospital a good fifteen minutes ahead of me, and David was in ER.

"No, ma'am. You can't see him right now. Are you his wife?"

"No, just a good friend." How did I elaborate on the relationship?

"Just have a seat over there." She nodded toward a row of hard, molded plastic chairs. "We'll call you when we know something. Can you put us in touch with his wife or next of kin?"

I shook my head. "He's divorced, no children. His parents are deceased. I'm as close to him as anyone."

"You willing to guarantee his bill? He didn't have any insurance information on him."

"Should be in his wallet," I replied, and then remembered his wallet was probably in the smoldering ruins of his house. "If I have to," I said stiffly. "I'm sure he has insurance. Can you give me a fax number so I can have proof sent to you?"

She looked a little surprised but jotted a number on paper, and I went off to call David's office. The new secretary screamed so loud the ER receptionist looked up, startled, and I wanted to say into the phone, "Stifle." Abruptly, her scream turned into a sobs, and I said, "I need your help." I told her I needed her to fax David's insurance information to the hospital and promised to call as soon as I knew anything. As I hung up, I wished I had learned her name at some point.

It was nearly five o'clock, and I could feel myself fading. A candy bar from a machine was a poor solution but apparently the best I had. That and a cup of really bitter coffee from a pot that I suspected had sat on the burner all day. I wished I'd uploaded a new book so I could read on my phone, but in reality I was too jumpy to read. Periodically I glanced at the clock but the hands barely moved. The receptionist beckoned me over, and I went eagerly, hoping for news. She merely said they had received David's insurance information.

A little after seven, the receptionist said impersonally, "You may see him now. Someone will be here shortly to escort you." Almost immediately a woman in scrubs opened the swinging door and called, "Family of David Clinkscales." She looked a little surprised but turned without a word and led me to a curtained cubicle on the other side of those mysterious doors.

David seemed to be sleeping. The nurse, if that's what she was, had left. I was alone, still with no one to answer my questions.

"David?" Soft and tentative.

His eyes fluttered for a moment, then closed again, and he reached out a hand. "Kate?"

"Yes, I'm here."

"Good." And that was all he said.

I sat in the chair, held the hand he'd offered me, and waited while time crept again. My cell phone vibrated, and I saw that Marj was calling. I didn't want to leave David, but I didn't want to disturb him by talking to her. I texted, "No news. Will let you know asap. Please close." She might check texts, and she might not. Then I texted his receptionist whose name I didn't know. No reply, but I figured in spite of her hysterics she'd gone home for the night.

Finally, about thirty minutes later, a doctor came in, not bothering to speak in hushed tones. Indeed, he was too hearty. "Your boy here has a broken ankle, a broken rib, mild concussion, but no internal injuries that we can tell. We'll monitor him probably for forty-eight hours to be sure. He's lucky. Someone wanted to kill him. Fortunately, that part's not my responsibility. Sheriff will want to talk to him, probably tomorrow."

I half expected David to rise up in indignation from his stupor at the condescension of being called "Your boy here." He didn't even budge. "He'll be in the hospital two days?" I echoed.

"Yes, ma'am. If all is okey-dokey then, we'll let him go, but he'll need care."

"Not a problem. Can I stay with him tonight?"

The doctor looked at me appraisingly. "You're not married, are you?"

What does that have to do with anything?

Before I could answer, he said, "I wouldn't advise it. You looked bushed. In fact, are you okay to drive home? Where is home?"

He was irritating me, or maybe I was just irritable. "Wheeler. And, yes, I'm fine, but I want to stay with him."

He shook his head. "He'll be out all night. We'll be sure of that. And we'll be in and out of his room checking his vitals. You wouldn't rest. Best thing you can do for him is go home and get some sleep. Come back rested in the morning."

And that is how I ended up sitting in a booth at a McDonald's in Canton, eating a sawdust hamburger at eight o'clock on a Friday night.

Chapter Four

Next morning I pulled myself out of bed reluctantly at six. Huggles, comfortable at the foot of the bed, didn't even want to move. Wynona, my aging cat, was curled at my feet and noisily displeased when I moved. But Saturdays were busy at the café, and I had to get those sticky buns started. I fed both of them and bolted for the café.

By the time I got to the café, it was almost light—that lovely hesitation between dark and day, and I was alone in the kitchen. Not something that bothered me at all. We didn't open until eight on weekends, so I had plenty of time. But an insistent knocking called me to the front door, and there, at six-forty-five, stood Chester Grimes, chief of police, in his spit-polished brown uniform. No day off for law enforcement, I guessed.

"I don't have any sticky buns ready," I said.

"And good morning to you too, Miss Kate."

"I'm sorry, Chester. Good morning. I guess my mind is elsewhere." Like about twenty miles northwest, at the Canton County Hospital.

"I thought you'd be here already. Just came by on a chance. Wanted to talk."

"Did Carolyn feed you? I've got my sticky buns rising, and I can scramble an egg or two."

"Lord love a duck! Do you think that woman would let me out of the house without breakfast? 'Course nowadays it's oatmeal with bran and raisins. A man gets a mighty longing for bacon and eggs."

"You won't tell Carolyn?"

He raised his hand solemnly. "Swear. But I need to talk to you."

"Okay. Come on in the kitchen while I cook."

And so Chester made himself at home on a stool while I fried bacon and scrambled eggs. "Sheriff was out to David's place yesterday after you left. Says what Huggles and I thought—arson. Someone poured fuel on that place to help it burn. And they beat David and left him inside, thinking he'd burn up with the house. That rainstorm we had ran their plans amuck, but David is one lucky man."

"I wonder how he got out in the shape he was in."

Chester looked long and hard at me. "I guess he wasn't ready to die that day."

My heart did a little flip-flop. Was it because of me? Or because David just plain loved life so much? I'd take either one. "So now what?" I asked.

"Sheriff will talk to him today, but somehow he's got to figure out who did this and why. I'm not part of it, but I told him aside that I wanted to be, and he said he'd keep me informed. He'll want to talk to you too. You got any ideas?"

I shook my head. "Not one. Far as I know, David had no enemies." To me, the idea that someone wanted to kill him was pretty extreme. "Sam Halstead still the sheriff?"

Chester nodded, his expression disheartened.

I'd crossed paths with County Sheriff Sam Halstead before when a boarder at my sister's B&B was murdered. Rick Samuels had been chief of police—and sort of my beau—at the time, and I guess his negative attitude colored my thoughts of Halstead. But I had found him overbearing and a bit misogynistic. "Oh, Lord, I better call Donna. But she won't be up yet."

"No need. Carolyn called her last night. Kept her calm, and Tom helped. You're okay on that front."

I sighed in relief. My sister Donna could be prickly.

Chester finished his eggs and my sticky buns came out of the oven at about the same time, both just when Marj arrived for the day. I filled her in on what I knew, which wasn't much, gave Chester a bun to take with him, and left for Canton, calling instructions over my shoulder. The day was too far under way for me to linger at the café.

* * * *

David was in a private room, propped up in his bed, contemplating a poached egg that looked cold and slimy, a container of orange juice, a sad-looking piece of toast, and a bowl of grits with butter floating on them. The grits were by far the best of the lot. His left leg was immobilized and both hands were lightly wrapped in gauze. He looked completely bumfuzzled about how to tackle this unappetizing meal with his hands all bandaged.

"Can I help?"

"Are you an angel sent from heaven?"

"Not quite, but I can feed you if you won't feel like a baby."

"Nope. I'm hungry enough to eat this, whatever it is."

I managed to butter the toast and get the egg onto it, whereby it broke, soaked the toast, and I cut it up into bits. I fed them to him one at a time. Drinking either water or juice he could handle on his own.

I had to ask. "What happened?"

"Damned if I know. I was at my computer fairly early in the morning when these two men literally burst in the doors. If there's anything left of them, you'll see where they pulled the sliding doors off the track. Who thought of needing a security system in a place like my cabin?"

I was glad to see that his sense of the ironic was back, but I prodded him to continue.

"They demanded my computer. Hell, I'm no hero. I gave it to them. Everything I do is automatically backed up, so it wasn't a big deal to me. Then they wanted my files. Told them they were all in Dallas. They didn't like that much and began using me as a punching bag. One guy used his fists, the other his feet. I guess I'm lucky I didn't get hurt worse."

"Did you recognize them?"

"Nope. Ski masks. And I didn't know their voices. But it's got to do with some case. They wanted computer and files. At least I'm pretty sure that's not my ex."

"How can you be sure? Is the divorce final, the terms settled?" It was a question I'd skittered away from several times, figuring it might make me look like a gold digger or something.

He looked away. "No, it's not final. I just think of her as my ex."

"Might she want to get her hands on something . . . I don't know, some papers or something . . . so she could get a better settlement?"

"I've offered a damn good settlement, but she won't sign. Her lawyer's holding out for more, and I'm not going to be bullied."

"Maybe you just were."

"No. I don't think that's her style, but I wouldn't put much past that lawyer of hers. Sleazebag. No, I think this has to do with a client."

"What client?"

"I don't want to point fingers until I'm sure."

Once, when I worked for him, I would have known all David's clients and been able to make an educated guess. Now I was at a loss, so I changed the subject. "How did you get out of there?"

David stared out the window a long time. "I'm not sure," he said hesitantly. "I came to smelling smoke . . . and, more strongly, kerosene. My brain clicked enough to know I was in deep shit. But my body wouldn't respond. I hurt everywhere, and every time I tried to stand my ankle told me that wouldn't work. Besides, my head was light." He paused. "I guess some deep instinct took over, because I crawled out of that damn place. Burned my pants and house shoes and my feet a bit, hands too." He held up the gauze-wrapped hands. "Some kind of salve."

I hadn't noticed the burns at all yesterday when I found him. I guess I focused on a breathing, living individual and his head.

"I rolled off what was left of the porch . . . and then I was afraid they'd left more kerosene that would explode, so I crawled toward the car. It was the only thing I could think to do. It was hard to pull myself up into it, but I did. And then I guess I passed out. Until you and Huggles woke me."

Horrified, I simply sat and listened. There was nothing to say. "I'm glad you're okay" was inane, because he wasn't okay. Finally, I said, "Bless Huggles. I'm not sure I would have looked in the car. He was so upset that afternoon, refused to let me go without him. Now I know why."

David grinned a bit. "He's our dog. We rescued him together, and he remembers." Then he sobered. "I need you to do something, like right nowwhile it's broad daylight."

"Okay?" I was puzzled.

"There's a fireproof safe under the bathroom sink. Did you see it?"

"No, but I didn't inspect that closely. Chester did, though, and didn't mention it."

"Good. Maybe the sink didn't burn away and expose it. I've been trying this morning to remember the combination but my head is still fuzzy. I think it's 4-48-28. If you could find my wallet, it's on a slip of paper in there. Wallet should have been in my pocket. Maybe it's in the car? Can you go look? I need the papers out of that safe . . . or I need you to take them home."

"Now?"

"Yeah. Maybe you should go get Huggles first."

My instinct to rebel was soon quelled. Huggles would once again be a good companion, even if it meant a much longer trip. "Okay." I leaned over, kissed him on the forehead, and felt him pull me down for a real kiss. I would have gone to the ends of the earth for this man.

Chapter Five

By the time I collected a wiggly, excited dog and made it to David's cabin, it was near noon, and I realized I was hungry. I had called Chester to make sure he didn't have the wallet, but I didn't give him any idea of what I planned. He'd have forbidden me. The cabin was, after all, a crime scene.

Even the yellow crime-scene tape across the driveway didn't stop me. I parked on the side of the road, and Huggles and I made our way around the tape and walked down the driveway. My chances of opening the safe were better than of finding the wallet, at least so I figured, so I gingerly stepped on one burned step and then another. Huggles bounded ahead of me, and I tried to figure out how to tell him to tread gently.

Around us the woods were eerily quiet, and suddenly my heart began to race. Here I was, out in the middle of nowhere, no neighbors close by, nobody knew where I was except maybe David. Who would ask him if I disappeared?

Gingerly, I made my way through the ruined house, checking every board before I put weight on it, trying to ignore the wet, burnt smell, urging Huggles to stay close to me. Luckily, the bathroom sink was in place, although a door hung open, exposing the safe. I knelt, with Huggles breathing on my neck, and tried the combination David had given me.

No sound of clicks, no reassuring final click, and no, the safe didn't open. Why did I think it would be that easy? Maybe my fingers were nervous. I'd try again. I cleared the dial and tried again, very carefully and slowly. No luck.

"We'll have to find his wallet," I said to Huggles.

We made our way off the porch and trudged to the car. A thorough search, pulling back seats, scouring the floor, looking everywhere I could think of—no wallet. Frustrated, I turned back to the house with no idea where to look. I scoured the ground on either side as I walked and then climbed carefully back onto the porch. Part of the porch floor had given way, so if the wallet was buried in the mud and slime under that gaping hole, it was beyond recovery.

I turned to the house. The stone fireplace was intact, though covered with soot, and the couch where David always worked had been in front of it; now it was a pile of ashes and melted iron. Huggles nosed around it whining, until I told him it was no use.

And then he came to me bearing the wallet in his teeth. It was virtually unscathed. Fire, I decided, was as capricious as a tornado. I'd never know how the wallet escaped the devastation nor how Huggles found it. But, praising him, I accepted it from his mouth; he gave it proudly as a prized possession.

My fingers nervous again, I pulled out the papers from the wallet. *How can one man keep so much stuff in his wallet?* I was careful not to drop any papers—who knew what was important and what wasn't? But I was down to the last few items when I came across a plain small strip of paper with the numbers: 4-38-28. David had only been one digit off.

Deep breaths to calm myself, and then I tried the safe again. This time I heard those small clicks, and then the final click. A turn of the handle, and the safe opened. I feared it would contain boxes of papers that would take me trips to the car to load, but it was only one armful. Gratefully, I scooped them up and said, "Come on, Huggles. Let's get out of here." The eerie feeling clung to me, and I couldn't be back at the café fast enough.

We started gingerly down the steps when there was a loud crack and a whistling sound. My country roots hadn't abandoned me—I knew the sound of a rifle shot, and I knew that a bullet had whizzed by not nearly far enough from my head for comfort. No hesitation. I pushed Huggles off the porch and jumped, landing on top of him with enough force that he protested. But I quickly began to reassure him in soft tones, petting him and urging him to stay still.

Two more bullets churned up the dirt, but not close enough to scare me. Whoever was shooting wasn't a good shot and may have been lucky with that first bullet. I heard two more shots but had no idea where they landed. After the fifth shot, the woods surrounding us became strangely quiet for a moment. Then I heard two men pushing through the brush. My guess was that they had waited to make sure I made no move, and now they were coming after me. My heart pounded in my ears, and I looked around desperately. No phone—it was in the car. No weapon. No shelter.

The only thing I saw was the porch that remained sort of intact. I inched Huggles under it, into the mud and muck, still keeping my body over his and whispering gently to him. He must have understood our danger because he kept very quiet. We had just managed to inch under the porch and a ways back, when two men in camouflage, carrying rifles, emerged from the brush.

"Where the hell is she?" one man demanded.

"How do I know? But she's here. Her car's still here."

"Miss, you better come out now. We have to look for you, we're gonna be that much more mad."

I held my breath. I'd learned several things—they'd been spying, so they knew they had a girl trapped, but they didn't know it was me. And they didn't speak good grammar. I assumed they were the ones who beat David and tried to burn his house. The next words of the first speaker confirmed that.

"It'd all be fine if that damn rain hadn't come through last night and dampened our fire. I did a good job of setting it, pouring kerosene in just the right spots." He was tall, stocky, with a dark beard on his face, fierce eyebrows, and an unpleasant look about him. I bet if I got close he'd smell bad too.

The other man was younger, slighter, and lighter in complexion. He looked a whole lot less intimidating, but I wasn't going to rush out and throw myself on his mercy. He didn't look quite that pleasant.

"Missy, you come on out now!" Urgency raised his voice to menacing levels. He was clearly losing it, and in a minute he did what no responsible gun owner would ever do. He threw the rifle down on the ground.

It exploded, a shot careening off in the direction of the younger man. "Holy shit! You do that again, and I'm out of here. What kind of bullheaded trick is that?"

I saw him rub his arm, where the bullet had apparently grazed him.

The other man remained silent and then said, "We better start searchin'. Now that we shot at this woman, whoever she is, we don't want her tellin' no tales."

I buried my head in Huggles' coat and he reached around to lick my face. I prayed. I talked to Gram. I sent urgent telepathic messages to David, though I was pretty sure he wasn't receiving. Overhead, I could hear the big man stomping on the porch, and I prayed it would hold and not send him crashing down to our hiding place. I had no idea how long Huggles and I stayed under that burned porch, but I saw the sun shift from one side of the sky to the other. The mud we lay in smelled bad, and in spite of the warm day, I shivered. I remembered how glad David had been for Huggles' warmth, and now I too welcomed it and hugged the dog closer.

Both men stomped their way through the underbrush and trees that hid David's house from the road. They were gone a long time, and then I could hear them down by the lake, though there weren't many hiding places down there. I wasn't about to wallow in the mud in those grasses that lined the lakeshore. I told David he should put a beach in there, but he scoffed at me and said someday he'd build a pier and get a fishing boat.

Eventually the men came back toward the cabin, arguing loudly with each other. Big One finally ordered, "You go off that way and see if you spot any sign. I'm gonna check what's left of this house—not that she could be there. But a woman and a dog can't just disappear into thin air."

I held my breath as he gingerly mounted what was left of the stairs, so close to me I could have reached out and grabbed his ankle. Actually, I considered it but decided it would get me in more trouble than I was already in.

He seemed to be picking his way carefully through the shell of the house. I tried to gauge from his footsteps where he was—in the kitchen, then turning toward the bedroom, and then into the bath where he yelled, "Well, lookee here! John, where the dickens are you? Get up here now."

John, apparently ever obedient, came running from the brush, jumped on the porch at the far end from where Huggles and I hid, and promptly crashed his foot through the floor, letting out a yell of "God damn!"

Big One, whose name I didn't yet know, yelled, "What's the matter now? Get in here."

"Can't. My foot's stuck in this hole in the porch floor, and I think I broke my ankle. You gotta help me."

If I hadn't been so scared and the situation so serious, I swear I would have laughed. As it was, I tried to figure out what might happen next.

Big One almost stomped to where John was—you'd think he'd have better sense, but apparently not. "How the hell did you do that?"

"Running at your command," John said, now with a touch of irony. "Help me outta here."

"I ought'a go off and leave you there," the other one said. "Of all the fool things to do. Here, pull yourself up by my arm."

There was a great deal of huffing and puffing and grunting. "I gotta see a doctor. I think it's broke. I don't wanna be a cripple all my life."

"Hands up, boys!" A new voice took command. "I'll see that you get a doctor and a nice long rest. Throw your rifles down off that way." Big One must have tried to aim his rifle because a shot sounded and he yelped, "Ouch! You dang near shot me in the head."

"Next time my aim will be better. Throw the rifle off to the side and get down here, lie face down in the dirt."

A lot of grumbling from both, and moaning from John, whose ankle was apparently hurting. "Last time I ever listen to you," he said. "'Come on, piece of cake,' you said."

Halstead raised his voice. "Miss Chambers? Come out, come out wherever you are. I could use your help right now."

I peeked out from under the porch and saw that he indeed had both suspects on the ground, face down, his foot planted squarely in the middle of Big One's back. I released Huggles, who rushed to stand over the two prone men and growl menacingly.

Big One suddenly turned the coward. "Get him away from me. I'm scared to death of dogs. He's gonna bite me, sure as shootin'."

I had managed to crawl out from the porch, stretch out what stiffness I could, and ignore the mud and slime that clung to me. I was sure I smelled and looked as bad as the burnt-out house. I made my way awkwardly toward the three men. "Not unless I tell him to," I said, knowing full well that Huggles had no such protective training but just might bite if he thought I was in danger.

Halstead wasted no words. "You and the dog keep that one down"—he nodded his head toward John—"while I tie this loudmouth up. Tempted to gag him too."

Not knowing what else to do, I planted my foot on John's back and pulled Huggles toward me. I reasoned John couldn't get very far at any speed with a broken ankle. His ankle did appear to be turned at an odd angle. While I stood there, I studied both faces as well as I could, though they were both flat down on the dirt. If I ever had to identify them, I wanted to be able to.

Once Halstead had the two men in the back of his car, handcuffed and seat-belted in behind a screen partition, with the doors securely locked, he came back to me. "I went to see Clinkscales in the hospital—Chester Grimes called me to report what happened."

"He did? Why?"

Halstead put on a patient voice. "Cause he understands what you don't. It's my jurisdiction. Anyway, Clinkscales told me he'd sent you out here and you hadn't been in touch—said it had been too long."

Too long? It seemed to me everything had happened in fast forward, and yet my morning visit with David seemed far distant. "I found what David wanted. Some files in a fireproof safe. Wait? I've got to get them." I sprinted—as fast as my cramped legs would let me—back to our hiding spot, crawled in, and got the files.

Halstead held out his hand. "Give them to me. Evidence."

Stubbornly, I held on to them. "I promised to bring them to David."

He sighed impatiently. "As long as they don't get into the wrong hands, he'll be okay."

"Tell you what," I said. "Let's give them to him together, and then he can turn them over to you."

He drew himself up in authority. "I have prisoners to check in, and I am ordering you to give me those papers. I don't want to get into a wrassling match to get them from you, but I will arrest you for obstructing justice. I remember you weren't too helpful last time I ran into you."

Last time he ran into me was when a journalist was found dead in her car in an old barn on my sister's B&B property. I didn't even want to think about it. I thrust the papers at him, wishing I could somehow inventory them. "I'm going straight to David's hospital room to report this," I said haughtily.

"You do that. I'll probably see you there later." A touch of his Stetson and he whirled around and left me. I thought he could have at least watched to see that I got out safely, but no, he slammed his car door and gunned it.

We tramped down David's road to the Farm-to-Market road where I'd parked, my legs complaining the entire time. I got Huggles settled in the back seat, got in, and locked the doors. Then I called David at the hospital and told him the story, downplaying the danger and emphasizing that the sheriff now had the papers.

"Damn!" his voice was much stronger than it had been. "Those papers needed to be confidential. At this point I don't know who's in league with who. Why did you give them to him?"

If he was going to be angry, I was prepared to give it back to him in spades. "It was either that or be arrested for obstruction of justice. At which point he'd be in possession of the papers anyway. I didn't really want to ride in the sheriff's car with those two goons."

"What two goons?"

I realized I hadn't told him the full story at all, and I repeated it in sketchy terms, minimizing the fright I'd felt, the danger I thought we were in, the agony of hiding in cramped, wet smelly quarters under the porch. When I told him, he was contrite but still angry — great mixture of emotions. Sorry to have sent me into danger but furious at the two men. No, he had no idea who they were but from my description they sounded like real trouble.

"Are they the ones who beat you?"

His voice was weary. "I have no idea. I don't know what the two you ran into look like, and the men who beat me wore ski masks. Halstead called just now and asked me the same thing today. Said they were brothers — John and Dan'l Smith. I'd say fake names, but who would make up the name Dan'l? Besides, Halstead said their IDs checked out. Neither one bright enough to think of this all by themselves."

"Which means someone else — someone smarter — is behind all this. Right?"

"Right."

"And it definitely has to do with a client?"

"Ninety percent sure. I may have to hire you."

"Thanks. I already have more than a full-time job." I wondered what was going on at the café.

My head was throbbing, and when I checked the time on my phone, it was nearing five o'clock. I hadn't eaten since breakfast, and I couldn't remember what I'd eaten then. "I'm going to the café to check on things and then I'll be in to see you."

"No," David said deliberately. "You go home and get some sleep. I think they're going to release me tomorrow, and I'll have to have a game plan. I'd much rather you be rested. And I know those goons are in jail, at least for tonight, but now I'm nervous about you on the highway at night. Go home, promise?"

I promised, with a bit of relief. Then I circled my car around in the road and headed to Wheeler.

* * * *

Even tuna salad, my perennial favorite, tasted like sawdust, and I wished for a glass of wine to wash it down.

Marj reported that the café was running smoothly. "You need to go home. I'll close. 'Course I been here since nine this morning, but I don't mind."

She knew I paid overtime. "Just log it in on your time sheet." I had honor system time sheets for the employees — Gram always said a time clock looked like you didn't trust them, and if you couldn't trust the people who worked for you, who could you trust? With one exception I could remember in my three years there, it worked pretty well.

"Oh, Kate! How could I forget? Mrs. Aldridge called four times. She sounded agitated, real anxious to talk to you. Here's her number." She handed me a slip of paper torn off an order pad and I pocketed it, just in case I couldn't find the card she'd given me before.

"I'll call tomorrow. Haven't got the heart for it tonight." And with that I went home, fed a starving Huggles, showered, and fell into bed. My dreams were of men beating bushes with baseball bats while I cowered under a rotting tree limb. Huggles apparently had bad dreams too, because he jumped, started, and barked several times during the night.

One glance in the mirror next morning told me that I looked as bad as I felt. I did my best with makeup, fed and watered Huggles, and left him outside, praying for a calmer day as I walked across the field to the café to make sticky buns.

By eight o'clock, the buns were made and in the warming oven, and I was eating a bowl of oatmeal, because I figured it would give me stamina for whatever the day held. Of course, my main agenda was to head to Canton and see about David's release. But before I could get out the door, the phone rang. Marj wasn't there, so I answered with as cheery a voice as I could muster. "Good morning. Blue Plate Café. How may I help you?"

"Kate, this is Edith Aldridge. It's even more desperate than ever that I speak to you immediately. Can you come to my home right away?"

Oops. What happened to yesterday's lack of presumption? "No, Mrs. Aldridge, I can't. I have to go right away to visit a friend in the hospital."

"Hospital! That's just it. I have found out, in a roundabout way that my lawyer has been badly beaten. I'm afraid he's dead."

I held the phone away from my ear and stared at it, as though I'd imagined that last statement. Distantly, I could hear her calling, "Miss Chambers? Kate?"

Finally, I put the phone back to my ear. "I'm here. You just startled me. What is your lawyer's name?"

"I'm not sure if I ought to divulge it."

Exasperation nearly got the better of me. "Mrs. Aldridge, how can I help you if you can't tell me things?"

A long pause. "I guess you're right. It's David Clinkscales, a Dallas lawyer who spends most of his time in this area now."

I drew in a deep breath. It was what I had been expecting. "Mrs. Aldridge, I do know him. He's a very good friend of mine. And he's not dead. He's recovering nicely. I expect the hospital to release him today."

"Oh, thank God. Can he come here as soon as he's released?"

This lady was really scared about something. "No, ma'am. He can't. He'll be frail and weak, and he'll need to rest. But I can give you his cell phone number. This might be a particularly good time to call."

"Bother," she said sharply. "I have that number. But if I don't get him, young lady, you tell him to call me as soon as he can." Gone was the obsequious polite lady, replaced by a demanding woman who apparently felt the privileges of the rich . . . or of being David's client.

"Yes, ma'am," I said and hung up quickly.

Chapter Six

I intended to be cheerful and caring when I went into David's hospital room. Instead, I barged in like a demanding harridan. My temper was blazing, and I imagine it was reflected in my eyes. "Why didn't you tell me Edith Aldridge is your client?"

David looked at me in a mild, slightly surprised way typical of him. After staring a minute, he said, "You had no need to know. You of all people know about client privilege."

"How long has she been your client?" I wasn't about to let go of my head of steam that quickly, although from afar I heard Gram say, "Now, child, you catch more flies with a teaspoon of sugar than a cup of vinegar." *Gram, I don't need platitudes right now!*

David said, "Long time. Her husband's unfortunate death was — what? Thirty years ago?"

"She was your client even when I worked for you, and you never told me?"

"She never visited the office, and we had little business to transact. Besides, she asked that I be extra careful about confidentiality, and I honored that. You can see why she was nervous." After a minute, he added lamely, "She's really a sweet lady."

"She was until about an hour ago. Then she nearly bit my head off."

"I know. She called me. She's upset about the beating and the cabin. Well, mostly she's upset that records are missing. Her file, which is relatively slim, is with those the sheriff confiscated, and no doubt he's reading it right now. He probably was ten years old at best when Walter Aldridge died. May look like fresh meat to a hungry dog."

I stopped short, baffled by his metaphor. "Fresh meat?"

"A cold case he can investigate." David rang for the nurse. "Edith was acquitted, but no one ever figured out who did kill Walter Aldridge. Shot him sitting at his desk."

"I know. I looked it up on Google."

He stared at me. "You could have just asked me." Then he began issuing orders. "Get my clothes out of that closet or wherever they put them. I've got to get out of here *now*."

"Why?" I wasn't letting him leave against medical advice if I could help it, and I was pretty sure at this point I was stronger than he was, if it came to that.

The nurse who responded to David's call—her badge read Alpha Jones—was crisp, efficient, and far too agreeable. "Mr. Clinkscales, you are scheduled to be dismissed today but you must wait for the doctor."

"That could be suppertime. I've got to go now, got business to take care of."

"Now, now"—she pushed him back into the pillows—"getting upset will only raise your blood pressure and alarm the doctor. I'll do what I can to hurry him, though heaven knows it's not much."

I truly thought about saying I had to go to the café, and I'd come get him that afternoon, but in spite of my bravado, I chickened out and sat back to watch.

David grabbed his cell phone and dialed. From the conversation, he obviously called Sheriff Halstead. "Sam, about those files you took for safekeeping yesterday. Would you bring them around to me?" Pause. "Yes, I'm still in the hospital but getting out today. Not sure where I'll be staying." He stole a look at me. "I'll let you know, but the files will be safe with me, and I need them for a client." Another pause. "You can't? Surely they don't have anything to do with what happened at my cabin. I'm sure they're not evidence." Pause. "Yes, yes, I imagine some of them are interesting reading." A pause during which David grew increasingly agitated. "Well, man, what do I do to get them back? Court order? They can't just sit in your file. I *need* them."

At length he hung up, looking totally discouraged. "He won't give them up. Seemed gleeful about reading the files, which makes me very nervous. I'm afraid he's got the law on his side, and he's smart enough to know it."

"Could the files on Mrs. Aldridge have anything to do with this mess?"

"They just might, Kate. You never know what greed or fear will lead people to do. Including the good sheriff."

Only then did I remember my resolve to be cheerful. I went to the bed, kissed him lightly, and held his hand. We both sat lost in thought for a long while.

* * * *

The doctor came in about three in the afternoon, semi-apologizing by saying, "My patients are always in a hurry to get out of here. Did the best I could." He leafed through the chart he held. "Hmmm. Blood pressure a little high at noon today."

"I was upset," David protested.

"Because I was late?"

"No, a professional matter. I'm a lawyer."

The doctor looked at me. "You his wife?"

I shook my head, refusing to remind him he'd asked me that question before.

"Can you make him take care of himself? His body's had a shock and, at his age, it won't respond as quickly as it once did."

David was probably forty-five, and out of the corner of my eye I saw the jolt the doctor's words gave him.

"I'll try. Can he drive?"

"No driving for at least awhile, and even then only as long as it's an automatic shift. We'll reassess from time to time. The burns on your hands and feet have to heal, and we need to be sure you're not light-headed anymore. And there's the matter of the broken ankle."

David protested immediately. "I'm not light-headed. I'm in full possession of my faculties, and I drive an automatic. It's my left ankle."

"Sorry, buddy, but it's for your own good. I'll see you in my office in one week. Call and make an appointment. Nurse will be in shortly to wheel you out."

"Wheel me out?" David said indignantly after the doctor left. "I can damn well walk out of this joint."

"Probably hospital rules," I said. I'd been out to a local fast-food place and gotten us BLT sandwiches—neither of us wanted a fast-food hamburger—so we weren't starving, and I couldn't blame crankiness on hunger. But David was the least cranky person I knew, and his out-of-character mood was beginning to affect me. I kept silent, even when his cell phone rang and his end of the conversation told me it was Edith Aldridge on the other end of the phone.

"No, Edith, I don't think it's as serious as you believe." Pause. "Really? You found what?"

Clear across the room I could hear her determined voice say, "A trip wire on the stair."

David paled. "Anything else?"

She must have told him about the papers in the office, because he put his head in his hands in an expression of defeat. "I think the cat is out of the bag," he said, "and on the prowl."

More conversation from Edith. Then, "The sheriff has already been to see you? Just tell him you won't talk without your lawyer present. I can be there for you tomorrow."

My heart sank. I couldn't spend my days driving David hither and yon—I had a café to run. I wasn't sure at all what to do, but first things first. David would have to stay at my house—in Gram's room. And I could already hear Gram pitching fits. And probably David too. Not that David and I were either naïve nor as pure as driven snow, but now did not seem like the time for romance or intimacy. Besides, what if I rolled over and hit his ankle? It was in what they called a soft cast, rather than being encased in rigid plaster. Much more comfortable, I'm sure, but just as limiting.

When he hung up, I asked a really dumb question. "David, how did the sheriff know to see Mrs. Aldridge?"

"The papers you handed him." His voice was almost accusatory, but he knew and so did I that I had no choice.

My questions were interrupted by a nurses' aide who was far too cheery. "So, we're ready to go home, are we? Let me just help you into this wheelchair, and if your wife will go bring the car to the ER doors, I'll wheel you down there. We'll have you out of here in no time at all." She was almost singing her words, all with this huge smile and too much use of "we."

David growled, "She's not my wife," and tried to stand to go to the wheelchair. But his ankle in a cast collapsed under him, and he fell, ungracefully, to the floor.

"See?" the nurse gloated. "We're not quite as strong as we think."

I grabbed my purse and ran for the car.

* * * *

The drive home was silent, with David staring out the window. I had decided not to talk unless he brought something up. Silence is sometimes hard for me, but I drove determinedly, watching the familiar landscape slip by. I studied farmhouses and antique stands that I'd seen a thousand times as though I'd never seen them, wondering when that house had been fenced and why that house had a cow in the front yard.

David got out his cell phone, stared at it, and then put it away. He too seemed absorbed in the landscape. Maybe he saw, as I did, the beginning of spring, the new green that covered trees and bushes.

At last I pulled in next to my house and grabbed the paper sack that contained the few things that were found on him—burned shoes (he was wearing slippers I bought in the hospital gift shop), and the clothes they'd torn off him to treat him. I'd had to go to Target to get the jeans and shirt he wore, and I admit the fit was all wrong and they were cheap and too stiffly starched—he looked like a marionette when he tried to walk. The pants were several sizes too big so they would fit over his cast. I suspected everything in the bag would go in the trash. I also picked up the sack of necessities I'd bought—toothbrush and paste, underwear, a couple of T-shirts.

Once in the house, David looked around helplessly, as though to ask, "What am I supposed to do now?"

Huggles couldn't get enough of being close to David, nearly jumping in his lap, but Wynona, never a sociable cat with strangers, looked at him with disdain and stalked back to her hiding place in the living room.

"Why don't you lie down and nap? Just getting out of the hospital is stressful."

He looked resentful for about half a minute and then said, "You know, you're right."

I pulled back the covers on Gram's bed and all but tucked him in. Then I left for the café, promising to be back with supper. Tired of hospital food, he requested chicken-fried steak and mashed potatoes.

I had to check on Marj and let her go home since she'd been doing double duty, but I also had to come up with a game plan for keeping David busy. After checking everything at the café and finding it was running smoothly without me, I called Roger Smith. He and his son, Cary, had lost their wife and mother in tragic circumstances that were of her own making . . . and almost led to my death. But when the dust settled, I counted Roger and Cary as friends.

"Roger? Kate Chambers. Does Cary have an after-school job these days or is he playing baseball all the time?"

Roger reported that Cary had given up sports, uncomfortable with other kids after what happened with his mother, and Roger was worried, wanted to get him out of the house and away from his books. I explained what I needed, and without consulting either David or Cary, we agreed on a plan whereby Cary could earn a little money driving David around after school. Some days Cary had school until three; twice a week, he was free at two.

I was back from the café by seven, knowing I'd have to go back one more time to collect charges and tally up. But I began to set the kitchen table, only to find I had to move David and his computer.

"I've been looking at house plans," he said enthusiastically, all his helplessness and anger of the day gone.

"Fine, but move the computer so I can serve dinner." I served up plates of chicken-fried steak, mashed potatoes, and fried green beans, a new dish for the café. It was good and went against everything I'd vowed to eat—or not eat.

I stacked the dishes in the sink without washing them, because David was insistent that I come look at the house plans he'd found.

"You know, tiny houses are all the thing these days. And some of them are remarkably efficient and stream-lined. That's all I need out there at the lake—a tiny house with a sleeping porch." He actually leered at me.

And so I found myself looking at house plans. Some were, indeed, neat, but I vetoed the ones where you had to climb a ladder to get to the sleeping loft.

I didn't mention Cary during our cheerful supper, but later as I did dishes, David said, "Kate, I need to go get some clothes—I literally have nothing but what's on my back—and I need to see Edith Aldridge tomorrow. I hate to ask, but can you . . ."

I took a deep breath and sat at the table, abandoning the half-washed dishes. "I've arranged for Cary Smith—you remember?"

He nodded.

"He'll drive you anywhere you want to go after school. I can usually slip away in the morning for a short while but as a routine thing, trips to Canton to buy clothes are out for me. Will that work for you?"

"Yeah, the Smith boy is a nice kid. How's he doing?"

I repeated what Roger told me and then added out of the blue that David might want to see about carrying a handgun. I knew he had a concealed carry license. "You never know," I said, trying to be flippant.

"Right."

"Besides, Big One and John are safely in jail. But obviously someone with more brains was behind their attack on you."

"Big One and John?" He was about to laugh.

"Big One is that one you called Dan'l. At the cabin he called John by name, but it didn't work the other way. So I called him Big One. And I can tell you he appears to give the orders, but John is the one with half an ounce of brains."

"Halstead said neither of them are right bright. Doesn't matter. They're facing two counts of attempted murder, arson, and resisting arrest. I bet Halstead can come up with more charges if he tries. But those two thugs are replaceable by someone who has the right—or wrong—connections."

That sent a shiver of worry through me. Who knew if the next ones might not be brighter?

"But here's the thing. Halstead said they've lawyered up—some slick lawyer from Dallas in Italian clothes and shoes. Expensive. Those two can't afford him. And the lawyer won't let them talk. Just tells them it will all be all right. And they listen. Halstead hasn't gotten one drop of information about them, except that someone told them to go get those files."

So who is pulling the strings?

On that note, we both went to bed. I heard David get up several times during the night, once to peer out the front windows, and I knew he was having as sleepless a night as I was.

Chapter Seven

Next morning I left the house at six, figuring David would call the café when he woke up. His ankle wasn't up to crossing the sloping, rocky lot between the house and the café, but I certainly didn't want to wake him. Sleep might restore the good nature of this man who I loved but who had almost become a stranger in the last forty-eight hours.

Gram counseled me. "He's been through a lot, Kate. Give him time. Give yourself patience."

"But . . . ." I started to reply but she was gone again. Aloud, as though I were calling after her, I shouted, "Patience is not my strong point!"

David did call. When I answered, there was no pleasant beginning. "Damn, I can't even get off this porch with this so-called walking cast on. Will you call Cary?"

I reminded him gently that Cary was in school and said I'd come get him. As I hung up, I heard a loud, "Blast and damn!"

In no hurry, I left the kitchen in charge of Benny, the wonderful young Hispanic cook I'd hired, and snuck out the kitchen door. Gus was sitting on the tree stump, having his usual morning cigarette.

"You be careful, Miss Kate. Somethin's in the air. I can feel it in these old bones. And it ain't good."

I put an arm around his shoulder and said, "I'll be careful, Gus. Don't you worry." I wished I felt as self-confident as I sounded for him.

David, apparently watching for me, hobbled out of the house by holding on to doorframes and the like. I helped him off the porch and over to the driveway so he could crawl into the car. Then we drove to the Blue Plate so he could have breakfast, but his telephone was already ringing. He looked at it and put it back in his pocket, but once he was settled at a corner table in the café, he pulled it out. I had no idea who he was calling and didn't linger to find out. He'd asked for scrambled eggs and bacon, and I went off to get them.

When I delivered his breakfast, I sat down and asked, "Okay, what do you need this morning?"

"Crutches and better clothes," he replied instantly. "And a private eye. But I've already taken care of that. Actually, he called me, looking for work, and I thought it was the perfect solution."

"A PI?"

"Someone's trying to kill my client, and I'm obviously not much help." He gestured toward his ankle.

For a moment, my nose was out of joint, a phrase Gram used a lot to tease us when Donna and I were jealous of something the other did or achieved. *Kate, you are not a private investigator; you run a café and that's enough to keep you busy!* I just stared at him, not believing this whole mess had escalated enough that he called in a PI.

"Maybe someone's trying to kill you."

"Possible. Kate, I damn near died that day, would have if it weren't for you! But you can't save me all the time. And you sure can't save Edith Aldridge. Someone out there is very serious. You may even be in danger since you can identify — what are their names?"

"Big One and John." I laughed. "Maybe it's her step-children? I'm sure that's what she thinks."

Shoveling eggs into his mouth as though he were still starving from hospital food, he managed to say, "Yeah. Greed is a powerful thing. But they couldn't, wouldn't have done what's happened to me and Edith. They've got hired guns."

I thought back to John and Big One. If they were the best the stepchildren could do, they were all in trouble. I tried to explain that to David, but he countered.

"They've done some pretty destructive things so far, Kate. Let's not dismiss the danger. A trip wire, an attempt-ed burglary, two attempted murders, arson. The Lord . . . or Gram . . . has been watching over us, but we can't count on that."

How does he know about my one-sided conversations with Gram? Did I let something slip sometime? He wasn't laughing at me, so I shrugged it off.

Business was a bit slower than usual that day and, against my better judgment, I ended up taking David to the Target in Canton, where he grumbled about the quality of clothes, etc. But between Target and a drugstore chain, we got him presentable clothes — no fancy dinners in Tyler in the near future — and the toiletries he needed plus a pair of crutches that were handed to him with the warning, "Careful. Lots of people hurt themselves falling off these things." Not reassuring, and David was indeed clumsy with them. I suspected it's a matter of coordinating crutch-es, feet, and arms.

I was back at the café barely in time for the lunch bunch. David had a tuna salad plate, after his large and late breakfast. He ate slowly, drumming his fingers on the tabletop.

"Is the tuna all right?" I asked on one pass by his table.

"It's fine. What time did you say Cary gets out of school?"

"Three." I looked at the clock, where the hands stood straight up at noon. Three whole hours. "Want to take a nap?" Part of me, a big part, didn't want him to wait for Cary, because I wanted to go with him to see Edith Aldridge. Curiosity got the best of me. But what if we met Big One and John?

David was watching me, trying to figure out what was going through my mind. Finally, he sighed and said, "I guess I'll have to wait. No nap. I need to think."

"Wait till lunch is over," I said. "If you promise on Scout's honor we'll be back by four thirty, I'll take you."

David knew me too well, and he grinned. "Just because you're curious."

I was glad to see that familiar grin back, even if it was temporary.

* * * *

On the drive to see Mrs. Aldridge, David was solemn again. "Kate, let me handle this. Don't ask a lot of questions."

"She asked me to help her," I said as calmly as I could. "And that was before you were beaten. She thinks you're the lawyer, and I'm the detective."

He was trying to be patient. "I've hired a private investigator, as I told you. He'll meet us there."

David was being devious. He'd known all along that I couldn't wait to drive him and had arranged this meeting without telling or asking me. I drove in silence until I blurted out, "David, how much money are we talking about? Is it worth all that whoever is doing?"

"I have no idea. She's been cagey, even with me. I'm wondering if there are hidden treasures in the house—art, rare books, stuff like that. Maybe there's a safe behind a huge painting. I honestly don't know, but it's got to be something for anybody to go to all this trouble."

"How valuable is this house?"

He almost laughed. "Location, location, location. It's not exactly in a ritzy setting, out in the country in East Texas. But city folks with money are beginning to be more interested in East Texas. Last comps I looked at were something like two million, mostly the land it's on."

I whistled.

From the road you couldn't see the house at all. David told me to turn when we reached an elaborate iron double gate. A bronze plaque on the stone pillar at the side of the gate read, "Peacock Mansion." A puzzling name. I pressed a button on a stone post at my side of the car, gave David's name, and the gates opened magically. The house sat at the end of a long, winding driveway with trees lining the road. Scrub oak and the like — this was no southern antebellum mansion.

Well-manicured lawns rolled away from the paver-brick driveway on either side. Far down one grassy slope I saw a huge pond with swans swimming along, their beautiful necks arched high. On the lawn beside the pond a peacock paraded with his feathers spread in all their glory. Now I knew where the name came from, but I had a hard time putting this picture together with rural East Texas as I knew it — maybe Highland Park in Dallas, but not outside Canton. And yet there was something creepy about it that sent a shiver through me.

David noticed. "You okay?"

"Yeah. Just something gave me a chill for a minute."

"Probably all the stories you've heard about this house. Put them out of your mind. It's a wonderful house — just in an odd place."

I wasn't sure I found that comforting. Besides, I hadn't heard stories except that Mrs. Aldridge told me she was accused and acquitted of her husband's murder in the house.

The house itself was faux Tudor in style. Brick on the first floor, half-timbered stucco on the second, with a tile roof. A double wooden door with elaborate brass ornamentation reminded me of an English castle.

Edith Aldridge greeted us in a tiled entryway that was like something out of a 1940s movie. She wore a hostess gown, the kind of garment I'd never in my life have use for but coveted immediately. Her welcome was warm and genuine. She took both my hands in hers and gave me a smile. Then she turned to fuss over David, saying we must get him off his feet.

A man stood as we came in, and Edith Aldridge introduced me to Steven Connell. He was everything I expected a PI to be—almost middle-aged, a bit overweight, casually dressed (in the extreme with a wrinkled shirt, corduroy blazer, and jeans over boots). But he was polite, even jovial.

"I hear you may be able to help me find out what's going on around here."

I blushed to the roots of my hair and said something stupid, like "I've just been in the right place at the right time once or twice." I didn't want to admit to nosiness.

"Or the wrong place," David added wryly, hobbling forward to shake his hand and greet him with a simple, "Steven. Good of you to come."

"Sounds like too much fun to miss," was the reply.

Edith Aldridge frowned a bit and cast a skeptical eye at this new figure. This was obviously not her idea of fun.

Steven didn't miss a beat. "Mrs. Aldridge showed me the trip wire. She cut it but left it in place, which was good thinking. No amateur job."

How much skill does it take to nail a trip wire across a staircase?

"High enough up she wouldn't yet be looking down and her fall would probably be fatal. Lower down on the staircase, she would have been looking down and the fall wouldn't have been so bad. And she left the office untouched—"

Edith Aldridge interrupted without hesitation. "David needs to sit down, and I'll order us some tea."

David was settled on an uncomfortable-looking Victorian sofa in the room she referred to as the parlor. I fetched a stool for his bad leg and then sat beside him and studied the room while Mrs. Aldridge—I wished I could call her Edith—rang for a maid.

The parlor had pulled plaster walls with paintings that were original and, to my only slightly trained eye, probably worth something. No old masters, no hidden collection of valuable art—unless it was in the basement. One wall held a large oil depicting the landscape of East Texas, with a small lake. I speculated about a hidden safe. The floor was varied width, pegged oak, mostly covered by a huge Oriental rug.

When a maid came and took the order, I sort of hoped we were in for watercress and cream cheese sandwiches, along with egg salad.

While we waited, Steven wanted to see the office, and I tagged along. Not to be left behind, David struggled to upright his crutches and follow us, a bit slowly.

The office was a dark-paneled room, walls lined with glass-fronted bookcases. A massive desk dominated, and two leather chairs offered cushy seats for visitors. Clearly a man's space. The desk drawers were pulled open, and papers were scattered as though they'd been tossed on the desktop and the floor around the desk.

"This is where I supposedly shot my husband," Edith said. "They never found a gun, and there was no residue on my hands. I called the sheriff as soon as I found him."

"You didn't hear the shot?" Steven asked.

I thought I detected a bit of skepticism in his question.

"I was out walking on the lawn, some distance from the house, with my dog. So, no, I didn't hear it. It was coming dusk, and I didn't see anyone. The staff—my cook, housemaid, and chauffeur—were all thoroughly questioned and cleared. I did *not* shoot my husband, though Lord knows there were times I was tempted."

That startled me, and as we trooped back to the parlor, I thought perhaps I was too quick to dismiss her as a suspect. She could have rigged the trip wire herself and made a mess of the office. But why would she have David beaten? The answer was obvious—to retrieve his files. And yet here she was fussing over him like a mother. Edith Aldridge was either innocent or a damn fine actress.

Tea distracted me. A three-tiered tray held the hoped-for finger sandwiches and apricot scones. Mrs. Aldridge poured tea into delicate cups with handles so small that you had little choice but to raise your pinkie to get it out of the way. Both David and Steven looked skeptical about the tea, but I loved it.

Steven asked when she'd last heard from "the children," and she said she never heard from them, and that was fine with her. No, she had an idea that they'd suddenly become upset all over again. She said they thought she killed their father and were angry that she didn't go to jail and forfeit her inheritance.

She handed each of us a sheet identifying the three children, with a brief paragraph about each. Rodney, the eldest, was a financial planner in Dallas—I shuddered because my family had already had one bad run-in with a financial planner. Rose, the middle child, was fifty-two, mother of one daughter, married to a lawyer, and lived well in Dallas, playing golf, going to bridge club and ladies' teas, and the like. Finally, James, an artist who lived in nearby Edom.

I immediately decided James was the usual starving artist and desperate for money. *Stereotyping, Kate!* Besides, artists were free spirits, or so I thought, and given to neither cunning nor brutality. Rose probably wasn't much along those lines either, though it might be instructive to find out about her husband. My money was on Rodney having the cunning, connections, and brains to try to outwit his stepmother. I was not going to explain my reasoning to David.

After we'd talked a while longer, Steven asked to explore the house, inside and out.

"I promised Kate we'd be back at the café in plenty of time for the dinner service," David said, "so we best be going. Steven, call me later and tell me what you found."

We made our polite farewells to Edith and were headed back to Wheeler.

"Didn't learn much, did we?" David asked.

"Oh, yeah, I think we learned a lot—the children, if nothing else." I bit my tongue to keep from fingering Rodney right away. David would have countered that the law is built on logic, not instinct.

"True, but we didn't find out why she's being so cagey about what the children could want. And we have no idea who really killed Walter Aldridge. That might solve the whole thing." He stared out the window for a minute. "While you're busy with the supper crowd, I'll go back to the house and do some online research into the murder. No use talking to the sheriff—he wasn't around then, and I doubt his records go back that far in any detail. Maybe I can find out who the lawyers were—like who defended Edith."

"You didn't?"

He pretended mock indignation. "Even I wasn't practicing law thirty years ago. I didn't know much about the case. It was a cold case when Edith Aldridge came to me, say, some twenty years ago."

"Why did she suddenly come to you? Was she dissatisfied with her current lawyer then?"

"I'd have to look at my records . . . and Halstead has them."

I drove him to the house, helped him get settled with his computer, and left for the café, promising to bring back meatloaf sandwiches.

Supper at the café was neither slow nor busy—just a steady stream of guests, most of whom I knew and stopped to chat with. It was a bit after nine when I closed up and took the receipts home with me. I could reconcile while David explored.

Opening the back door, I called cheerily, "I'm home," only to see that though lights blazed in the kitchen, David's computer screen was dark, which meant he hadn't touched it in a while. A moment of panic receded when I found him sound asleep in his bed. He never woke up until morning, and I ate a lonely meatloaf sandwich that night.

Chapter Eight

Rodney Aldridge, the oldest of the "children," came into the café a few days after our visit to Edith Aldridge. Of course, I didn't know it was him. I just noticed a man who didn't look like he belonged in the Blue Plate Café. Stocky, slightly overweight, with a pasty face and dark hair slicked back from his forehead, he looked like a used car salesman to me. I seated him at a table in the front room and brought a menu, asked what he'd like to drink.

"Coffee, please." He studied the menu with great care. "Is your tuna salad fresh?"

I really mostly serve tuna for the women. My men customers want chicken-fried and meatloaf and a hearty midday meal. "It's canned tuna." I wasn't sure if he meant one of those fancy salads with a filet of tuna over it.

"No, no. Was it made today?"

Sometimes I carried tuna over to a second day, but this time I could truthfully answer, "Yes, it was."

He ordered the tuna salad plate, with a side of cottage cheese. Then he asked, "Is Miss Kate Chambers available?"

"I'm Kate."

He rose to hold out his hand in greeting. A limp handshake. "I hope we can visit while I'm here."

"Of course. Just let me turn this order in."

I did, alerted Marj, and went to sit down at his table with a muttered, "May I?"

He rose again, obviously well trained in gentlemanly ways. "Please do."

During this little interchange I studied him. His eyes were brown, small, and a bit puffy, as though perhaps he'd had too much to drink the night before. They didn't sit well with his pasty complexion. I decided I would not buy a car from him.

"I'm Rodney Aldridge," he offered by way of introduction, "and I know full well who you are. My stepmother has talked of you recently."

"All good, I hope." I was a bit at a loss what to say.

"I want to talk to you about Edith. I'm afraid she's losing it."

"Losing what?" I knew full well what he meant. *Why are we playing cat and mouse here?* His next statement made it plain.

"Her mind. She's seeing things that don't exist, threats to her that are pure fabrication. I am no longer comfortable having her live in that house."

What he's really saying is that he wants her out of the house, and he doesn't care where she goes. "You could hire a daytime nurse, and doesn't Lucy, the housekeeper, live in the house with her?"

"All that is true, except Lucy doesn't stay at night. I'm afraid Edith would never stand for such an arrangement. She's a very independent woman. I've tried to suggest that for years, but she wasn't buying it."

Smart woman. More in control of her faculties than you are! I was saved from having to reply by the appearance of David, hobbling on his crutches. He did so much better on them after a few practice sessions. Still, this was his first solo trip from house to café. I knew he'd come around the front way to avoid the steep meadow in between, but still I was surprised to see him.

He was equally surprised to see me with Rodney and his good morning was brusque till I asked if he wanted to meet Rodney Aldridge. Then he made his way to the table, held out his hand for a shake, and said heartily, "Nice to meet you. Mind if I join you?"

Rodney, who had stood for the greeting, looked definitely skeptical.

"David is your stepmother's lawyer," I explained. "I'm sure you'll want to share your concerns with him."

David was back to the cagey man I knew. I smiled inwardly. Rodney Aldridge had met his match.

"Concerns? She seemed perfectly well when I saw her yesterday." He was almost too hearty. "'Course there've been a couple minor problems in her household. You knew about the trip wire, of course."

Rodney was tight-lipped. "Of course."

"Interesting," David said. "How did you know about it?"

Rodney tried to appear urbane. "She told me, of course. We're quite close."

David raised an eyebrow. "Do you have any suspicions about who might be interested in harming her?"

Rodney appeared thoughtful, drumming his fingers on the tabletop. At long last, he said, "That Lucy who stays with her. She has a disreputable brother. Hangs around the house a lot. Always thought he was mooching a free meal."

David carefully took a pad out of his pocket along with a pen. "Brother's name?"

He stammered again. "I'm not sure. I just know he's Lucy's brother. Don't trust either of them."

"Pity," I said. "Edith seems to have so much faith in Lucy." I rose to refill coffee cups and check on what else was going on in the café, but as I turned away, I heard Rodney say, "She never was a good judge of character."

I wondered if that was a derogatory reflection on his father or a comment on her failure to appreciate Rodney.

I got busy on the cash register, every once in a while casting a look at the two men. David had what I called his lawyerly look on — skeptical, bemused, and utterly unconvinced. Well before noon, Rodney stood to leave. David remained seated but reached out to shake the other man's hand, and Rodney stalked out the door.

"You're welcome for the coffee," I muttered under my breath. We had both forgotten his order for tuna and, after David arrived, Rodney never mentioned lunch. He probably would have found something wrong with the tuna anyway.

David stayed for lunch, and as soon as I could get away I plonked myself down at his table. "Well?" I demanded.

His eyes were laughing as he looked at me. "You tell me."

"A big bunch of hot air and bluff."

He leaned over and kissed me right there in front of Gram, Marj, and the whole café. "I always knew you were smart. I called Edith. Lucy has no brother, and when quizzed said no man has been hanging around her kitchen.

Said, and I quote, she 'wouldn't let any trash hang out here.' There is a groundskeeper, who's there a lot of the time."

I took a deep breath. David was back, and we could work on this together. I forgot about Steven, which was my mistake.

"I've called Steven. He'll do a complete background check on all three stepchildren."

Steven, I decided, was going to take all the fun out of the game.

* * * *

That evening about five thirty, Donna came into the café, all aflutter. Donna's my twin sister, but we haven't really gotten along since the day we were born. Totally different personality types, though Gram raised us with equal love and discipline. Donna was always in rebellion, but it never turned out well for her. I was the quiet one who never caused trouble, but I was the one who left Wheeler for the big city of Dallas and had a career — Donna resented that. In recent years, Donna had gotten into a few scrapes — like suspicion of murder, just a minor thing — and I was there to help her husband pull her, kicking and screaming, out of danger. Sisters are sisters, after all, and there is a bond there. We just don't spend much time together.

"Kate, I've got the most exciting new guests coming tomorrow. A Mrs. Middleton and her daughter, from Dallas. I think they're sort of — you know — high society."

After several false starts, Donna now operated a B&B that was doing pretty well. She'd never make back her initial investment — she used her inheritance from Gram for that — but she broke even most months, according to Tom, her husband. She offered guests either a bare-bones breakfast plan or a "deluxe" plan under which she'd serve a formal dinner every evening. Trouble was that Donna's not much of a cook.

"Mrs. Middleton chose the deluxe plan, so I have to plan several meals." She looked at me coyly, but I knew what was coming. "I need your help."

"Of course you do, Donna. I'll be glad to make suggestions and give you directions, but I can't cook a gourmet meal in this kitchen while we're handling the dinner crowd. What do you want to serve?"

"I don't know. I sort of hoped you'd tell me."

"Donna, it's five thirty, dinner hour. Can we do this at nine tonight or in the morning?"

"I'll be back at eight thirty tonight. In the morning I'll have to grocery shop and make up the beds. I have a lot to do!" She shook her head so indignantly that the brown ponytail bobbed up and down. As usual, she was dressed in high style—leggings, three-inch heels, and a long tunic with a sweater casually thrown over her shoulders to ward off the evening chill. Of the two of us, Donna was definitely the fashion plate.

"Okay," I said.

"While I'm here, could you fix me five meatloaf plates to go, with mashed potatoes and I guess the green beans?"

Donna had never gotten over the idea that the café was her own personal dining service, and she never offered to pay. For me, it was a small price for friendship. I turned in the order, handed it to her a few minutes later, and sent her on her way. All evening, while I waited on customers, checked them out, and saw the business of the café, I was reviewing menus in the back of my mind. I didn't give another thought to Mrs. Middleton.

By eight thirty only a few customers lingered, and the wait staff was taking care of them. Donna and I settled at a table near the cash register so I could pop up to check people out when needed. I generally didn't let the staff handle the cash register—a business policy that I thought good insurance.

"For the first night, how about a good chicken Divan with haricot vert and oven-roasted potatoes?"

"What's chicken Divan and whatever in the world are harry-coat verts?"

My sister lived in a chicken-fried world. I explained, gave her the simplest chicken Divan recipe ever, and told her how to roast potatoes with rosemary. She could get the rosemary out of my yard.

"Tom and the kids will love this too," I said.

"Oh, Tom will have to cook for them. I'll be Little Miss Domesticity in a clean white apron, serving dinner at Tremont House."

Tom and the kids will be at the café tomorrow night, I told myself gleefully. Tom was like the big brother I never had, and I adored my two nieces and nephew. They adored Huggles and me.

The next morning I got two frantic phone calls from Donna, but pretty much I put her cooking problems out of my mind. I'd left the house long before David woke, so I didn't see him until he came in at noon and asked if it was too late for eggs and bacon. Normally, I turn down such requests—breakfast is over at ten thirty—but I filled his order myself.

"Steven called. He's fast, and he's already located Rodney's siblings. No background checks yet, but they don't sound like killers to me."

I waited.

"Edith said the other day that James, the youngest Aldridge child, the one that's an artist, lives in Edom. Just down the road. He's got a gallery, lives above it. Single but has a live-in girlfriend. Lives modestly. Steven suspects he still has much of his inheritance left, whereas Rodney has blasted through his. He'll dig deeper to find out."

"And the daughter?"

"Married well. I suspect Walter Aldridge would have seen to that. Lives in Highland Park in Dallas—can't get much tonier than that. Name is Rose Mitchum. One daughter, a deb next year. Lives the upscale life. Husband's a big-time lawyer. I've met him. Probably will all pan out well."

For just a second there, I thought he was going to say her last name was Middleton and a big alarm bell was ready to go off in my head. I guess I was too used to seeing conspiracies everywhere I went.

David watched me. He knew me well enough to follow my thought process. "What?"

So I told him about Mrs. Middleton checking into the Tremont House, and he laughed out loud. Such a good sign.

"Kate, haven't you learned that life is full of coincidences but it doesn't usually tie up that neatly in a pretty package?"

I blushed. "Let's go for a ride," I said, glad to change the subject. "You need fresh air, and it's a lovely spring day. Wish I had a convertible."

"You're right. Let's go. We spend too much time on Edith Aldridge's affairs. Let's go check on my house."

Not exactly the kind of outing I had in mind, but I dutifully headed the car toward David's burned-out house.

You could smell the ruins as you turned into the driveway — an acrid smell, mixed with damp and mold. Not pleasant at all. We'd brought Huggles with us, and he barked in displeasure. I pulled into the clearing, and we both sat and stared — the porch had now fallen in, helped I supposed, by James' plunge through it. The shell of the lake side of the house still stood, looking ghostly in its emptiness. His car had been towed to a garage in Canton.

David struggled out of my car. "I didn't come here to mourn the loss," he said. "I want to begin planning the future."

Three cheers for optimistic thinking! I scrambled out of the car and released Huggles, who bounded off to the water's edge. David followed him, and I tagged along behind, though I couldn't rid myself of the feeling that someone was watching us. *Nonsense, Kate. Get your act together. Big One and John are in jail, and Rodney would hardly stoop to hiding in the bushes.*

"Here," David said. "It's where we'll put the house." The site was slightly to the right of the burned ruin. "They won't overlap, but I'll have to do some investigating to see how to treat the soil under the burned stuff. Does ash make things grow?"

I shrugged. I needed Dave Millican to help me with that question. Dave had owned a wonderful nursery in Wheeler, across the road from the café, but he hadn't put his past completely behind him and was eventually arrested for dealing drugs. A part of me still hoped he'd been set up, because he was one of the kindest, gentlest men I've ever met. On his last day of freedom — and he surely knew what was coming — he'd spent the day building a fence for me. I briefly thought myself in love with him, and though that feeling had long ago fled, I still grieved for him.

"Earth to Kate! Are you listening to me?" David called so loudly that if anyone was hiding in the trees they heard him clearly.

"Sorry. I got carried away for a moment."

He grinned. "I was saying I want to build one of those small houses here — the kind that are really efficient in their use of space. I've found some plans I'd like to use, you know cherry-pick from this one and that one. But there's one that has a sleeping porch at one end, and I figured that would face the water. Can't you imagine sleeping out in summer with a slight breeze?" He positively glowed with excitement.

I didn't tell him what I imagined was oppressive heat and bothersome bugs, especially mosquitos this close to the water. And throw in the possibility of a snake.

"I'll show you the plans when we get back to Wheeler. But then I want to grow vegetables where the old house was. That's why I have to find out about treating the soil. This will be a whole different place, one that I built from scratch by myself."

I was aghast. "You're going to build it?"

He laughed. "No, of course not. I'll hire someone, but I'll get Cary to drive me out every day so I can supervise. Blast this ankle. I can't wait until I can drive again." He looked sheepish. "Not that you haven't been really sweet about it."

I was used to hearing myself described a lot of ways. "Sweet" wasn't one of them. "I better get back to the café," I said almost brusquely.

When we were back in the car, I still had that eerie feeling of being watched, and in that moment before I turned the key and started the motor, I heard another motor start—on the farm road, by the turn into David's driveway.

Someone had followed us and spied on us. Who and why? I didn't bother David with those questions because he had other things on his mind. Before I could put the car in gear, he turned and enveloped me in a huge hug which led to a passionate kiss. I felt myself responding, realizing how I'd missed this side of our relationship.

Shakily, I said, "We better get back to the café." But I drove with what Gram would have called improper thoughts, not held at bay by the fact that David had his hand on my thigh.

Gram? Just look the other way. Please?

68

Chapter Nine

Edith Aldridge hadn't called in several days, which I took as a good sign. Maybe nothing—or nobody—was bothering her. But she came to the café one morning about nine, ordered a sticky bun and coffee, and sat and waited until I could visit with her.

Once I sat down at the table, she wasted no time on preliminaries. "I understand Walter's children are all in the immediate area. They must be planning something." She was quite matter-of-fact about it, but a frown of worry knit her eyes closer together.

I thought for a moment. "Yes, I believe Rodney is staying in Canton temporarily and, as you know, James lives in Edom. Has a gallery there. How did you know that?"

"It's part of my precaution. I keep up with their whereabouts most of the time. James is the sweetest of the three, but I doubt he has much of an artistic future. He's waiting to live off that fortune he's never going to get."

"Have you seen his work?"

"No. I haven't wanted to get close to any of the children. I know Walter thought James' work was good, but he was hardly an unbiased observer. Or an art critic. What do you know about Rose?"

"Nothing, except that she lives in Highland Park. As far as I know, she's not any closer than that. But I'll talk to

David—his investigator, Steven, can probably find out more."

"That would be good. I'm sure, with them circling around, they're plotting something. It makes me uneasy. I've doubled my security measures at the house."

Those measures were already so strong, I had no idea how she could double them. But at the same time, I thought for the first time that she sounded a little harsh about the "children." Had she ever tried to get to know them, or had it been an antagonistic relationship all along? It also occurred to me that she was so anxious to save her life, but what kind of life did she have, living alone in that mansion and never venturing out?

She stayed a while longer, inquired about David and why she hadn't seen him.

"I just can't drop the café and drive him wherever and whenever he wants to go. He has a teenager who drives him around after school, and I'm sure if you need him, he'll come any afternoon. But right now he's wrapped up in plans for rebuilding at the site of his burned-out cabin. You know, those small houses people are so crazy about these days. He wants one of those."

She snorted. "Not good for people to live on top of each other in small spaces. You need room for privacy. Lord knows, I value mine."

Well, there was the answer to one of my questions. But I still wondered what went through her mind when she woke up and thought, "What shall I do today?" Aloud, I reminded her that David lived alone, which earned me a long, knowing look from her.

After Edith departed—I refused her offer to pay for her bun and coffee—I sat there for a long time puzzling over her. She was abrupt, but I guess after all she'd been through, she had the right. And if I felt my life was in danger, I'd be abrupt too. I suddenly knew what I was going to do next—and I wasn't telling David.

* * * *

He came in for lunch but hurried back to the house. He was talking to a contractor he knew in Dallas and an architect. They were planning the small house. I tried hard to raise some enthusiasm, but the house seemed remote when Edith Aldridge was worried about her life and her stepchildren seemed to be closing in on her.

"Have you talked to Edith lately? She was here this morning and mentioned she hasn't heard from you."

He was startled, as though he'd forgotten all about her. "No, she hasn't called. Does she need me?"

"No. I just think she'd like you to hover over her a bit, show some concern. She thinks her stepchildren are in this neighborhood."

He slapped his forehead. "I've been so wrapped up in this house business . . . and keeping up with my office that I didn't even think of it. Thanks, Kate. I'll call this afternoon. And if you can slip up to the house, I'll show you some plans." Then he stopped himself. "There I go again. Are those wicked stepchildren nearby?"

I shrugged. "We know Rodney has been here. Ask Steven about the others." I wasn't telling him about James. He'd want to go with me to Edom.

"About those house plans, maybe tonight. I have an errand to run this afternoon," I said.

"Okay." He was off, blowing a kiss to me as he pushed open the door with one crutch.

These days he moved pretty fast on his crutches and was really feeling better generally. His bruises had mostly faded, and, blest be, his disposition had returned.

As soon as David was out of sight, I told Marj I was running an errand and would be back in about an hour. I still had to do menu plans for the next week and pay some bills.

The drive to Edom was all of about ten minutes, and I was soon on the main street—the state highway that ran through the middle of the small town. Before Wheeler was rejuvenated, Edom had long been an artists' colony with pottery shops, a leather worker, a ceramics studio, a gentleman who crafted handmade jewelry—the expensive kind. I spotted James' studio, new to the artists' strip, by its plain sign: Art Gallery.

I opened a creaking wooden door—like most of the studios, this was in an old building, once a part of a commercial strip, I supposed. Inside, all four old brick walls were hung with abstract paintings. I know nothing about abstract art, being almost of the bluebonnet school of paintings myself, but I thought these were probably pretty good. At least, they didn't look like a chimpanzee had been turned loose with the paints. Nor were they the kind of work where thick layers of paint substituted for artistic quality. The colors of several drew me. When I came in, I called "Hello?" but got no answer, so I stood and studied the paintings for a few minutes. Every once in a while I thought I caught a fleeting glimpse of a shape—the figure of a woman, a face, a rough indication of an animal. I liked the absence of hard lines and sharp corners.

"Just looking, or may I help you?" He was slight, not much taller than me, and had the requisite long hair of an artist. His pants and shirt were stained with paint—acrylic, I would later learn. But his face was gentle and friendly.

"James?" I asked.

He wasn't startled, just amused. "Yes. Sorry, you have the advantage of me."

I held out a hand, hoping the paint on his was dry. "I'm Kate Chambers from the Blue Plate Café in Wheeler."

"Looking for some art for your café?" He was still amused. "I don't think my stuff exactly suits your customers."

I laughed nervously and agreed. "No, I wanted to talk to you. I've been talking to your stepmother."

Now he was just a bit wary, shifting from one foot to the other. "This might get tiring. Let me drag a couple of chairs in."

He returned with two folding chairs. Yes, they were paint-stained, but he assured me it wouldn't come off on my clothes.

"What does Edith want now, except for the three of us to disappear into thin air?"

"Oh, I don't know that she wants that. She simply wants to be safe . . . and she's felt threatened lately. A burglary. A trip wire across the stairs. She thinks one of you . . . or all of you are trying to kill her for your inheritance."

He hooted. "Do I look like a steely-eyed killer?"

There was no holding in my grin. "Hardly, but you never know."

He had the habit of stroking his chin, like a philosopher deep in thought. "True, but I don't want her money or that godawful house he built her. I'm happy where I am, doing what I want—which is not, of course, what the old man wanted me to do."

Curiosity won. "What did he want you to do?"

"Practice law. Maybe go into politics."

"Oh, you've had made a miserable lawyer!" It came out before I could stop the words. "But that's another thing. My boyfriend"—what a strange word for my ex-boss who was now my lover!—"is a lawyer. Has an office in Dallas but does most of his business from a cabin on the lake. Or did, until two thugs beat him half to death and left him to die in a burning house. He's on the mend now, and the two are in jail. They tried to shoot me, too."

He jumped from his chair and began pacing. "You're not making this up, are you?" His worry and concern seemed genuine.

I sighed. "No. I wish I were. I gather you don't have any idea about it."

"No. I'm not fond of Edith, mostly because she didn't like us. But I wouldn't wish her harm. As for the inheritance, I don't know how much will be left after she's barricaded herself in that mansion for all this time. Rodney might have a better idea. We each got a nice chunk when Dad . . . er . . . died."

"Are you close to your sister and brother?"

His laugh was almost harsh this time. "Not hardly. They became the people the old man wanted them to—contributing citizens, he called it. I'm the oddball out. And I couldn't care less. They both make me uncomfortable." He sat back down and stared into space for a moment. "Sometimes I've thought about going to see Edith, trying to reach out to her. I suspect she needs friends, although I'm probably not good friend material for her."

"You're right, she does need friends. She denies being lonely, but I think she is."

"I guess now isn't a good time."

"No, probably not," I agreed. "But keep the idea in mind."

We talked a little more. James even tried to explain his art to me, though he ultimately said if it needed explaining, it wasn't successful. If I'd been a rich woman, I'd have gone home with a painting, just as a way of saying thank you.

As I left, he said, "I've never been to your café, but Shelly"—he jerked his head toward the back—"is always after me, saying we should go out. I think she gets tired of her own cooking. Maybe we'll come one night. Are you always there?"

"Yes, and I'd be delighted to have you be my guests."

"Oh no!" He raised his hands in protest. "I pay my way. I'm not a starving artist."

We both laughed. I drove back to Wheeler in a relieved and happy frame of mind. Now I knew about Rodney, who I didn't trust, and James, who I liked a lot. What about Rose?

* * * *

Mrs. Middleton, Donna's new guest at Tremont House, came into the café the next day for lunch. I'm not absolutely sure how I knew it was her, except that she was matronly looking—I couldn't think of another way to put it. She had on a stylish pantsuit with a ruffled blouse, gold earrings, and clattering gold bracelets. The pantsuit looked like it was from a catalog for "ladies of a good size." Her brown hair waved in curls that must have been set the day before, and she'd slept on them and then dressed without brushing them out. You know, that flat, hair-sprayed look. Heaven forbid that we should disturb the hairdresser's careful work.

With her was a bored young woman, maybe nineteen or twenty, with long straight brown hair, carefully done makeup, and a layered outfit that spoke of the latest style.

I waited on them, after signaling Marj, and as I handed them menus, Mrs. Middleton said, "My goodness. We are starved for some good food. That place we're staying is lovely and comfortable, but our dinner last night was . . . well, not acceptable. Breakfast this morning was all right but who can mess up oatmeal with brown sugar and raisins?"

Way to go, Donna! How did you mess up chicken Divan?

"I'm so sorry. Would you like a light lunch today?"

The woman looked at me with pity. "Not on your life. I'll have chicken-fried steak, mashed potatoes, and turnip greens. Melissa?" She turned to the daughter.

"I'll have the tuna salad plate," the girl said languidly, looking up for a moment from her cell phone.

When I delivered the lunches, Mrs. Middleton asked, "Do you know that Mrs. Bryson who runs the B&B? I believe her name is Donna. You look a lot like her."

I couldn't hold back a grin. "She's my twin sister. Fraternal, not identical. She's the good-looking, stylish one."

I swear that sophisticated woman blushed to the roots of her hair. "Oh, now I didn't mean . . . the chicken Divan wasn't that bad. Just maybe a touch overcooked."

"I'll try to help her do better," I said. "How long will you be staying?"

She waved a vague hand in the air. "No idea. I've some business to take care of, so we'll stay for however long that takes."

Melissa sighed heavily. "Mother!"

"Oh, you may go home any time, dear. But since I have the car, I don't know how you'll get there except bus."

"Isn't there a plane?"

I really did laugh at that. "Not from Wheeler," I said. "The bus would be faster."

"Josh will come get me," she said.

"Not if I have anything to do with it," her mother said rather harshly.

Melissa looked down and began to poke at her tuna salad, and I found it an auspicious time to leave them.

When I returned to bus their dishes, Mrs. Middleton raved over her meal. "I grew up eating chicken-fried steak, and I haven't had any this good in years. I may just tell Donna we'll take all our meals here."

"Let me talk to Donna," I suggested.

"I'd be grateful. We may be here a while. Meantime, thank you for a delightful lunch. I like the . . . ah, casual . . . atmosphere." She offered a smile, a gracious handshake, and then she followed her daughter out the door.

I imagined she didn't eat in what she called "casual" places and I called "down-home cafés" very often. I could more easily imagine her at Neiman's Zodiac Room or the posh restaurant at The Mansion on Turtle Creek.

I didn't have to call Donna. She called me, distraught. "I've been making beds and cleaning the kitchen all morning. Just got time to call now, Kate. My dinner was a disaster last night. Neither mother nor daughter did more than pick at it, and I tasted the serving I'd saved for myself. It had okay flavor but the broccoli was limp and the chicken tough."

"Sounds like you overcooked it, Don. What's for tonight?"

"Oh, Lord, I have no idea. You have to help me."

No, I don't have to, but I will, because we are sisters and that's what sisters do for each other. I wondered if she'd ever figure that lesson out for herself.

"We need ingredients you can get locally, since you don't now have time to get to Canton and back in time to cook. Let me think. I'll call you back." I hung up and went through possibilities in my mind — coq au vin was out, because we didn't want to do chicken twice in a row. My favorite quail recipe was out, because there were no quail available in Wheeler. I ruled out salmon croquettes — not upscale enough — and decided on my favorite meatball recipe. Large meatballs, baked in the oven, served with a rich brown sauce and mashed potatoes with spinach. When I called Donna, she said, "I can't do that."

"I'll do it for you. Come pick it up at five thirty." And that's how I spent my afternoon cooking meatballs. I made enough for David and me for dinner.

When Donna came to pick the meals up, I said, "I'm tucking in a recipe for scrambled eggs with ranch sauce — just stop and get the ingredients on your way to Tremont House. You can't go wrong — unless you cook the eggs too long."

She blew me a kiss. "Bless you, Kate. You are the best sister ever!" She ran out the door, carrying her prize meals.

You don't always feel that way! Gram, are you listening? I'm following your orders to take care of my sister.

Chapter Ten

Donna called on that Friday morning. "Tom is taking Henry camping and fishing tomorrow afternoon—won't be home until Sunday night. I was wondering . . . ." Her voice trailed off in hesitation, then regained strength. With a sudden burst of quick words, she said, "Could Ava and Jess spend the time with you? I thought I might run to Dallas for a quick getaway."

My radar went up. Donna's quick trips to Dallas used to be to see her lover—we were just all a little slow to discover that. But he was now gone, murdered at Tremont House, and Donna and Tom seemed to have turned their marriage around. She was even a better mother than she'd been almost since the children were born—and Ava was now nearing fifteen.

She, of course, noticed the pause before I answered and went on, "The girls want a girls' night with you. Of course, I realize David Clinkscales is staying with you, but I assume it's all proper and above board." She let her implication float in the air.

I wanted to snap, "Of course, it is!" but it wasn't a position I'd always be able to defend. "He's sleeping in Gram's room, and our rooms—yours and mine—only have single beds. Can they bring pallets or sleeping bags?"

"Of course. They'd love to sleep by your bed, with Huggles."

Huggles would love it too, though I didn't tell her he'd been sleeping by David's bed since David had come home for the hospital. Nor did I tell her I'd slept in Gram's bed the last three nights. She didn't need to know any of that.

"I want to get off early so I can get a full day of shopping in. Can I drop them at the café around nine? I figure they'll be fine at the house with David. What does he do all day anyway?"

"He works." My answer was clipped. There went Donna again, arranging everything for her own convenience, with little or no thought of how she was putting others out. Fortunately, David was fond of the girls — he'd never had children of his own — and it would really be kind of fun. I just didn't want Donna to know that.

"Don, what about dinner for your guests at Tremont House?"

"I'll steer them toward that Currents place in Tyler you're always talking about. Sorry, but I don't think they'd like the Blue Plate. They're not the chicken-fried steak kind."

* * * *

Donna actually brought the girls to the café a little after eight thirty, gave me a slip of paper saying she'd be at the Adolphus Hotel, hugged the girls briefly, and was out the door. A whirlwind.

Ava had brought a book she was reading, and I got crayons and a coloring book for eight-year-old Jess — which she promptly told me she was too old for. Fortunately, David hobbled in about that time and sat with them, the three planning what they could do for the weekend. I brought them all scrambled eggs, bacon, and biscuits with gravy without bothering to ask what they wanted, and then I tended to my other customers. David and the girls disappeared about nine.

Eleven thirty found me busy prepping main courses for lunch and dinner. The Saturday special was, as always, fried catfish, something that could not successfully be done before ordering. But we had to have catfish and batter ready, plus mashed potatoes, greens, and salad makings. Saturdays were busy days. With thoughts of a fun evening with the girls filling my mind, I was almost on automatic as I whirled potatoes in the giant mixer and put a huge pot of greens on to simmer.

I was totally unprepared when Marj came into the kitchen and whispered, "Mrs. Aldridge is on the phone for you."

Wiping my hands on the nearest towel, I went to the desk that doubled as my office and where it was a little quiet. "Good morning, Mrs. Aldridge. What can I do for you this morning?"

Her reply was brusque. "You can get out here as soon as possible. There's been another . . . ah . . . incident."

"Are you all right?"

"Yes, I'm not physically hurt. But there's something you need to see."

"Did you call David?"

"No, I preferred to call you. He's my lawyer. You're my investigator."

And just how did I earn that title? "It's Saturday, and the café is busy, but I can be there about three or a little after. I'll have to bring David and my two nieces. I hope that's all right."

"Your nieces may not like what they see, but that's fine. I'll have a high tea ready."

High tea sounded fine, but the caution that my nieces might not like what they saw didn't sit well with me. I figured, however, that I didn't have a choice. I wasn't sure why but Mrs. Aldridge didn't seem to request things; she demanded them. So visit we would.

David and the girls didn't come for lunch, which alarmed me. About twelve thirty I called him at my house. "The girls are tired of your menu. They're making me peanut butter and mayonnaise sandwiches with lettuce. It's a treat I admit I've never had before."

Laughter spilled out of me. "It's something Gram fixed us when we were kids. I love it. Enjoy." Then I told him where we were going at three.

"No! I planned to take all three of you ladies to Currents in Tyler for a fine supper. About time these girls learned to eat upscale food, and they're excited about it. Think they'll eat escargot?"

"No. And neither will I. Caviar, yes. Escargot, no." Still I thought the idea of a fine meal with the girls was enticing. But I said, "David, Edith Aldridge is upset about something. Even if she made it sound like a casual tea. I told her we'd have the girls."

"Is there such a thing as a casual tea?"

"Hush."

"I don't want the girls to ruin their appetites for supper."

"They can split something." My practicality came to the surface. If David didn't care about the bill, I did.

"I can tell how Gram raised you." David sounded just a bit put out. "Frugally. It didn't take with Donna, but it sure did with you."

I changed the subject. "Have the girls dress in the best clothes they brought. I'll come change about two." If I had time to run by Donna's, I'd get them Sunday clothes.

The lunch rush died down, and I escaped a little before two, asking Marj once again to cover. Then I rushed to Donna's to get clothes for the girls, going through their closets and dressers like a mad woman. Donna would have to straighten up behind me.

In the end my choices weren't bad — leggings and short skirts for both girls, longish shirts with cropped tops to go over them, and any kind of shoes I could find that weren't athletic shoes. When I got home and laid out their outfits, there were only mild groans, and I told them I'd not stand for any complaints. Then I went to see how I could match them, and finally chose black leggings, an ecru silk artist's shirt, big and blousy, and gold chains — okay, faux gold.

Once we were in the car, with me still driving, Ava groused. "Why do we have to go see this old lady?"

"Because she's David's client and she has something she wants him to see."

David interrupted. "Correction. Something she wants you to see."

"I should have brought my iPad," Ava said.

"I wouldn't have let you pull it out. I bet you have your cell phone, and that's enough."

Jess piped up. "Is this the house with the swans and peacocks? I really want to see those."

I guess she'd heard David and me talking about the Peacock Mansion. "Yes, it is. And girls, we're going to have tea, which means tiny sandwiches and cakes."

"And tea?" Ava asked.

"And tea. Even if you don't drink it, you will sip politely. Because, no, it won't be iced."

When we pulled into the driveway, the girls were both awed by the grounds. I pulled the car smartly up in front of the entrance, got out, walked around the car, and nearly lost my lunch. "Girls, stay there. Do NOT get out of that car!"

David quickly opened his door, got out, and uttered something I wished he hadn't said in front of the girls.

In front of us lay one of the peacocks, those wonderful birds that gave the mansion its name, an arrow piercing its chest, blood congealed around the wound. It was dead as dead can be. David poked at it with a stick, and said it had long ago stiffened.

"Can we get out now?" Jess called impatiently.

"No. You stay there."

I looked at David. He interpreted the look and rang the doorbell.

Mrs. Aldridge answered quickly. "You've already seen what I called you here about."

"Yes, and it's horrible. But my nieces are in the car, and I can't let them out to see this carcass. Can your hired man come move it?"

"Pshaw! He's not around. Now that you've seen it, I'll move it." And she did. Dressed in another elegant at-home gown, she picked up the dead bird's feet and began dragging it around the house and out of sight.

Inside the car the girls were clamoring. "What's wrong with that bird?" "Is it dead?" "Why is she dragging it?" "Can't it fly like most birds do?"

I got them out of the car and into the house through the door Mrs. Aldridge had left open. Fortunately, there were no bloodstains where the bird had lain. A tiny corner of my mind registered that meant the bird had died elsewhere and been dragged to the front door. For display for us? It was too much to puzzle on when I had to think of the girls.

Edith Aldridge came back inside, closing the door behind her. "Make yourselves comfortable in the parlor. I'll just wash up and be right back."

And she was. Ever the gracious hostess. I introduced the girls, and she asked, "Would you like to wander across the lawn to the swan pond?"

Ava looked temped, but Jess hung back. "No. I'm afraid."

"Whatever of?" Mrs. Aldridge asked.

How could she be so oblivious? Jess was afraid of dead birds and people with bows and arrows and who knew what else?

Edith Aldridge did not hug Jess or say any of the comforting things I thought she would. Instead, almost briskly, she said, "You girls come with me. Lucy has made chocolate chip cookies and lemonade in the kitchen, especially for you. And she'll give you a tour of the house, after she serves our tea."

Jess looked at me hesitantly, but I hugged her and gave her a gentle pat on the behind so she followed Ava, who was apparently eager to see the house. Jess looked over her shoulder once, but I gave her a slight hand wave and what I hoped was a reassuring smile. If I thought too much about it, I'd realize this house was enough to frighten anyone. At least there were no mounted game heads—not in the part of the house I'd seen.

Edith Aldridge was all charm as she strolled back into the room. "Sorry about that. I didn't realize the dead peacock would upset the girls as much as it did me. I am, after all, very proud of those fowl . . . and fond of them. I had John L. put it in front of the door so you wouldn't have to traipse all over the lawn. Thoughtless of me."

"The girls will be fine." David said that with more bravado than I felt. "Tell me what happened and why you wanted us to see it."

She looked surprised, as though it was obvious why she wanted us to see it. I still wondered if she couldn't tell us over the phone. "Why, I wanted you to see what lengths someone will go to in scaring me. I found Peter—that's my senior peacock—on my morning walk, down by the swan pond." She looked away for a moment. "Lucy was gone last night, and I was here alone, all safely locked and tucked when, when I heard a terrible scream, like a woman in great pain. I was afraid, naturally, to go investigate, but I did go at first light. And that's what I found."

David's look was intense. "Why would anyone shoot a peacock . . . especially with a bow and arrow?"

"To scare me, of course. Rodney Aldridge is an archery expert. And also a falconer."

What that had to do with anything was beyond me, but an archer? Rodney, the uptight businessman?

"Who is John L.?" David asked.

I knew he was thinking of Lucy's worthless brother, as described by Rodney.

"The man who does my grounds, keeps them in good shape. The fowl are his responsibility too, and he was heartbroken this morning."

Tea arrived. As I hoped, we once again had small sandwiches of egg salad, cream cheese and cucumber, and thinly sliced smoked salmon, along with a tray of petit fours. I didn't want to overeat because we were going to dinner, but I wanted to eat enough to be polite. And, besides, the smoked salmon was out of this world. I reached for a third sandwich as David gave me a sideways look.

"How do you know Rodney is an archer? I thought you had nothing to do with the children all these years."

"Steven Connell told me. He reports to me sometimes, and I called him this morning."

David's face turned red. "I thought I hired him for you, Edith."

"You did. But I have confidence in him, and he came out first thing this morning, looked at the bird, and called me before noon to say archery was one of Rodney's interests."

My mind flashed back to the time she said she knew the children were in the area and dismissed our curiosity by saying she made it her business to keep up with their whereabouts. Did she know Steven before David brought him into this mess? Something was funny here.

I excused myself to go check on the girls. Edith gave me directions to the kitchen — go down the great hall, through the dining room, and through the swinging door to the butler's pantry. I did, agog at what I saw. The long dining table was set for six with what looked to be authentic Imari china and matching gold flatware, with gold-rimmed goblets and wine glasses. A vision of Miss Havisham from *Great Expectations* flitted through my mind. *Is she always hoping to host a dinner party on sudden notice? She's lonely, this convinces me.* I pushed through the swinging door, with one-way glass so, I supposed, the staff could watch for when they were needed but guests couldn't see them.

The butler's pantry held glass-fronted shelves with rows of various size and purpose glasses, all arranged like soldiers in a perfect army. There was an automatic ice machine — surely a recent addition — a small sink, a stack of perfect white linen towels and a cutting board. Edith Aldridge was prepared to entertain but she never did. Was it fear that kept her from it? For a moment I forgot my questions about her and was filled with sympathy.

Beyond me, I could hear the girls chattering, so I called, "Hello" to announce my arrival.

"Aunt Kate, we are having more fun. Lucy let us cut some cookies out of dough ourselves and now we're decorating them. Here, I saved the prettiest one for you." Sweet little Jess handed me a cookie shaped like a rose and decorated with two shades of red and pink icing. It was a sugar cookie with orange flavoring, delicious!

"Hello, Miss Kate. I'm Lucy, and I've heard a lot about you." She carefully rinsed the flour off her hands, dried them, and then held her hand out in a welcoming handshake.

"It's good to meet you, Lucy. I've enjoyed your teatime treats, especially the smoked salmon."

"It's special, isn't it? Missus gets it flown in from the Northwest." She looked at the girls. "Fine pair of nieces you have here. I'd love to have them come back sometime. Maybe we could make a cake."

Even Ava, who'd grown too sophisticated lately, seemed interested in that idea.

"Lucy, pardon my inquisitiveness, but do you stay here every night?"

"No, ma'am. I have a husband and children of my own, grown though they might be. I go home every night after serving the missus her dinner, but I'm back by seven in the morning. I take Sundays off so I can see that my brood go to church."

An irrelevant question hit me. "Does she eat at that dining table?"

"Yes, miss. Just as though there were guests, and I serve a formal meal."

How sad!

"One more question, if you don't mind. Is John L. your brother?"

She laughed aloud. "That man? No way, miss. He's a good sort, he is—makes the lawns look good and takes good care of the birds and rabbits, but he's no kin of mine."

Another puzzle.

The girls fixed on another fact. "Rabbits?" they squealed almost in unison.

"We want to see," Ava said.

"No, ladies. You'll have to wait until John L. is here. The rabbits are his responsibility, unless one ends up in my kitchen for rabbit stew."

She said it matter-of-factly, but even I was taken aback, and Jess looked like she might cry. In fact, I could see tears inching down her cheeks. For us, rabbits were cute cuddly pets; in this household, they were a food source, like cattle and hogs. I wasn't going to make that comparison to Jess and Ava, but it told me a lot.

"Come on, girls. Time to thank Lucy and get out of her hair. David will be ready to go."

We went back to the parlor, thanked Edith and said our good-byes, assuring her she was safe, and left as quickly as we could. The minute we were in the car, David announced, "It's not dinnertime I'm ready for. It's a drink."

Jess piped up with, "Who was that man standing in the trees watching us as we drove away?"

David asked, "What man?"

"I don't know. That's why I asked."

Ava's look clearly said she thought her sister had made the story up, but I took it far more seriously. David tried to drag details out of her, but she simply couldn't describe him except to say he had one of those things that you look through and see things up close. I never said that I'd seen the man too. It was Rodney. I just filed that fact away in my mind. No reason to scare Jess any more than she was already.

"I thought it was like that whole place—creepy. I don't want to go back, even to make a chocolate cake." Jess' pronouncement had an air of finality about it, and I knew she would not be going back to Peacock Mansion.

Ava made a face at her, and at the same time David made a face at me. They were different faces entirely. Ava's was one of scorn. David's was one of alarm and concern. I shared his feelings, but we couldn't talk in front of the girls, and I couldn't tell him I recognized Rodney. So I tried to make light of it.

"Maybe he's a bird watcher."

"Or maybe he shoots peacocks with a bow and arrow," Ava responded.

Big help. Jess gave her sister a dirty look and moved as though to punch her.

"Don't hit me, little sister, or you'll be sorry."

"Girls, shall I take us home instead of to Tyler? I won't take quarreling sisters to a nice restaurant."

They chorused "no," and by the time we reached the outskirts of Tyler, the incident—and the man—had been forgotten. Except I hadn't forgotten.

Chapter Eleven

The girls were primly proper when the waiter seated us and whisked napkins onto their laps. They studied the menu carefully, until David teasingly asked, "Who wants to join me for escargot?"

"What's that?" Ava asked.

"Snails," I told her, and she made a face.

They decided on shrimp cocktail, which was pretty adventuresome for them. David did order escargot, and I chose the smoked salmon carpaccio. David ordered wine for us—white because he knew that was what I liked, in spite of the truth that red would have gone better with the grilled duck breast he ordered. I had splurged and asked for lobster; the girls agreed to split the pasta of the day— which was linguini with an Alfredo sauce. David ordered Shirley Temples for them, but Ava was a bit downcast.

"Couldn't I have a wine spritzer?"

I assured her she could not, but I also realized David had to stop thinking of her as a little girl. And so did I.

We were midway through our appetizers when the maître d' showed two women to a table on the other side of the restaurant. I gaped so long that David surreptitiously poked me.

"Earth to Kate. What do you see?"

"Mrs. Middleton."

"Oh, good. That clears everything up. Thanks."

Ava contributed, "She's mom's guest at the B&B. She and that snotty daughter of hers."

"Ava!"

"I don't care, Aunt Kate. She is snotty and all stuck up just because she's four or five years older than I am."

I gathered there'd been a social rebuff somewhere along the way.

David turned, without too much subtlety, and stared. "I can see why you thought she might be Rose Mitchum. Same type—rich lady from Highland Park or someplace similar. Odd that she's in Wheeler."

"Isn't it?" I tried but couldn't tell what they ordered, not that it would have helped me much. I did see that the daughter still seemed bored, and I thought maybe Ava was right in her assessment, even if she shouldn't have said it.

Our dinners were as good as I expected. I shared bites of lobster with the girls—Ava said she didn't like the texture, but Jess liked it, especially when I dipped it into the melted butter. For dessert, we all had parfaits.

And then we were on our way home in a silent car. Everyone was too full and tired to talk. We left Mrs. Middleton and her daughter behind, except that I remembered Donna told me she had recommended Currents to them.

I dropped David and the girls off at the house so I could go back to the Blue Plate to close and pick up the cash and receipts.

"Hate to have you walk across that meadow alone after dark."

"David, I'll be fine. I do it every night."

"I know. Maybe it's just been a funny day."

"I'll see you shortly." I closed the car door and crossed the open area to the café. The high heels didn't help at all. It rained during the night the day before, and the ground was soft. My heels sank into it, and I came close to falling. Finally, I dug out my cell phone and turned on its flashlight, focused on the ground in front of me so I didn't misstep. I didn't look up until I got close to the back door to the café and the motion detector light went on.

A few customers lingered, and a young waitress named Sallie was wiping down the empty tables and collecting condiments, getting ready to close. I set about helping her but then had to stop to check out a longtime customer.

"Looking mighty fancy, Miss Kate. High heels and all."

"Thanks, Mr. Sumner. I've been to Tyler for dinner. I couldn't work all day in shoes like this. I'm afraid you'd see me barefoot."

He laughed, and I counted out his change.

When the restaurant was empty and Sallie had gone on her way, I put the receipts and cash in my bank bag and then took paper and pen and made a list of the things that had puzzled me today:

Edith Aldridge said she never heard from the children; Rodney said they were close.

How did she know they were in the area if she didn't hear from them?

How did Steven Connell fit into things? Why was Edith in touch with him, when David hired him? How much does David trust him?

Why was Rodney in the bushes at the mansion? I thought I knew the answer to that one: he was spying. But on Edith or on us?

Why hadn't Steven reported on Rose's whereabouts? If she lived in Highland Park, that should be easy to verify.

Edith Aldridge seems contradictory in her attitude toward her stepchildren.

I sat so long pondering this list that I was afraid David would worry, so I stuffed the paper in the bag, turned out the lights, locked the front door, and slipped out the back door, locking it behind me. Grateful that I'd installed a motion detector light out there I headed home across the great open space. Something made me want to run, but the high heels prevented that, and it seemed to take forever to reach the gate, my way lit only by my phone flashlight.

The motion detector light outside the back door came on, and David stood there watching for me.

Wait! That's not David. No crutches, a ski mask, not his familiar face. This man was heavier and not quite as tall.

I screamed with all the power I could muster and kept screaming. The moneybag flew in one direction, the cell phone in another, and my heels tripped me up so that I went splat on my rear end. My first thought was if the man wanted the day's take, he was welcome to it. For a moment, stunned, I simply sat there awaiting my fate.

But the scream must have frightened him as much as he frightened me. He bolted around the other side of the house, jumping the low fence to the driveway with more agility than I thought a man his size would have.

All hell broke loose. Lights went on in the kitchen, and the girls burst out the door, screaming, "Aunt Kate! Are you all right? Where are you? Aunt Kate!"

David came behind them on his crutches, bellowing for them to get back into the house with one breath and calling me with the next.

Struggling to my feet I managed a weak, "I'm over here. I'm okay. Just frightened."

David made his way off the porch and over to me where I stood holding on to the fence to support myself, my knees shaking. "You fall?"

"Yes, but that wasn't why I screamed. There was a man in the yard, wearing a ski mask."

"Are you sure? Maybe you just thought you saw something when you fell."

That angered me enough that I got over my shakes. "I am definitely sure. Call Chester *now*!"

"I don't have my phone," he said. "Give me yours."

"It's over there on the ground somewhere," I said.

The girls had come outside by now, carefully looking around, waiting to be scolded back inside.

"The receipts! And my phone. We can't leave them out here all night."

The girls immediately began to search. Ava found the bank bag near the gate and handed it to me. Jess, meantime, was down on hands and knees, patting the ground, looking for the phone. At last she called triumphantly, "Found it. But it's muddy."

"I don't care," I said, holding out my hand. I gave David the phone, saying, "Chester is number two on speed dial."

As he punched the button, he asked, "Who's first?"

I was tempted to hit him.

Ava and Jess followed us into the kitchen. Ava remembered to lock the gate, for all the good it would do.

David was on the phone. "Chester? David Clinkscales. Kate saw a man in the backyard wearing a ski mask . . . . no, no, he's gone . . . . yes, we're all back in the house, doors locked . . . . okay, thanks."

At least he didn't say, "Kate *thinks* she saw!" I would have whacked him in the head with the bank bag. Instead, all my anger disappeared into fright and great sobs. I leaned against his chest, almost throwing him off balance on his crutches, and cried into his shirt, soaking it with my tears.

David steadied himself and stroked my hair, crutch still under his arm.

"It must have been the man Jess saw in the woods today. It was Rodney in the woods. I knew it and didn't want to scare the girls. But why is he here? What does he want?" I got the words out between great, heaving sobs.

"We don't know, but I swear we are going to find out." He turned to Ava. "Would you pour your aunt a sip of the bourbon on the high shelf in the cupboard?"

"Why does she keep it there?"

"Guess."

But Ava was climbing up on the counter, reaching for the bourbon bottle. She got a wine glass, so David reminded her, "A bit more than a thimbleful."

I crossed that fine line between tears and laughter and began to giggle. "I hope Gram isn't watching." Shouldn't have said that.

"Gram? What about Gram?" Jess tuned in at just the wrong moment.

"Oh, sweetie, just an expression. You know Gram watches over us from heaven."

"And she wouldn't like you drinking whiskey," Jess replied. She earned one of Ava's condescending looks.

Gram was looking . . . and listening. "Kate, you'll figure this out. Just be careful who you trust."

"I don't know *who* to trust," I wailed. But she was gone, and both girls and David looked at me as though I'd taken leave of my senses.

Noises in the driveway drew our attention, and through a window we could see a flashlight. "Chester's here," David announced unnecessarily.

And in a minute, Chester was at the back door, scraping his shoes on the outdoor mat. "Guy must have taken a heck of a jump and landed hard. Found big holes where his heels dug into the gravel on the driveway, and a few prints of him running down the driveway. Must have had a car parked close by." He looked me carefully. "You okay?"

"A bit shaky but okay."

"Tell me every little detail. Start with closing the café."

I did, leaving nothing out as far as I could tell. I even told him I was pretty sure it was Rodney. Then I waited for his response.

"I suspect this Rodney was trying to frighten you. If he'd been intending to hurt you, he wouldn't have run. But this is a warning. A fairly serious one." He turned to David. "You got a gun?"

"In Dallas." David's tone was wry. "Didn't think I needed it out here in the peaceful country."

Chester scoffed. "Hah! City boy, don't know much about East Texas. You licensed for concealed?"

David nodded.

"I'll get you a pistol. Keep it with you all the time, and stay by Kate as much as you can. I'm not sure which one of you is in danger. Maybe both."

Jess began to sob quietly, and Chester turned to her. "Little lady, you're perfectly fine. Nobody's gonna hurt a fine child like you." His voice was soothing, but Jess looked skeptical.

I sat down and drew her, gangly as she was getting, on-to my lap, stroking her hair and talking softly to her, and she calmed. Ava looked bored.

Chester declined offers of coffee or beer—"Carolyn would shoot me with my own gun!"—and left shortly af-ter. "If you hear my siren briefly, don't be alarmed. Just my way of telling Carolyn I'm on my way. Don't hurt either to let your masked friend know I was here. Lock all the doors and windows and leave some lights on."

We obeyed, and then I made the girls hot cocoa and tucked them in bed. Jess begged to sleep in my bed, and Ava volunteered to put her sleeping bag on the floor. I sat with them until Jess was gently snoring.

David sat at the kitchen table. "Let's talk."

My list! I'd forgotten all about it. And I was too tired to talk about it.

"Tomorrow. I'm too tired tonight. I made a list tonight at the café, and I'll go over it with you tomorrow. Right now, my money is on Rodney, though I'm surprised he's agile enough to jump that fence." I stared off into space for a second, beginning to doubt my sure identification of Rodney. "Could it have been Steven Connell?"

"Steven Connell? Kate, he's a licensed PI, not a thug."

"He's for hire, isn't he? I've been uneasy about him ever since Edith Aldridge said he sometimes reports to her. You hired him, didn't you? But how much do you know about him? How long have you known him?"

"Come on. He was recommended by a lawyer friend, and I've been using him about three years. Reliable. Trustworthy. Let me see the list."

"Okay, but I'm going to bed." I knew if I didn't go right then, we'd talk all night. And I was about to fall over.

That night, curled around Jess, I thought about these children and what a difference they'd made in my life. In Dallas, I could never have imagined myself with such protective feelings about children, but now, if anyone threatened them, I'd fight bear to keep them safe. Sometimes, if you let children into your heart, they have a softening effect. *I wonder if Donna feels that way. How will she react when she hears about tonight?*

* * * *

Tom and Henry came back from camping earlier—a spring rain dampened their enthusiasm for fishing, although I reminded them fish bite best in the rain. Tom looked glum, and I surmised it was Henry's idea to give it up. They joined David and the girls in ordering chicken-fried pork cutlets, David's new favorite. I was nibbling on mine between taking orders and running the cash register.

"When's Ma coming home?" Henry asked.

"It's Mom, not Ma, and I have no idea." Tom took another bite of his pork cutlet.

Donna didn't get to Wheeler until almost six Sunday night. She came straight to the café, bursting through the front doors just after Henry's question. Her hair done, her makeup professional, her outfit new and stylish. She almost glowed with self-satisfaction. A huge bag from Neiman-Marcus hung on one arm. "Hi, everyone. Miss me?"

They were good kids. They answered with a chorus of happiness, and I hoped they really meant it.

"I've got goodies for everyone." She pulled out adorable matching outfits of short tops and miniskirts for the girls. Jess was delighted, Ava less so. She did not need to match her little sister. *Ah, Donna, when will you learn about your girls?*

For Tom and Henry, she had matching heavy wool sweaters, obviously on sale now that sweater season was over. "Mine looks awful big," Henry said tentatively.

"It will just fit next fall," Donna assured him. "I believe I'll have the tuna salad plate. Watching my figure, you know."

"So am I," Tom retorted, leaving in the air whether he meant it as a criticism or compliment.

Donna, of course, took it as a criticism and huffed a bit.

Jess had poured out the story of our adventure last night to Tom as soon as she saw him. Nothing would do but that she repeat it for her mother, in spite of Tom's efforts to hush her.

"What?" Donna's voice rose octaves. "You put my daughters in danger?"

"Not purposely." I was more than a little defensive.

"I should have known. Trouble follows you like a magnet. After this, Tom, we can't both leave town at the same time."

I sighed. *There go Tom's fishing and camping trips with Henry, and Henry needs them so much!*

"I want to spend the night with Aunt Kate." Jess' look challenged her mother directly.

Donna looked at me, then at her daughter. "No, darling, it's not safe. What if that bad man comes back?"

"David will keep us safe. He has a gun now."

Out of the mouths of babes!

Donna shrieked. "No, no one may stay there if there's a gun in the house." This time she glared at me.

David kept silent through all this, but he finally spoke to Jess. She was sitting next to him, and he reached out an arm to hold her closer. "The bad guy will go away pretty soon, and I'll get rid of the gun. Then you can come back. Okay?"

Jess didn't look happy, but she nodded.

Donna looked at David with resentment, and I knew she was thinking he wasn't family and should be interfering.

Dinner was effectively ruined. Conversation fell flat, and we all picked at our food. The Bryson family left shortly after, Donna striding out the door as usual with no mention of payment. As he passed me, Tom gave me a hug and said, "I'll settle up tomorrow. You don't have to feed us."

How did my difficult sister get such a good guy? And why did he stay with her? I knew the answer to that question. He loved his children beyond measure.

* * * *

David went along home, and I stayed to close. This time David gave me strict instructions to call when I was leaving and handed me a flashlight.

"Better than that puny thing on your phone. You could use this one to club someone if necessary."

"I sincerely hope that won't be necessary." I gave him a quick kiss and said, "I'll call in about an hour."

Less than forty-five minutes later, the last customer left, Sallie had cleaned the tables while I counted the day's take and put the credit receipts in order. After she left, I locked the front door, turned out the lights, and called David from the kitchen to tell him I was leaving. Then, kitchen lights off, and I slipped out the back door, locking it behind me.

I had on better walking shoes this night, and the flashlight created a wide arc of light around me. Made me a great target, but it also made me feel safe. I couldn't help but wonder if beyond that circle of light, someone waited in the shadows. *Stop scaring yourself, Kate!* I looked up to see David, crutches propped under his arm, standing at the gate waiting for me. I assumed the gun was handy . . . but it was concealed. Huggles stood beside him, barking a welcome.

When I reached the gate, David gathered me in a big hug while Huggles jumped, anxiously to be in on the loving.

"Me first, buddy," David said.

We turned, and he led me into the safety of my own kitchen.

Chapter Twelve

David and I finally had a chance that evening to go over my list privately. He agreed that both Rodney and Edith were contradictory and probably both distorting the truth on each side. He even seemed willing to take my opinion of James on good faith. But he remained stubbornly convinced that Steven Connell was to be trusted.

"What about Rose? Why hasn't Steven found out more about her? Surely that can't be hard."

"He's determined she's away from her residence. Since she left before he came on board, he's had no chance to trace her."

"Can't he check her cell phone, get her license plates, check the home phone?"

"I'm sure he's done what he can—phone records require a warrant, and we have no reason to request a warrant. I think he has the license number—most PIs can get such information easily. But where would he look? He's checked airlines—she hasn't used her passport. She could be anywhere."

"What about her husband?"

"He goes to work every day, says 'No comment' when Steven tries to talk to him. So does the rather large house staff."

"She can't stay away forever." One niggling thought was in the back of my mind, and I hatched a plan but I didn't tell David.

"You've already decided he's unreliable and are on a fishing trip to prove it. It's supposed to work the other way around."

"What about Halstead?"

David sighed in exasperation. "He's obsessed with Walter Aldridge's murder. Thinks if we solve the old murder, we'll prevent a new one and solve this mystery. But he's also convinced that Edith Aldridge did murder her husband and got away with it. Makes no sense—why would she ask you to investigate and work with Steven if that were true? She has been uncooperative with Halstead."

"You know," I said, "I just might dig into that myself, see what I can find online. Does your office have the court records?"

"They were in the file you gave to Halstead."

"Can they get more copies?"

"I suppose so. I'll probably have to go to the city to do some digging. Wish this darn cast would come off." He didn't sound at all enthusiastic. "Can we please talk about my new house now—our new house?"

Oops! The possessive pronoun had gone from his to ours. I spent the next hour looking at architectural plans. The architect had sent them to David by courier, and David was excited about them—but of course I couldn't make heads or tails of them, and David had to explain everything to me.

The house was wooden inside and out, with a tin roof and double-paned windows for energy efficiency. It was a thousand square feet, plus an added sleeping porch for summer with sliding double-paned glass doors that could be closed in cooler weather.

"When it's really cold, we'll have to sleep at your house, of course."

He has all this planned out! While I'm worrying about men in bushes and conniving stepchildren, he's been focusing on this house. Seemed I had two choices—I chose to put my arms around him in a huge hug.

"See? There's a stairway to the loft. It's pretty skinny, I admit, but it has a railing and real risers. It's not a ladder."

He wanted so badly for me to like it, how could I resist? He showed me where his office would be and outlined plans for a small but really efficient kitchen, cleverly disguised storage space that would never hold enough to suit me for permanent living, a seating area around an old-fashioned wood stove. I would always be a guest in this house, but that was okay.

"Security?" I asked.

"Alarm system, deadbolts, motion-sensitive outdoor lights. And it's not on wheels so nobody can cart it away when I'm not there. It will sit on a concrete pad."

I didn't mention that alarm systems were of minimal use when help was so far away.

"So when do you start?"

"Demolition people are going to bulldoze the old house tomorrow. Cary's promised to take me out there in the afternoon."

At last, talked out, we went to sleep. But as I drifted off, I thought, *Gram's house is probably 1,700 square feet! I'm glad I won't have to leave it.* I also sketched out in my mind a plan for the next day. It would be busy.

* * * *

Next morning David asked about my plans for the day. He would be home all morning doing some work but would go to see his cabin demolished as soon as Cary could go after school . . . unless, of course, I wanted to go earlier.

"David, I love that you're so excited about this, but I'm not much into watching bulldozers at work. I'll go when the new house begins to take shape."

"You're sure?"

I put my arms around his neck, kissed him soundly, and said, "I'm sure." I had plans of my own but I didn't say that.

David usually didn't get up early enough to see me off to the café, but he had this morning, so I wasn't surprised when he showed up early—seven thirty—for his breakfast. By eight he was headed back home. "Going to do some work," he said.

"Researching Edith's husband's murder."

He looked startled. "Maybe a little, but I do have other clients, you know."

"Okay. See you at lunch."

The morning kept me busy with orders and inventory checking. Lunch was upon us before I knew it, and the café got unusually busy. When David came in, I didn't have time to check with him on his morning's work—besides, he probably would have thought I had no need to know. We talked briefly, and he went back to the house, suggesting I bring supper home when I could, rather than both of us eating at the café. I readily agreed, and he left the menu choice up to me.

"I'll be late," I said. "Can't ask Marj to close too often."

"No problem. I'll open some wine."

"Sounds good. I can hardly wait." I blew him a kiss as he left.

In truth, I had an errand on my mind. I'd already called Edith Aldridge to ask if I could come by about two or a bit after. She'd protested it was awfully early for tea, but I assured her I didn't need tea. I just had some questions. All this, of course, after asking how she was and making sure she hadn't had any more scares.

"I don't scare easily," she said, once more adopting that frosty tone. "But there have been no more incidents."

I left the café, promising to be back well before the supper rush, and arrived at the mansion just after two, armed only with a pen and the small legal pad I'd stuck in my bag.

Edith Aldridge greeted me as cordially as always, but this time she was dressed in a gray pantsuit—maybe ten years out of date, but what was once an expensive pantsuit. The jacket topped a lilac silk shirt, and heavy silver beads hung around her neck. Perhaps she instinctively knew that gold wouldn't have worked with those colors—but I liked the silver.

"I've an early dinner appointment," she explained, "but I assume we'll be well through by five."

"Yes, ma'am. I have to be back at the café before then. But I just have some questions. I've given this a lot of thought, and I think if we're going to figure out why the stepchildren are all back in the area, we need to find out the truth about your late husband's murder."

"The truth?" she murmured. "I told you. I was acquitted."

"Of course, but if we're going to figure out what's going on today, we need to figure out who did kill him. After all, Mrs. Aldridge, I have a stake in this too. David Clinkscales is a very special person in my life. And he was nearly killed. His house was destroyed."

She looked at me with what I thought was honesty. "I guess I've been so wrapped up in my own troubles, that I hadn't realized the enormity of what happened to David."

Without an invitation, I settled myself in a chair, whipped the pad and pencil out of my bag, and said, "How did you meet Mr. Aldridge?"

She didn't sit but began to pace. When I asked my question, she let out a sound that was half laughter, half harshness. "How did you meet Mr. Aldridge?" she repeated, as though the irony of the question amused her.

"I was a cocktail waitress at the old Baker Hotel in Dallas. Dirt poor, but they gave you what I'd call skimpy cocktail outfits, and I was good-looking in those days, if I do say so. But nobody had taught me manners or grammar, until Walter took me on as a project. You might say I was Eliza to his Henry Higgins. He taught me to dress, speak, eat properly, even dance—he made a lady out of me, and I was always grateful. But once I was 'finished'—his term, not mine—he found other Pygmalion-like subjects. In other words, he cheated on me, including financially, and railed that I couldn't run the house on the reduced budget he gave me. And the older he got, the more he drank. I suspected all along that he was in financial trouble.

"I used to lie in bed and listen to him roaming about downstairs, sometimes throwing things—I always hoped it wasn't the Limoges he'd given his first wife, Alicia. Several times I thought I heard him fall. His best friend at night was a bottle of bourbon."

"What happened to Alicia?" It was an interruption but an important one.

"She committed suicide. She was the mother of his children, and he drove her to that point. I know he did. I think they should all hate him, but they hate me."

I squelched a "Wow!" and managed to say calmly, "Let's get back to the night he was killed. What did you see or hear?"

"That night I woke and realized he hadn't come upstairs. By then I kept a derringer for self-protection, and this night I grabbed it and put it in my pocket. I found him slumped over his desk, a pistol lying in front of him. It was a stupid move that I regret to this day, but I picked up the gun and smelled it. It had been fired recently—what else could I have expected?"

This tale was getting more bizarre. I itched to check it out on the web, but for now I was a captive audience and, I admit, mesmerized by the calm recital of her story. "What happened next?"

Her gaze had gone far away, and it took a minute for her to call herself back to reality. "I called the police, of course. They told me not to touch anything, but it was already too late for that. Walter usually kept his desk neat as a pin, no stacks of paper, nothing to indicate that he ever did any work there. But this night, papers were strewn everywhere. Even his checkbook was open, and it appeared he'd started to write a check. It was dated, and he'd written in thirty-thousand dollars—I was appalled. But he hadn't yet made it out to anyone. I looked without touching, though it was a terrible temptation."

I let her rest a minute as she seemed lost in her own thoughts. At last, after a glance at my watch, I urged her to continue.

"The sheriff came—I don't remember what his name was, not this persnickety young fellow we have now—and a couple of deputies. They went over the entire house, gathered up lots of Walter's papers, and told me no one could enter the office, put that awful yellow tape all across the door like a spider web. Then they questioned me until the wee hours of the morning—what had I heard? Seen? Didn't I know my husband had at least one visitor? What was unusual? I told them about the mess on the desk and the unsigned check."

"They didn't arrest you, did they?"

She smoothed one pant leg nervously. "No, not exactly. They advised me to call my lawyer."

"David?" I squeaked.

"No, this would have been Walter's lawyer, but he was the only one I knew. I fired him after the trial and hired David much later when I thought I needed a lawyer."

I wanted to ask how she found David, but I was getting ahead of the story . . . and the afternoon was flitting away. "Did you call the children?"

"Rose and James were at home; Rodney was away, and I asked the sheriff to notify him." She looked at her watch for the eighth or ninth time. "I don't know that any of this has been any help, but I really do have to be on my way. We can talk again if you want."

I wanted. "Yes, I'd like that. May I call you?"

"That would be fine. One other thing. They did find signs that someone broke in through the French doors behind Walter's desk."

Major information! "Was Walter shot in the back or" — I hated to say it — "in the face or chest?" *In other words, did he see it coming?*

"There was a single bullet hole in his chest." She said this as impassively as she'd recounted the rest of the story. "Sheriff said it was a well-placed bullet. The shooter knew what he was doing."

I was relieved he wasn't shot in the head. A single well-placed bullet in the chest by a skilled shooter. A professional hit? Questions ran through my mind, but I knew when it was time to leave, and I rose.

"I don't want to keep you, and I have to get back to the café. But thank you, Mrs. Aldridge. You've been a huge help, and we'll get to the bottom of this yet."

In the car, I reviewed my unasked questions. Where was a recluse going for such an early dinner, and why was it so important? Where was Rodney when his father was shot? Was Walter a gambler, with debts? Did he associate with what Gram would have called "the wrong kind of women?" The head of a high-priced call-girl operation

might have sought overdue payment. Definitely we needed to look into Walter much more thoroughly. What was
Steven Connell doing to earn his keep? A vague memory
came to me with a start. Hadn't she told us before she was
out walking with her dog and didn't hear the shots? What
dog? None in sight now. Did she forget her first story? Oh,
what a tangled web we weave . . . .

Back at the café, I put on an apron, sent Marj home, and
threw myself into dinner prep. Supper hour was well under way when Mrs. Middleton and her daughter walked
into the restaurant . . . and right into my trap, although she
almost sidetracked me by greeting me before I could say
"Welcome."

"Hello, dear, how are you? Your sister was going to
serve us meatloaf tonight. And I thought we were getting
gourmet meals. I never ate meatloaf in my life, and I don't
intend to start now."

Thrown off a bit, I said, "You should come here for
lunch tomorrow and have a meatloaf sandwich. There's
nothing better. I use the same recipe Donna does." It
occurred to me to wonder what this unlikely
mother/daughter duo did all day. I'd have to ask Donna.

Meantime, Mrs. Middleton dismissed my sandwich
suggestion with a wave of her hand. "We came to have
that pork cutlet you've added to the menu. I used to eat
those as a child, and I want to see if yours hold up."

Nothing like putting me on the spot.

Melissa almost interrupted her mother to say, "I'll have
a chef's salad. Oil and vinegar, please."

Now there was a girl watching her weight. Probably
didn't want to grow pudgy like her mama.

I went off to turn the orders in, and when they were
ready I came back carrying two plates. "Chef's salad for
you," placing the salad in front of Melissa, "and chicken-
fried pork for you, Mrs. Mitchum."

I almost dropped the plate she jumped so suddenly. She was halfway out of her chair, when she sank back down, looked at me blankly, and said, "What did you call me?"

First smile I think I'd ever seen from her daughter.

"You are Rose Mitchum, aren't you?"

She looked at her plate and muttered, "Rodney will kill me." Then she looked up at me and asked how I knew.

"An educated guess. I'm a friend of your stepmother's."

"Hah! That woman has no friends, young lady. Beware, she's using you for something."

A thought that had definitely occurred to me before.

"Rodney was in a few days ago, and I know James lives in the next town over. What brings you all together? A family reunion?"

"You might say that," Rose said. "If Rodney comes in the next few days, please don't tell him I was here."

I practiced my surprised look. "Really? Why, I got the impression from him and from Edith that all of you were close." The use of the casual reference to Edith was a brilliant touch, I thought.

Melissa piped up for the first time. "Like vipers in a pit," she said without expression and dove into her salad. I noticed that she had impeccable manners and figured she was off to the modern equivalent of finish school, although so many women's colleges, like Sweetbriar, were closing these days. I was sure Mama Rose would find something for the darling daughter with whom she had a difficult relationship.

I left them to finish their dinner. During a lull, I thought about the Aldridge family—sure there was money and a big house involved, but they were the prickliest people I'd ever met. They made Donna and me look glued at the hip.

When I cleared their table, Rose Mitchum had the grace to say that her pork was every bit as good as she remembered.

"Thank you. Because you've been such good customers and so helpful to me, your dinners are on the house tonight."

"Oh, no, you mustn't do that." All the proper protests.

"I'm the owner, and I can do that. Y'all come back for meatloaf sandwiches tomorrow."

Rose Mitchum smiled vaguely, murmured "Yes, of course," and reached for her sweater. After they were gone, I found she had left me a ten-dollar tip. Not as sophisticated as she wanted to be or she'd have known you don't tip the owner. On the other hand, maybe she thought I really needed the money.

The next morning Donna called to report that the Middletons, mother and daughter, had checked out, without paying their bill. "Mrs. Middleton stiffed me, Kate." Donna muttered something about meatloaf, and said, "I think I'm giving up the gourmet dinner option."

"Good plan, Donna. By the way, her name is Rose Mitchum."

"What does that mean? But I was already was already pressing end on my cell phone.

Chapter Thirteen

Normally, I would be in a hurry to get home and tell David all that I'd learned that day. But a part of me was angry with him. No, that wasn't the right word. I was resentful. I resented his absorption in his new house and his lack of interest in the affairs of Edith Aldridge. He was the one who got a retainer fee from her, who was her legal representative, and I was the unpaid one doing all the work. And wondering about Edith and truth. I would go into a brightly lit kitchen with pictures spread all over the table, along with architectural plans, and a man semi-drunk on excitement. I took a deep breath, opened the gate, and stomped my way to the back door.

Instead, the kitchen was almost dark, the stove light being the only one on. With a clutch at my heart, I opened the door and called, "David?"

He answered quietly. He was sitting at the kitchen table in the gloom, a half empty glass of wine in his hand. "I'm right here."

Relieved, I asked, "What are you doing in the dark?"

"Thinking."

"About?"

"About you and Edith Aldridge and my new house. Sorting out my priorities."

And who or what comes out on top of the list? I didn't ask aloud but waited for him to respond.

His voice was low and soft. "I've had them all wrong. Jennifer always told me that I got carried away with what interested me and didn't pay attention to what those around me cared about. I thought she was selfish, because she didn't care about the things I did. But now I think I was the one who was selfish." He stood and stretched. I noticed he didn't have the crutches. A cane hung on the back of his chair, but he placed one hand lightly on the table for balance.

I set down the supper I'd brought — two BLT sandwiches — and poured myself a glass of wine. Then I sat at the table.

"Cary took me to the doctor today. No more crutches. He says it's time I learned to walk again on my own two feet." He gestured toward the cane. "And I can drive. I drove us home, just to get the feel of it again, while Cary was in the car. Cary said an interesting thing. Said he guessed it was the last day he'd be driving me, and he'd miss it, but he was glad I could get back to being me. That struck me, that phrase: 'back to being me.'"

I waited, almost holding my breath.

"I haven't been me. I've been some guy I wish I didn't know, some guy who thought the world owed him because he'd been beaten up and his house burned. I used plans for the new house, like a spoiled child demanding his own way. I ignored Edith, who is my professional responsibility, and I ignored you, letting you do whatever had to be done with Edith. If you left me, now that I'm almost whole again, I wouldn't blame you. But I'd be devastated."

I was stunned. But I didn't think I should say, "Oh, you haven't been that bad," or "It's all right." Because it wasn't, and it was the truth. I'd been waiting for David Clinkscales to come back. "I won't leave . . . or ask you to leave."

A wry chuckle. "That's right. I'm in your house. And I have no other house to go to."

"You have an apartment in Dallas, but don't go there."

"As a matter of fact, I am going there for a day or two. I need to get the Aldridge records, and I want to check with Steven. You're right. Something's funny there." He wandered over to the counter, keeping close enough to furniture that he could steady himself if necessary. "What's for supper?"

Now I wished I'd brought a real supper. "Sandwiches. BLT."

"Perfect. Let's eat. I'm famished."

And so we ate and talked. He couldn't believe that Rose Mitchum had been right under our noses for almost a week.

"And Steven didn't find that out? I presume she had a car, with a license plate he knows. He knew she was in the area. How could he miss?"

"That's one of my questions: how did he know they were in the area? How did Edith know? I didn't ask today because I'd overstayed my welcome."

"Today?"

"Oh, yeah. I didn't get to that part yet. I went to see Edith, asked her to recount the night of her husband's murder. She told an interesting tale, compared herself first to Pygmalion and then portrayed herself as an abused wife — emotionally, not physically, though she claims she lived in fear. Her story held together — at least it was consistent. She says the French door to Walter's office was broken, and that as he was shot he was writing a check for thirty thousand dollars."

"I've heard some of that before," David said. "After all, I am her lawyer. Even if I haven't been acting like it."

"I have so many questions, I need to make another list."

He clapped a hand to his forehead and said, "God help me." But he was smiling — sort of.

"Can't you get court records in Canton? And shouldn't the sheriff have records of the investigation?"

"Who knows, after thirty years? And the question is, will he share them? I can poke around and find out. If court records are in Canton, why did John and whatever-his-name is beat the shit out of me to get them?"

I shook my head. "Maybe they didn't know that. Maybe they thought you had more. Maybe they're so disreputable, they didn't think anyone would let them look. I didn't even think that those records might be so close, so probably they didn't either."

"I didn't think of it either. But I still need to go to Dallas, check in at my office. I'll get copies of the copies there and bring them back. Better than sitting in the courthouse studying them. I'll stay overnight, maybe longer, but I'll keep you posted."

"I'm getting on the Internet tomorrow to see what I can find out about Walter Aldridge. You know, Edith has kept us so busy with threats and the children's conspiracies that we've — at least I've — lost track of the original question: Who killed Walter Aldridge and why?"

We turned in shortly after that and had a glorious reunion. But I thought it was good that David was going to Dallas. He was taking responsibility, which was the David I knew and loved.

* * * *

I stayed at the café almost all day the next day, running home only to give Huggles some food and a bit of exercise and feed Wynona. The cat hadn't taken to having David in the house — cats can be so choosy with their affections. The result was that she hid a lot and didn't get the attention she craved. She seemed to know that he was gone and purred and posed, wrapping herself around my leg as I knelt to feed her. I stroked her velvet head and loved on her, but then, to her disgust, went outside to throw a Frisbee for Huggles.

Back at the café I typed Walter Aldridge's name into Google and came up with several entries. Alas, no Wikipedia page, which was where I always liked to start when looking something up. Not reliable, I know, but great for an overview.

I read the obituary, even an entry in the *Handbook of Texas* history, assorted other newspaper clippings, and gradually a picture of Walter emerged. I almost laughed when I realized that I had spent so much time wondering who killed Walter that I didn't even know how he amassed his fortune. He was a banker with a big bank in Dallas, now defunct. From the obituary I learned that he had been a civic leader, active in Rotary, the Elks, the Republican Party, and the Presbyterian Church. But I also learned that he was born on a North Texas farm and clawed (well, they didn't use that word but it was clear) his way to the top, doing a variety of menial jobs, each one a step up the ladder. He and Edith had been married twenty years when he was killed. Sounded to me like twenty years of misery, perhaps for both of them. He was older than she — fifty-two when he died to her thirty-eight — and was preceded in death by his first wife, Alicia Campbell Aldridge. He was survived by his wife and three children.

There were the expected stories with headlines that blared, "Prominent banker shot at country home" and the like. It tickled me to think of the mansion, as we had begun to call it, as a country home. Inevitably, they concluded with something like, "The local police have no leads," or "Law officials are questioning Mrs. Aldridge." Of course, the spouse is always first in line. No mention of the broken French door, the desk, the check he was writing, none of what Edith had told me.

But there were other articles—one with an image of what I presumed was Walter hiding his face with his fedora as he was led away. The headline read, "Banker caught in gambling raid." One of my suspicions confirmed.

Another article, without an image, led off with the line, "Is embezzlement a problem at a local big bank?" The bank wasn't named, but the article was clear enough, stating that the bank president had gambling debts. The picture of Walter that was emerging wasn't all that pretty.

A few pictures showed Walter at various banquets, receptions, museum previews, and the like—places a prominent citizen would want to be seen. Often as not, one beautiful woman or another, all younger than Edith was at the time, was seen standing quite close to him, never clinging, never touching, but always there.

About four I turned off the computer, locked up the copious notes I'd taken, and told Marj I was going for a walk to clear my head.

"You been at that thing all day. Something serious?"

"You might say that, but nothing to worry about." *At least not for you, but a lot for me to worry about.*

I walked for half an hour, wandering down one side of the main street, almost to the edge of town, and back up the other. I thought of dropping in on Donna at Tremont House, but I figured she'd blame me for the loss of her guests, so I just kept going. It felt good to stretch and be out in the fresh air.

I did a lot of thinking, but mostly what I came up with was that another visit to James should be next on my agenda. I wanted some honest memories about growing up in that household, what his father was like, and what he remembered about the night Walter was killed. I didn't think James would play games with me.

Back at the café, I put on a clean apron and prepared for the evening. Nora was the main cook, and Sallie was on duty, so I alternated between taking orders and plating dinners. It wasn't a busy evening, but there was a steady enough run of customers to make me happy. To my surprise, James Aldridge came in about six fifteen with his girlfriend.

"James. This is a nice surprise. Must be mental telepathy."

He ducked, like a shy boy. "Oh, oh. Shelly here wanted to go out to dinner, and I told her this is as fancy as it gets. Kate, this is Shelly. Shelly, Kate, who owns this place."

We exchanged greetings, said the usual "Nice to meet you," and I showed them to the corner table, where many infamous conversations had been held. No, I wasn't going to grill James tonight. I just wanted them to have a quiet, happy evening.

"Can I have a beer?" James asked.

"Sorry. Not unless you want to take your dinner to my house next door. I don't make that offer to all customers."

He laughed. "I'm sure not, but I'll settle for iced tea."

Shelly chimed in with, "Me, too."

They both studied the menu. Shelly asked for chicken-fried steak with mashed potatoes and greens, and James followed, saying "Sounds good to me."

"Just like your sister. She loved it too when she was here."

"Rose? Here?"

"Under an assumed name, but I figured it out. Said you all grew up eating chicken-fried."

"We did. Dad had a thing for it, and we had a country woman for a cook."

"Well, let's see if mine can live up to that." I went to turn their orders in.

When I came back with their orders, James asked, "Can you sit and visit a minute?"

Ordinarily, it was against house rules to visit with customers, other than family, while they ate, but I made yet another exception. It was slow enough Sallie could handle things if I took the cash register. I sat down, saying, "Just for a minute. I want you to savor your dinner."

"We will," he promised and cut off a bit of steak. He chewed with his eyes off in the air, as though he were making an important decision. Have you ever watched the expression on judges' faces on those TV cooking shows? That's how he looked.

I waited for his verdict.

"Better than what I remember," he said. "Shell?"

"Absolutely delicious." She twitted him on the nose with her fork, leaving a blob of gravy. He grinned, wiped it away, and they shared a private moment.

I looked away, then took a deep breath and asked, "Shelly, what do you do in Edom?"

"Clean up after James," she said with a laugh. "It's a full-time job. Painters are notoriously sloppy, but he's the worst. He'd paint in the buff if I let him. No, I clean, cook, do the laundry, all that mundane stuff."

James took her hand. "She's actually a pretty good poet, beginning to get some stuff published in small literary journals. I'm really proud of her."

I watched them. They were happy and devoted to each other. I doubted that was true of his brother and sister and their spouses. *Kate, stop judging.*

"James, I want you two to enjoy your dinner, so I don't want to ask you any questions tonight, but might I come see you tomorrow, either right after the breakfast rush or the noon one?"

"Of course. Afternoon might be better. I usually do my best work in the morning. Say, about two? I can come here if you want."

Better to be on his turf where he's comfortable. "No, I think your studio will be fine. If it's as nice as today, we can walk and talk."

"Sounds like a deal. I'll look forward to it . . . well, maybe, depending on what you want to talk about."

"There's only one elephant in the room right now," I said as I rose to leave.

They lingered over dinner, but when I could see they were almost through I brought them two pieces of chocolate thunder cake a la mode. "On the house," I said.

"You don't have to do that, Kate," Shelly protested.

"No, but I want to make sure you come back."

"We will. I'll prod old stick-in-the-mud here to get us out of our routine. I like to eat at home but not every night."

They left after finishing their cake. "See you tomorrow," James said, and Shelly said, "I hope I'll get a chance to say hello."

"Me too."

She held out her hand and said, "Truly nice to meet you. James liked you the day you came to talk to him. Usually he doesn't tell me anything about visitors."

"I liked him too. And now I want to get to know you better." I reached and gave her a huge hug.

After they left, the crowd really dwindled. I ate one piece of chicken-fried chicken—the thigh, my favorite—and a salad, bussed the tables with Sallie and collected the day's tickets. We were out of there early, eight forty-five, but it was still dark when I started across the meadow, and I got out my flashlight.

I had that eerie feeling of being watched again, but I put my head down, watched where I planted my feet, and kept going. Huggles was waiting by the gate, which was immense reassurance to me. He was wagging his tail, so he sensed nothing awry in the night.

With relief, I let us both into the kitchen, locked the door, and turned on the alarm system. Safe and snug in my own home, though I missed David. I knew all along I'd get too used to him being there at night.

I hadn't been home too long when he called. We exchanged news of the day, with me reporting on my web explorations of Walter, his gambling and womanizing, my unexpected visit with James and Shelly, and my plans to talk to James. He countered that he had court records in a new briefcase, ready to bring back, and had cleared up some things on other unrelated cases.

"It's a good thing I came in. I've let too many loose ends slide. Settled a divorce case out of court, and got approval on a new will from another client. I have a lot of work to do when I get back."

"Hmmm. When is that?" My voice was sleepy and probably unintentionally had a "come hither" sound to it, as though I could ever be that provocative.

"Kate, don't do that to me. I'll do all I can to be home tomorrow night. I have to clean up a few more things at the office."

I liked his use of the word "home." We talked longer that night — about an hour and a half — than we had in the whole time since he was beaten. And he didn't once mention the new house. I went to bed with a happy feeling.

Chapter Fourteen

Huggles barked and woke me about two in the morning. There's something about a dog's bark — when he's telling me there's a critter in the backyard, I murmur, "Good dog," roll over, and go back to sleep. But this bark was different — a deep growl in his throat, followed by frantic barking. He ran to me in bed, licked my face, and then ran back to the dark kitchen. I stumbled along behind, just in time to hear someone try the doorknob. Who would think I'd left it unlocked?

In panic, we don't always — ever? — act with good sense. Without thinking I flipped on the lights, only to realize that meant I couldn't see whoever was out there and they had a full view of me in my T-shirt and underpants. Flipped the light off again.

Huggles ran to the front of the house, and I did the first thing right. When Huggles woke me, I'd thought to grab the cell phone by my bed. Now, in the dark of the hall, I pushed the speed dial button for Chester.

"Chester Grimes," he mumbled.

"Someone outside my house, Chester."

He was immediately alert. "On my way."

I huddled in the hall, listening and watching as my canine protector went from one end of the house to the other, still growling, still barking. Wynona sensed the unease and crept out of the bedroom to sit close to me.

I wondered if this person would break in this time. Lord knows it wouldn't have been hard in that old house—a tap on a window and he was in, though I'd installed a dead bolt on the kitchen door and hung the key on a hook slightly out of reach. The front door had two dead bolts, and the only keys were on my key ring. Chester had warned me about fire hazard, and I kept meaning to get extra keys.

I held my breath, waiting for sounds from outside. Sometimes I thought I heard footsteps; other times I told myself it was my imagination. The night seemed perfectly silent, and Chester seemed perfectly slow. Then, like a merciful sound, I heard that slight "bleep" that law enforcement calls give as an announcement they've arrived. He came quietly, not giving whoever it was time to get away but putting him on alert. In retrospect, I thought maybe he shouldn't have even done that, but I would never tell Chester.

There were running sounds, Chester shouting, a motor gunned, and then Chester turned on his siren full blast and they were off on a chase.

I moved to the kitchen and sat shaking in one of the chairs. By now I'd turned all the lights on, inside and out. Wynona, probably figuring the excitement was over, stalked back to the bedroom, but Huggles came and sat with his head on my knee, eyes looking up at me intently, as though trying to tell me what he heard.

"I know, boy. You're a good protector, and I thank you." I buried my face in his thick coat, and he rewarded me with lavish kisses to my face. Then I ran to put on a pair of shorts before Chester came back.

I waited for what seemed like forever. The siren sound had faded, and the night was once again silent. I was too scared to even stand up and look out the kitchen door. Finally, Chester called my cell phone.

"Lost him. But I got his license number. I'll be there in ten minutes."

Ten minutes! He must have followed that guy a good ways out of town, probably twisting and turning on back roads, which made me think it was someone who knew those county roads. When Chester did come to the back door, he was winded and flustered. I opened the door, got him seated at the table, and asked, "Coffee or beer?"

"You got whiskey?"

"A bit."

"Two fingers. Neat. And don't tell Carolyn."

For the first time I grinned. "Of course not." I gave him his whiskey — more like three fingers — and sat waiting.

"I'm too old and too slow for this kind of thing," he said sorrowfully. "Makes me think I should turn in my badge. Whoever he is, he's a damn good driver. And he knows this county, the back roads. I couldn't push myself or my car to keep up with him."

"Maybe it was the car," I said. "You need to request a better one." This wasn't answering my questions, but I could tell Chester was filled with self-doubt, and I felt sorry for him. David would have said, "Get to the point, man!"

He did, finally, get to the point. "Maybe I shouldn't have announced my arrival. Maybe I was afraid of a confrontation — a shootout."

"Chester, you can't second-guess yourself. Tell me what you did see and learn." You'd have thought I was interrogating him, instead of the other way around.

He took a deep breath and another sip of whiskey. "Tall guy, not thin, not really good shape. Must've been in the backyard because he jumped the fence, but it's a low fence.

Even I could jump it. And I was out of my car by the time he hit the highway. Had my gun ready but, hell, I just really don't want to use it. Yelled for him to stop, but he jumped in a dark car parked not far from where I was. I jumped in mine, made a U-turn, and followed him. Godamighty, I bet we got up to ninety miles an hour, on twisty back roads so that I wasn't even sure I could find my way back."

He fumbled around in a pocket and pulled out a crumpled piece of paper. "But here's his license. L5X 6T2. I can run it in the morning. But by now, he's probably gotten rid of the car." Chester pulled a huge, pure white handkerchief out of his pocket and mopped his brow. Then he took another sip of whiskey. Then he sat in silence, and so did I.

Finally I ventured, "What next?"

"I don't rightly know. I'll report this to Halstead. I also think we have to put a watch on your house. For instance, I don't want you coming from the café alone after dark."

Yes, I was afraid. But at the same time I didn't want someone watching me all the time. I didn't want to be tied to someone else's time schedule for when I left the restaurant.

"David will be back tomorrow, and he's off his crutches."

"Still can't run very fast," Chester mused.

"No, but he can shoot straight. He's got your pistol and will probably bring his own back with him. He'll protect me."

"No doubt. I'm just not sure it's enough."

Chester nursed his whiskey, and we sat in silence, though I wouldn't exactly call it companionable silence. We were each trying to figure out what was going on.

Finally he took a last sip. "You goin' to call David tonight?"

"Yes." I needed to talk to David and was just waiting for Chester to leave, though I didn't want to seem ungrateful or impatient.

"You'll be alright tonight, Kate. Take a sleeping pill or drink another glass of wine, and get some rest. I'll be in touch in the morning."

"Thanks." I stood and walked around the table to give him a hug. "Don't tell Carolyn I'm half in love with you."

He chuckled. "She'd be glad. And I am too. Now lock me out, set your alarm, and call David. He needs to know what went on."

As I could have predicted, David was sound asleep, and it took him a minute to come to his senses. "Kate? Is something wrong?"

"Not any more. But I wanted to tell you what happened tonight. I'm sorry to wake you, it's purely selfish. But I'll feel better if you know."

His voice deepened, and I could almost see him clutching the phone tightly as he demanded, "What happened?"

So I told him. Every detail as I remembered it. Every frightening moment. "Huggles is the hero of the day. And Chester."

"Damn. I wish I'd been there."

"No, it's all okay. And now that I'm talking to you, I'll be able to sleep."

"Well, hell, I won't," he shouted. "I'll drive back first thing in the morning."

"No, stay and finish your business. I'm okay in the daytime. It's nights that scare me. And you'll be back tomorrow night."

"For damn sure. I'm not sure I even like you being in the café during the day."

"David, there are lots of people around, and I bet some of those farmers are carrying. I'm safe. Besides, I have an errand to run in the afternoon."

"Oh yeah, you're going to talk to the artist son."

"Yes. I told you I have some questions for him."

"I don't like that. Don't trust anyone in that family." Earlier that evening, when I'd mentioned visiting James, David had no reaction. Now he was afraid . . . for me.

"He's perfectly trustworthy. A lovely man, in fact."

"Your instinct," he growled. "Okay, I'll be there midafternoon."

We hung up, I checked doors and windows and alarm system one more time, and went to bed, where I slept soundly all night. David would tell me the next day he never went back to sleep, but I didn't believe him.

Next morning I had just pulled the first batch of sticky buns from the oven when Chester came in, looking dejected.

"Your timing is perfect. Here, this will cheer you up." I gave him a plate with a bun and a cup of fresh, black coffee. I couldn't stand café coffee that wasn't freshly made. I'd been known to throw out half a pot when it began to get that stale, slightly burned smell and taste.

"That car the guy was driving last night was a Lexus—no wonder I couldn't keep up. Stolen in Canton, ditched in Tyler some time before six this morning. So that's a dead end."

"I didn't expect it to tell us much, Chester. We'll just have to keep digging."

"You're more cheerful than I am. You sleep well?"

"I did. Did you?"

"Nope. Carolyn smelled the whiskey on me and kept me up half the night haranguing about how I shouldn't ever drink it. I told her this was an exception because your safety was involved, and now she's all worried about you and won't leave me alone. Wants me to glue myself to your side, but I explained I have other things to do."

"And much as I love you, I don't want you to be at my side all day long."

He put his face in his hands. "Now, I am really crushed. Okay, if that's how you feel." He turned serious. "Kate, you be careful. And call me if you feel the least bit threatened. When will David be here?"

"Midafternoon. And, Chester, stop worrying. I'll be okay."

On a fine spring morning with the sun shining — it would be hot soon — and the birds singing, I felt optimistic. Of course I would be fine.

After the lunch rush I set off for Edom and James' studio. I followed familiar back roads, enjoying the drive. James was waiting in the front part of his studio, critically studying his own work, adjusting one and then another as though they hung not quite straight. He didn't hear me come to the open door.

"James?" I spoke softly, hesitant to disturb him, but he whirled around.

"Kate! I've been waiting for you. How about if we take a walk? There are some shaded benches on the old fairgrounds, and that might be a perfect place to talk."

I agreed and we set off, though I lingered to window-shop at the potter's place, the store where they sold hand-crafted jewelry, and the leatherworks. James finally laughed at me.

"We won't have time to talk if you keep dawdling."

"Yes, sir. Coming right along."

He had brought thermal cups of green tea, slightly sweetened with honey. I sipped and sighed and thought I could easily forget about the puzzle of Walter Aldridge and who killed him. But I knew better than that. I pulled out my ever-present steno pad and began.

"James, tell me what you remember about your father when you were little."

He stared off in space. "When our mother was alive, he was a great father, a lot of fun. He played games with us—hide-and-seek, softball, all kinds of things. Taught Rodney and me to fish—doubt Rodney cares to try it, but I can still catch and clean a bass or catfish for dinner—and sometimes I do. Dad read to us, said prayers with us at night, saw that our clothes weren't too awfully mismatched."

"Where was your mother? A lot of those sound like things moms do."

"Mom was sick ever since I can remember. And when she died, Dad changed. We had several nannies, and Dad didn't spend much time with us. After he married Edith, he spent all his time . . . well, coaching her. We'd peek around doorways and watch and listen. He was trying to fix—his word, not mine—her East Texas speech. He taught her to stand and sit tall, how to walk, all that stuff."

"How long did that last?"

"Oh, probably a couple of years. Remember, I was pretty young. Seemed like forever to me. I didn't miss my mom so much because we all saw little of her, but I missed the laughing, loving friend my father had been. And then, they started to quarrel. I thought it was completely unlike him—he'd yell at her, literally yell, about the house staff or the grocery bill or something else. When that began, I always ran away and hid, but Rodney told me Dad had just realized what he'd married. Rodney didn't mean that in a good way."

I thought about Rose. She obviously hadn't benefited from the walk and sit tall lessons and all, though her speech was more Dallas than East Texas. I didn't ask about Rose because something much more important was on my mind. "Tell me what you remember about the night your father died."

He poked at the dirt with a stick. "I was fifteen. Rodney was twenty, and he'd stayed in Dallas with a friend. I can't remember why we were at the mansion, except that Dad was in a yank to be there. Rushed us all around, kept trying to hurry us. So there we were. Lucy had fixed us dinner, and Rose and I had gone to our rooms. She was barricaded, listening to music and mooning over pictures of movie stars; I was supposed to be asleep, but I was drawing. I closed the door and hoped Edith wouldn't see the dim light from my worktable under my door. I heard her come upstairs and go to their bedroom, but what's funny is I didn't hear Dad. By that time of night he usually had too much to drink and was ranting and raving around downstairs. That night, he was quiet. He'd been sort of quiet at dinner too, but I was just thankful for that and didn't think any more about it."

I flexed my fingers, tired from writing too fast. And I thought to myself what an awful childhood these three had. What would have happened if Alicia Aldridge had lived?

"It got pretty late, and the house was still quiet. I may have fallen asleep, because the next thing I remember I was at my desk, and there was a lot of commotion downstairs. I crept to the banister to look, and almost instantly Rose was beside me. She asked what was going on, and I didn't know. But Edith was down there, dressed in a gorgeous robe like she always was, talking to some kind of law officer. And then suddenly she screamed."

"Did she say anything or just scream?"

"Something like, 'Dear God, no!' Of course Rose and I went flying down the stairs, only to be told to go upstairs to our rooms, shut the doors, and go to bed. We did. Lucy told us next morning at breakfast that Dad was dead. But she didn't answer any of our questions. No one ever did. Certainly not Edith. I think she was in denial."

"Did you stay with Edith after that?"

"Not really. She shipped us off to various boarding schools. Rose liked Hockaday in Dallas so well that Edith arranged for her to live with a friend. Rodney and I got sent to a military school. I hated it—couldn't draw for six or eight years. He loved it. It was his thing."

I knew that eventually, with funds left by their father, Rodney went to Princeton, and James studied at the Art Institute of Chicago. Rose married, almost as soon as she was out of high school. Melissa was the only child, so bridge club and tea at the Adolphus and book clubs and golf were mostly what Rose did with her life.

"Have you heard from Rose and Rodney lately?"

He rose, stretched, and wandered off a way. Then he came back and sat again. "Yep. They've got their knickers all in a knot over Edith spending our inheritance in lavish ways. I told them I didn't want to talk about it. I don't need the money. Rose was snappish, said everyone needs the money. Far as I know, she doesn't. Her husband's beyond wealthy."

"Rodney?"

He shook his head. "Rodney's a risk-taker. He may have taken one risk too many. I don't know, and I don't want to know." He stood up again. "Want more tea before you head back?"

I looked at my watch. Three forty-five. A ten-minute drive back to Wheeler would put me in the café just in time for dinner prep. "Thanks, but I'd better not. Give Shelly a hug for me."

"My pleasure," he said and grinned.

He walked me to my car, hugged me casually, and watched while I drove off.

Chapter Fifteen

Driving on back roads again, I was musing on what James had told me . . . and what I hadn't learned. I was more convinced that Edith didn't kill her husband, but I had no clue as to who did. Surely Rodney wouldn't have done the deed, and I couldn't imagine Rose doing it. For that matter, where had Rose gone from the Tremont House? And why hadn't Steven Connell tracked her?

With a sudden movement, my car jerked to the right edge of the road, almost throwing it in the ditch. I straightened but found the car hard to control, steering a straight line almost impossible. No novice to flat tires, I stopped and got out to look. Not one but two tires were flat. Since they were fine when I drove away from James, I could only assume that someone had loosened the valve or done something else to create slow leaks.

But two tires! I only had one spare — one of those bubble things that don't go too far. I'd have to call Chester to send a tow truck. I rummaged around in the well between the front seats and came up with my cell phone. Turned it on — and nothing. A blank screen. I pushed buttons, did everything I could think of — and nothing.

Swell, I was stranded on a country road with little traffic and no communication. I scolded myself for thinking I was smart and taking the back road when I could have been on the state road where someone would have noticed me. I looked at my watch—almost four o'clock. Too soon for Marj to worry about me or wonder where I was. How long would it take her?

I sat in the car for a while, plugged in the phone but that did nothing. Then I got hot and restless, and I got out and paced up and down the road. Everything around me was quiet and still. Some cows stood watching me from a pasture on the other side of the road, but they would do no good. I was bored, frustrated, and mad as hell.

It was a long time before another vehicle came down the road. A dusty, rusty old pickup. The man driving it wore a baseball cap and a plaid, short-sleeved shirt, with one arm out the window on his side. He'd have a farmer's tan on that arm at least. He pulled up next to me and said, "Howdy. Looks like you need some help."

I desperately needed some help, but how did I know who he was? How did I know I could trust him? His face was wrinkled and his teeth yellowed—he looked like a man who didn't take care of himself. But his smile was friendly enough, and his eyes seemed to light up. He jumped out of this truck. "What we got here?"

He bent down by first one tire and then the other. "You do something to make someone mad? They've punched small holes in both tires—leave you enough air to get out here but not to get wherever you're goin'. Where *are* you goin'?"

"Wheeler. The Blue Plate. You ever eat there?"

His face lit up. "Best fried catfish anywhere. Me and my wife, we go every Saturday night."

He was beginning to sound more and more okay, but what if this was a ruse and he was in cahoots with Rodney . . . or who knew who else? "I own it," I said.

"Shut up! Really! I'm mighty impressed and glad to help you."

"Do you have a cell phone?"

"Nope. Never did truck with them things. You got one?"

"Yeah, but it doesn't work."

"That's why I don't bother with them. I'll give you a ride into town — either Wheeler or Edom, your choice."

I debated. Was I safe getting in a truck with this man? Could I trust him? I'd trusted in the past where I shouldn't, and no one knew where I was, who I was with. On the other hand, I could be out here all day if I didn't go with him.

"I'd be grateful. My name's Kate Chambers."

"Go on. You Ms. Johnny's daughter? I'm Jimmy Baldwin."

"No, I'm her granddaughter."

He took off his hat, slapped it against his pants, wiped his hand on his pants, and offered it to me. "It's a real pleasure to meet you. Let's go. Wheeler or Edom?"

"I think Wheeler, if that's not too inconvenient."

"Sure. I got a small auto garage there. Off Main Street. You just ask anybody about Jimmy Baldwin."

Well, good, now I knew that. But why had I never heard of Jimmy Baldwin and his repair shop? I was still bothered that no one else knew where I was or with whom. If I vanished into thin air, nobody would know that I'd ridden with Jimmy Baldwin. I climbed into the passenger side of his truck and scooted as close to the door as I could. Then I laughed. I reminded myself of early shy dates, the kind boys used to call "Damn door huggers."

Jimmy Baldwin proved to be a talkative sort who asked a lot of questions about the café, where I lived, where I grew up, that sort of stuff. I began to hedge on my answers because he was getting too much personal information.

"You know," he said expansively, "I had a lady from Dallas in my shop the other day for engine trouble on her big Buick. Said she was staying at the Tremont Inn. Don't your family own that?"

I nodded. "Sort of." So Rose had been in his shop. I'd verify with her, if I ever found her again.

He told me he'd go back and fix those tires, but he "just don't mess" with tires. Strictly worked on engines. Said my tires could be a problem unless a tow truck with a flat-bed was available, because you couldn't hoist up the front end of the car and tow it on a flat tire — ruin the tire, the rim, everything.

I had a vision of the entire car collapsing like the one-horse shay. But his patter reassured me — if he were a steely-eyed killer, he would have revealed himself by now. I'd been holding my body stiff with tension, but I gradually relaxed.

"Might could fix those tires with Fix-a-Flat, least long enough so you can get some new tires from Canton. Doubt anyone has the right tires in Wheeler."

I was learning too much about tires and cars. "Fix-a-flat?"

"Oh, yes, ma'am. It's stuff you put in the tire and it seals those tiny holes. Someone wanted you to have a lot of trouble, 'cause they made several holes in each tire."

With that scary bit of knowledge, Jimmy Baldwin deposited me safe and sound at the door to the Blue Plate Café. I thanked him profusely. He waved his hand as though to way it was nothing and said, "See you Saturday night for catfish."

Marj greeted me almost stridently. "Where have you been? I was getting worried. Not like you to be so late for the supper hour."

"I'll explain later. Let me get in the swing of things." I took over the cash register and was instantly busy making change, inquiring about how this one or that liked his or her meal, greeting friends, being the hostess with the mostest. Things finally calmed down about one thirty, and I sat at the counter.

"So tell all," Marj demanded.

"I had a flat, two flats actually, on a back road. Someone poked holes in my tires in Edom and somehow sabotaged my cell phone. It wouldn't work."

"So how did you get here?"

"Fellow came by in a pickup, offered to bring me here or back to Edom, whichever I wanted. I wanted to be here."

"You got in a truck with a strange man." Her hands were on her hips and her pose was one of indignation.

"It's okay. His name is Jimmy Baldwin. Says he has an auto repair shop here."

"Never heard of him, Kate. I've lived here since before you were born, and I never heard of Jimmy Baldwin. Only one auto mechanic in town that I know of. His name's Bill Cook."

My mind's eye flashed to talkative country boy Jimmy Baldwin. Was that an act? If so, he was a darn good actor, but he didn't threaten me or try to harm me. What was the point? But I remembered how much he'd talked about our Saturday night catfish, and I was pretty sure I'd never seen him in the café on a Saturday night. I'd watch this weekend. And he had seemed awfully curious about me and my life.

David came in just about then, bringing with him a man I'd never met. "Kate, meet Brian Gallagher. Brian's the architect who's designing our new house . . . and acting as contractor too. He wants to go out to the property, now that it's cleared. You haven't seen it either—want to go with us?"

I noted right away that he called it "our new house," and just as quickly I saw that his feelings were hurt when I said "Not right now." I hurried on. "David, I had a bit of trouble this afternoon, and I need to tell you about it."

"You okay?"

"Now, yes." I repeated the whole story that Marj had just heard.

First thing he said was, "Give me your cell phone."

I got my purse from behind the cash register desk, fished out the phone, and took it to him.

He fiddled a minute and handed it back to me, working as perfectly as it ever had.

"What did you do?"

"Turned it on. Someone turned it off, and you never do that. So you didn't think to turn it back on."

My face flushed, mostly because David was laughing and even Brian Gallagher was smiling.

But David sobered quickly. "Call Halstead and tell him about Jimmy Baldwin. I don't suppose you got a license number. Make of the truck? Model is too much to hope for. Color? Age? Extended cab?"

I finally came up with a description: it was an old truck, no extended cab, leather seats were ripped and patched with duct tape, paint had once been dark blue, now sort of a nothing color. Probably a Chevy or Ford—looked like any old pickup around Wheeler. Rear bumper was loose and complained when Jimmy drove over potholes and the like.

"Better," David said.

"But we've got to get my car off that road!"

Marj came up behind me. "Call Bill Cook. He's got a tow truck."

"Does he have Fix-a-Flat?" They all stared at me, and David began to laugh.

"Where'd you hear about that stuff?"

"Jimmy Baldwin." I didn't want to look at any of them. "Or whoever he was or is."

David was back to his efficient self, and I let him take care of everything. Bill Cook would tow the car; flat tires were not a problem; he'd let us know if he needed to order new tires; no, he'd never heard of Jimmy Baldwin.

Halstead was angry about the car but said he could do nothing about it. I wanted him to take fingerprints, go to the scene of the crime, canvass people in Edom to see what they saw. In short, I wanted him to acknowledge I'd been a victim. Instead, he asked if I could give a description of Jimmy Baldwin. I wanted to tell him not of the *real* Jimmy Baldwin, only of an actor in disguise.

"Do you have a sketch artist in your office?"

He snorted. "Nothing so fancy. I just want to know what he looks like."

I did the best I could over the phone.

"I know him," Halstead said. "Jimmy Baldwin is kin to John and Dan'l," he said. "I don't know what he wanted, but he didn't break any law, and I can't go after him."

"He's right," David said. "There's not much he can do. Brian and I are going out to the house now before it gets dark. Want to come along?"

"No, thanks. I've had a full day already and been away from the café too long. Take pictures for me." Pictures of a scraped, blackened patch of earth. Whoopee! I just couldn't work up to David's level of enthusiasm about this.

"Will do." He kissed me on the forehead and was gone. Brian, trailing behind him, gave me a smile.

* * * *

To complete my day, Edith Aldridge came in about six and seated herself at her usual table. I went to greet her and ask if she needed a menu.

"No, just tea and talk, please. I suppose you only have tea bags."

"Yes, ma'am. That's all we have. But we do have English breakfast tea as well as Lipton's."

She shuddered at the mention of Lipton's and said she'd take the English breakfast. "I don't suppose you have biscotti?"

I shook my head. *Who even asks for biscotti in a small-town country café? I was tempted to tell her no, but we had chicken-fried steak. But Gram had raised me too well to be that rude.*

When I delivered the tea, I pulled out a chair next to her and asked, "May I?"

"Of course. I came to talk to you. What progress have you made?"

"Not as much as I'd like. I've studied everything I could find online about your husband and his death. And this morning I talked to James about what he remembers about the night of the murder. From everything I've found, I think Sheriff Halstead is wrong to even begin to suspect you."

"I knew that," she said flatly. "You've not made progress in the right direction, though. Who did it? I'm convinced if you find that answer, we'll know who's threatening me."

She was so demanding I almost asked if she wanted to talk about billable hours. Edith Aldridge had been charming the first time she'd come to call. I guessed now that I agreed to help her, pro bono, she thought I was part of her staff and she could be demanding. There were several quick responses to her question.

"I thought you suspected your stepchildren."

"Rodney was twenty-something and supposedly away for the night."

"Have you decided you don't suspect the children?"

Suddenly, all defenses gone in an instant, she put her face in her hands. "I don't know what I've decided. Another one of my beautiful peacocks was by the front door this morning. Someone wants me out of the house. All my birds are being killed." She was almost keening.

Out of the corner of my eye I saw Marj start and look our direction. I reached out a hand to Edith and almost patted her on the shoulder, as I would comfort a young child. I gave her a minute to compose herself and asked, "Did you call Steven Connell about the peacock?"

"He didn't pick up, and I left a voice message. He hasn't called back."

I tried a new question. "If you think Walter's children are behind this, why is it so important to find out twenty years later who killed him?"

She went quickly from desperate to fierce. Looking me straight in the eyes, she said forcefully, "Because I think it is, and because I'm convinced it's all connected."

I couldn't make sense of that tangle, but before I could worry about what to say, she said, "James came to see me this afternoon."

"He did?" I know my voice almost squeaked. "What did he want?"

"To be friends."

I have never seen so many expressions on one face. Now she looked bewildered. "How can he want to be friends after all these years?"

That I could answer. "Because he's a kind and gentle soul. He always felt you didn't want anything to do with him or his siblings, but he felt bad about it."

"How do you know?"

"I've talked with him, and I really like him. And his girlfriend. I don't understand his art. I'm pretty much a bluebonnet painting kind of art fan."

Honest, she shuddered just like she had when I mentioned Lipton's.

"But I think he has talent. He's had works in shows, a few in museums, and some in galleries. I think the gallery in Edom is incidental. He works, or paints, in Edom but he knows his clientele is not there."

She stared at me. "Maybe you have made progress. Shall I invite him to bring his mistress to tea?"

Now it was my turn to shudder. Surely even twenty years ago she wouldn't have used that term. "Why don't you meet them here for supper? They both came in one night, and we had a good visit."

"You've been conspiring with him without my knowing it." Back to accusations.

"No, I've been investigating, as you asked." I wanted to say angry words to her, ask how I could investigate if I didn't talk to people without her permission. But I didn't.

"I'll think about all this." She swept up her purse and made as grand an exit as she could manage.

I felt sorry for her.

Chapter Sixteen

David was high on excitement when he and Brian came in just before closing. "Brian had some great ideas. The old house sat on the only sunny part of the lot, so we're going to make that the garden—vegetables and stuff—and angle the house so it focuses more directly on the lake. We can hear the lake when we sleep on the porch."

That blasted sleeping porch again! "Can you grow plants on burned-out soil?"

"For sure," Brian said eagerly. "It's been tramped on and packed down. David will have to plow it and treat it but it should be great."

"Make a list of the vegetables you want," David said.

I'm sure he had visions of a lush crop the first year, but I knew better. Hadn't I struggled a couple of summers just to get herbs started and keep Gram's poke salad alive? From my deep store of knowledge, I suggested April was a little late to plant.

"Oh, sure, some things. No potatoes or onions or things like that this summer, but we can have them in the fall. But it's a good-sized plot—we can have squash and tomatoes and lettuce, green beans, spinach, I guess even kale, though I don't much like it."

"I'll make a list," I promised.

"The house will be wonderful. Maybe a little bigger than I first thought—slightly over a thousand square feet. But all the conveniences of home."

I wanted to shout. "David, I have a home!" Instead, I asked what they wanted for supper.

"Can we have to-go? Brian brought a wonderful bottle of bourbon and some good wine."

I agreed. David raved about the chicken-fried steak, and Brian readily agreed to have that. I put their orders in along with my own, and since it was late sat down with them, wondering if Brian would spend the night. I supposed he could sleep in Donna's old room, but then I'd feel awkward and probably have to sleep in my own bed. *Go on, Kate, bring that bridge right up here and jump it.*

"Edith Aldridge was here today, really upset."

David slapped himself on the cheek. "I had a call from her and forgot to return it. What's up?"

"Another peacock was shot and killed."

"At least it wasn't a threat to her."

"David Clinkscales, it is a threat to her! To her sense of well-bring, her pride in her home, all kinds of things. Get your head out of house plans and pay attention to your client." The minute the words were out of my mouth, I wanted to say, "Kate Chambers would like to withdraw that last message."

Brian turned tactfully away, and David looked sheepish. "You're right. I'll call her."

"What have you heard from Steven Connell?"

"Nothing. I guess he has nothing to report."

"Well, he might start by finding Rose Mitchum. I know what I think of Rodney, and we know he's probably back in Dallas . . . ."

"We do? How?"

"I don't know, but why would he hang around Canton when he has a business in Dallas? And we know James is in Edom—he went to see Edith today. I think she's relaxing a bit toward him. But he doesn't remember much helpful about the night his father was killed. He was fifteen and lost in his art, drawing in his room after he was sent to bed.

"Rose is the missing piece now. Steven could at least find out if both Rose and Rodney are back in Dallas. If there's any collusion between the children, it's those two. James is out of it. They came to talk to him, and he wanted no part of it."

"I'll call Steven tonight," David said.

"And I think you have a story to tell me." Brian's curiosity was written all over his face.

I felt silly calling David to meet me at ten or so, with Brian there, but I had promised. I had my heavy flashlight and didn't sense or hear any danger. As it turned out, Brian had headed back to Dallas and left a gracious note, thanking me for dinner.

"I called Edith. She's calmed down since she was here, but she's thinking about donating the remaining three peacocks to the Caldwell Zoo in Tyler. Says she can't stand to have any more killed."

"Aren't they like watchdogs? Sounding the alert?"

"Yes, but she didn't hear them last night, although she heard that scream the night the first one was killed. Today she just found the dead bird. She's determined to stay in her house and find out who killed her husband."

"Two different problems. She told me that today, but I don't know why she waited thirty years to get so anxious about who killed him."

"I don't either, but I also called Steven and told him to get it in gear, find Rodney and Rose. He suggested Rodney killed his own father."

"Edith and I considered it, but I think it's unlikely. What does Rodney's record look like since? If he would kill his own father, I doubt he'd stop there."

"Good point. Like kids who abuse animals and go on to abuse people."

We went to bed shortly after that, but I might as well have slept in my own bed. There was a gulf between us. For my part, I was frustrated at the inaction of David and Steven and also feeling like a bit of a nag for keeping after David. What David thought, I didn't know, because we didn't talk.

* * * *

By noon the next day, David called from Canton to say that Rodney and Rose were in adjoining rooms at the Holiday Inn Express. *Quite a comedown from the mansion!*

The most surprising news was that Rose had apparently sent Melissa back to Dallas—which I would have done a long time ago—and was sharing a room with Steven Connell. David found that out when he called the motel number Steven had given him and Rose, answering the phone, had blurted out that her name was Rose Middleton. Talk about sleeping with the enemy. Trying to picture svelte Steven with—forgive me—dumpy, matronly Rose just didn't work out in my mind. She surely didn't look like a cougar. And I couldn't figure out who was telling what truth—Rodney told me he was close to Edith, which Edith denied; Edith told me she communicated privately with Steven—but when he was sleeping with the step-daughter she thought wanted to kill her? Probably she didn't know that.

"Did you talk to any of them?"

"Just Steven, who was a bit sheepish about it, says he can explain. I told him it better be a damn good expla-nation. But even without his story, it explains why we haven't heard from him. He's off the payroll. I may contest his license if this gets any worse."

"I'm glad. I'm coming to Canton."

"Hold on. As you keep telling me, you've got a restaurant to run. And Steven said Rose wants to have more chicken-fried steak—and to talk to you. She's headed your way now. I have no idea what she wants to say, but I'm staying out of this and leaving it a girls' talk. In fact, I'm going to Dallas. Be back late tonight. Love you."

And he was gone.

Rose came in early, along about eleven fifteen. She was not the coiffured Highland Park matron I'd seen before. I thought her hair probably hadn't been done by a stylist since she left Dallas, and it showed. She'd obviously finally tried to brush it out herself, but the results were dismal. Her face was made up but not as carefully as before. Whereas the first time I met her I thought maybe she was in her early forties, now I thought she looked fifty or beyond.

"Chicken-fried steak?" I asked brightly as I seated her.

"Yes, and some talk. Can you be free?"

I looked around. It wasn't busy yet, and Sallie was working with Marj. "Let me find out," I said. I asked Marj if she and Sallie could handle things, and she, always willing, agreed.

"I need to talk to this woman privately," I said.

Marj, always intrigued by my intrigues, said of course. She knew she'd get the story later.

I went back to Rose and suggested we take our lunches to my house next door. She brightened at that, and I ordered her chicken-fried with all the trimmings and my tuna salad plate to go. Then I led her across the meadow to my house.

"My goodness. How handy that you live so close." She was panting a little as we crossed the steep rise of the meadow.

"Yes, mostly it is."

I'd left Huggles out that morning since it was a pleasant day and I anticipated no trouble. He waited for us at the gate, wagging his tail and barking enthusiastically. She misunderstood the bark and pulled back.

"I'm afraid of dogs. Really afraid."

I saw that she was trembling and turning pale.

Really afraid is an understatement. "Huggles will only love you to death, but I tell you what. Can you make it around the house to the front door?"

She looked at the uneven ground but gave me a positive, "Yes, of course."

"Then I'll go in through the kitchen, leave Huggles outside, and come let you in the front door. I hope you don't mind cats."

"I don't much like them, but I suppose I can handle one. You don't have a houseful, do you?"

Good heavens! What a wimpy lady. "No, just one. I'll meet you in a minute."

And so I left a disappointed Huggles outside, went through the house, and let Rose in the front door. Wynona didn't even make an appearance, which I took as a relief.

We sat at the kitchen table, and I poured iced tea for two, then unpacked our lunches, and served them on proper china, not the Styrofoam boxes they'd come in. A touch of Gram's nicety.

"I'll just reheat yours a bit in the microwave."

"Thank you." She sank down in the chair, and I do mean sank. Her shoulders were slumped, her head sunken on her chest, and her whole body seemed to have lost its uprightness.

With forced brightness, I put on lunches on the table and said, "Cheers to you," lifting my glass of iced tea.

"Thanks," she said, responding limply.

What has happened to this woman? I didn't have to wait long.

"I've made a terrible mess of things," she said, picking at her food but not really eating. "I don't really know where to begin."

I thought a minute and then said, "Begin with Rodney."

"Ah, Rodney. My big brother, my protector. Always there for me. But this time I think I've listened too much to Rodney and not enough to myself."

"How?" I took a delicate bite of tuna and noticed she really wasn't eating. I could always microwave it for her again, but it would lose crispness and flavor each time I did that.

"I listened to him when I shouldn't. He's always thought we would inherit a lot if we just got Edith out of that house. He'd go for years without mentioning it, and then it would come up again. I never paid him much attention. I didn't much like Edith, but if she wanted the house and was happy there, so be it. I don't need money."

"And this time?" I prodded.

"He caught me at a bad time. My husband has filed for divorce, ordered me out of the house. I have no place to live and no money. Oh, I'm sure I'll get some when the settlement is finalized, but for now I have nothing."

He can't do that! There are laws, even in Texas. How gullible is she? This was a case for David, but I kept listening.

"Rodney must have known, or else it was pure coincidence, but he called me again with that wild notion about getting Edith out of the house so we could inherit it."

"I thought it was hers as long as she lived."

"No, only as long as she lived in the house. He thought we could make it so unpleasant that she'd leave and forfeit it. Frankly, I think Rodney underestimates Edith. But I was desperate, and I listened. I agreed to come to East Texas."

I said nothing, waiting for her to go on.

"I'm not sure how Rodney thought he'd convince her. He says he's close to her, but I know that's not true."

"So did he plant the trip wire and shoot the peacocks?"

She shook her head. "No, Rodney's conniving and scheming, but he's not that mean, and now he doesn't know what he's started."

"Okay, so let me get this straight. You're in Canton because you have no home in Dallas, right?"

She nodded. "Geoffrey said he'd welcome Melissa, but I was banished."

Tempting to ask what she'd done to precipitate banishment, but I held my tongue. "I'm no lawyer but my companion is, and he may be able to advise you on that. Unless you had a prenup, this is a community property state. But moving on, why is Rodney still in Canton? Doesn't he have a business to tend to in Dallas?"

She shook her head. "Rodney's business went bust, and he's being hounded by creditors. And his wife sued for divorce, but he has no money for a lawyer or anything else. He thinks he and I could live in the mansion, on the money Dad left Edith."

"What does he plan to do with Edith?" Seemed plain to me.

Her eyes grew wide with fright. "I don't know. I told him I didn't want to have anything to do with it. Edith was always fairly nice to me."

David is going to go ballistic over this! Or else say, "Not my circus, not my monkeys!" Oh, but David, they are, because I've taken them on.

She hadn't touched her lunch, and I had only nibbled on mine between questions. "Where does Steven Connell fit into this? I thought he worked for David, who works for your stepmother. In fact, I thought she sometimes confided in Steven, which made it awkward for everyone."

She pushed her steak around and finally cut a bite. "Steven . . . he . . . well, I guess he plays both sides. I think he takes care of Steven, and right now he takes care of me. That's all I care about. I certainly wasn't going to share a room with Rodney." Indignation flashed across her face.

All I could think of was that old line, "What tangled webs we weave/When first we practice to deceive." Instead, I said, "Eat your lunch. It's getting cold."

Once she started to eat — and I left her alone with questions — nothing seemed wrong with her appetite. I could barely finish my lunch, and outside Huggles barked, letting me know he'd finish it for me.

When Rose finally wiped her mouth and pushed her plate to the side, she had one simple question for me. "What should I do now?"

Have I suddenly become the mother of a middle-aged woman? Had she always had someone to tell her what to do next? Probably so. I sighed in frustration.

"I'd move out of Steven Connell's room for starters," I said.

"Where? I left Tremont House because I had no more money — and because you knew who I am."

This one was a long shot. "Go back to Tremont House. I'll tell Donna. You'll have to fix your own meals, do the cleaning, and so on. If she gets other guests you'll have to help her."

"I was never trained in housework," she said softly, "but I suppose I can learn. In fact, I suppose I may have to."

"I think so." I hope the bitter irony didn't show in my tone, and once again I blessed Gram for all she taught me. I only wished Donna appreciated those lessons as much.

She left, assuring me she was going to get her belongings out of the Holiday Inn in Canton and would tell neither Rodney nor Steven where she was going. She only hoped—and I did too—that she saw neither of them. *I've eliminated two of the stepchildren from those wanting to kill Edith, leaving only Rodney. But that wasn't what she asked of me. She wanted me to find out who killed Walter, and I've made no progress on that front at all. Still, I guess keeping her safe is the foremost concern.*

I rinsed the dishes, cleaned up after lunch, and called David. To my everlasting frustration, he was too busy to talk—his voice was clipped when he said this, as though he were talking to a barely remembered stranger. "We'll talk tonight," I said, "but you'll want to hear this."

I called Donna.

"You did what? She stiffed me. Didn't pay her bill, after all the trouble I went to—and you too—to fix those special meals for this hoity-toity Dallas matron."

"The hoity-toity Dallas matron has no money and is in fairly desperate circumstances. I told her she'd have to work for her keep."

"Good. I need someone to clean my house, do the ironing, that sort of stuff. I'll figure out a rate of pay. She can work off her debt too." A pause. "She bringing that snooty daughter? I could put her to work too."

"No, the daughter's back in Dallas. And, Don, remember there's a minimum wage law. She's not exactly an indentured servant."

Donna snorted and cut off our conversation.

Chapter Seventeen

Rose returned to report that Steven Connell beat her to it—he'd moved out of the motel and, she assumed, left the bill unpaid. She didn't see Rodney but presumed he was still there.

I wondered if Connell had moved out because David fired him. If he'd gone back to Dallas and more profitable pickings, that suited me fine. One less person involved in this mess.

"Donna's expecting you. Hasn't even changed the linen on your bed yet. And she says she can work out a payment arrangement."

Rose wailed. "I have no money to pay her. I can't even buy food or gas."

The poor pitiful act wasn't going to work with me. "David will help you. Come on, let's go." I all but had to drag her to the B&B. She was like a reluctant puppy who saw no other way out. She followed my car in her Buick gas-guzzler. *No wonder she can't afford gas!*

Donna loved nothing better than having someone to lord it over, especially someone who had previously intimidated her. Her surface graciousness covered a streak of downright meanness. "Mrs. Middleton! Or is it Mrs. Mitchum? Either way I thought I'd never see you again. I'm so glad you're here."

Rose by contrast was nervous as a wallflower at her first dance. "Uh, I'm sorry, Mrs. Bryson. I'll see that you're paid . . . eventually. I . . . that was unforgiveable. I should have explained the circumstances to you."

The Dallas matron melted before my eyes into a puddle of stammering insecurity.

Nothing fazed Donna. "Oh, dear, do call me Donna, and I'll call you Rose. Now let's get you settled. You can take your suitcase right on up to your old room. I'm so sorry that darling daughter isn't with you." She led the way, without even offering to help Rose with her baggage.

"I'll just run on back to the café," I called after them. "Rose, be sure and come to the café for supper. Say about six?"

Rose flashed me a look, which I assumed to be a yes, and I left, careful to quell the instinct to slam the door behind me. I think I wanted to slam the door on the lot of them. I also wanted to put my next plan into operation, which I hoped wasn't a big mistake.

Once at the café, I asked Marj if she could cover dinner once again. "I'll be back to close." She agreed.

Next I called James Aldridge and asked if he and Shelly could come to dinner at my house. "It's important," I said.

James hesitated only a nanosecond before agreeing. They would be there at six fifteen. Finally I called David. "Dinner guests tonight at six. Can you be here?" If he couldn't I'd wing it without him. But I really needed to talk to him first.

"On my way now. Sorry I couldn't talk before. Big new client had just come into my office in Dallas, and I was Skyping with him. As good as a conference, and a lot less trouble."

I was incredulous. "Where were you that you could use Skype?"

"iHop in Canton."

"Weren't you afraid of being overheard?"

"Kate, no one's in iHop at ten thirty in the morning. It's as empty as the café. Will you be at the house when I get there . . . about fifteen minutes?"

"Yep. I'll be cooking."

I took enough for salad from the café and went home to examine my cupboard. Found spinach fettucine, canned artichokes, lemon, garlic, pesto—everything I needed but mushrooms. I raced back to the café, grabbed about half a pound of fresh mushrooms and headed home.

When David came in, I decided it wasn't the smartest thing to hit him immediately with all my news. I gave him a quick kiss and continued setting the table. "Who's the new client?"

"You'll never guess. Big-time lawyer from Dallas named Mitchum. Filing for divorce on the grounds of infidelity."

Silverware clattered to the floor, and I was only lucky I wasn't holding a stack of plates. "Mitchum?"

"Yeah. What's wrong with you?"

"David, Rose Middleton is really Rose Mitchum, Walter Aldridge's daughter." And so I launched into the whole long story, including the fact that she was penniless and her husband wouldn't give her money nor let her come home. "You'll have to recuse yourself or whatever that term you lawyers use is."

"You're kidding, right? Mitchum is an important man and a friend of mine. Well, maybe that's overstating it but we've played golf, and we're in Rotary together. I don't know Rose Mitchum or whatever she calls herself, so I have no investment in her. No conflict."

"You're meeting her tonight. She's coming for supper. So are James Aldridge and his Shelly."

"Kate, what have you done?"

"David Clinkscales, how could you take the case of a man who turned his wife out of her home and made her penniless? She doesn't even know that the law says the home is common property and so is his fortune. She needs your help a lot more than that big fat rich banker does."

"He's not fat," he muttered.

"Maybe not, but his bank account is." David was losing this argument, and he knew it. He also knew that if he met Rose at dinner, he'd have to give up the case.

"I guess Steven Connell was a bad idea."

I turned back to the stove.

* * * *

Rose Mitchum arrived a bit early and came to the front door as I'd suggested. I met her, seated her in the living room, offered wine which she gladly accepted, and sent David, her wine in hand, to introduce himself.

"I feel awkward about this," he muttered. "Lawyers don't force themselves on clients."

"You're not forcing. You're offering to help."

He kissed my forehead. "If I didn't love you . . ." The sentence wandered off as he headed for the living room or, as Gram would have called it, the parlor.

In the kitchen I heard murmured voices, although I couldn't make out the words. Still, the quiet sound made me think all was going well, until I heard a shrill, "You don't mean it!" from Rose. I wondered which part of her rights David had just told her about. Her voice continued shrill as she said, "That skunk! That lowlife skunk!" Then the talk subsided.

James and Shelly came to the back door soon after—another suggestion on my part. I was beginning to consider myself a great conniver. But they heard the low voices the minute they came in, and James cocked his head toward the living room.

"We have another guest." I poured wine as I explained. "Your sister, Rose, is talking to David, my . . . uh, companion. She's in a world of trouble."

"Trouble?" James snorted. "What kind of trouble could she possibly be in with that rich husband and big house and spoiled brat of a daughter?"

Nailed it, James! I put a finger to my lips to indicate whispering. I explained the whole situation in soft tones and they listened quietly until I came to the part about Steven Connell.

"She what?" James almost exploded, but then he lowered his voice. "Miss Righteousness hooked up with some guy? I don't believe it." He apparently didn't know whether to laugh or cry. Finally, he said, "I've lost no time weeping for her, but she's my sister, and if she's in trouble I want to help." Then he looked around, counted the places at the table, and said, as if to confirm, "You didn't ask Rodney to dinner?"

"Nope."

"Good."

"I think besides reuniting you and Rose, we have to figure out who killed your father. Then we'll know what's going on now. I'm not sure Rodney would be . . . ah . . . a helpful part of that."

James just looked grim.

For too long, James and Shelly sat in silence, sipping their wine, and I fiddled, unnecessarily, with my pasta, re-tossed a salad that had already been tossed. The silence grew uncomfortable, but at long last David came into the kitchen, dragging a reluctant Rose by the hand.

She stopped in the hallway. "James!" She stared as though to pinch herself back to reality. "I know you don't much like me, and I'm sorry."

James was rapidly becoming one of my favorite people. He opened his arms, came toward her, and wrapped her in an embrace. "Rose, you're my sister. How could I not like you?"

She pulled back, looked at him, and said, "Because you thought I was in a scheme with Rodney to get the mansion from Edith."

"Were you?" His tone was gentle.

"Yes, I was. And now I'm so ashamed. But I was desperate."

"If you're desperate, you come stay with us. We'll shelter you and put you to work."

She laughed nervously. "Kate's sister is going to do that. I have a feeling I'll be learning skills I never thought I'd need."

While they talked, I toasted the garlic bread and then announced dinner was ready, serving up huge bowls of pasta. For a few minutes there was silence, and then they began to talk about what I'd hoped—Rodney's plan to get Edith out of the house.

"He was going to scare her out of the house. I pointed out she could have tripped and gone down those steps to her death, but he seemed unconcerned. Steven told me Rodney shot the peacocks."

"Did he have help with this?"

She nodded miserably. "Steven."

David startled visibly, and I could only think that Steven Connell was playing both sides of the game. I only hoped he'd lose this time. The one thing I couldn't pin on him was Walter Aldridge's death. Steven was younger than Rodney. Which brought my thoughts back to Rodney.

"James, what was Rodney's relationship with your father?"

His half laugh had a bitter quality to it. "Rodney was the fair-haired boy, ready to follow in Walter's footsteps. He would talk stock market and banking with Dad at the age of twelve . . . and I gather talk pretty knowledgeably. I didn't pay any attention. It wasn't my kind of deal."

David stepped in to the conversation. "Was Rodney greedy, even at that young age? Would he have snuck back home and killed his father, believing as the older son he'd inherit the house and the majority of the fortune?"

James and Rose stared at each other until she shook her head, and James spoke. "No, I don't think so. Even back then, I don't think there was that much to inherit beside the house, which was apparently paid for. We had some spare dinners in those days—lots of soup, stew, none of the roasts and steaks I remember from my mom's day. I don't know if Mom's money disappeared when she died or if Dad gambled or whored"—he cast a glance at Rose—"away the money. But it didn't seem to be there. I suspect Edith lives frugally. She only heats and cools a few rooms in the house; she never invites guests to dinner—always tea, which is easy and cheap."

I thought of that sad, formal dining room. "What about Lucy and the groundskeeper?"

"Loyalty," James said. "They know Edith is dependent on them, and she's generous with the bounty of the property—eggs, vegetables that John L. grows. I think he shot a deer on the property last year and they took it home to butcher. And look at Edith's clothes—a bit out of date, a bit shabby."

"So it's not greed that killed Walter and threatens Edith now. What is it? Revenge?" David looked at him with his best lawyerly look.

Rose suddenly broke into the conversation. "I think it was all over Edith. Has anyone looked into her background?"

I was so surprised I could only stare. I'd studied Walter up one side and down the other and found lots—gambling, womanizing—but all I knew about Edith was that she was his Pygmalion, the woman who'd been a cocktail waitress and he'd groomed to be a lady. I almost slapped my hand to my head.

Rose continued. "I remember once when I was still very young, when Edith had just come to live with us. It was the middle of the night. I woke up and was scared. I wanted my mother, and of course she wasn't there. Edith wasn't the sort of person I'd run to for comfort. So I crept down the stairs toward Daddy's office. He was different since Edith was there, but I remembered a man who would take me on his lap and comfort me, lull me back to sleep."

She paused and wiped a tear away. "When I got close to his office, I heard loud voices, men's voices, arguing. I wanted to turn and run up the stairs, but it was like I was frozen there, listening."

James reached out an arm to put around her shoulders. "What were they saying, Rosie?"

It was the first time I'd ever heard that affectionate nickname.

"This other man—I never did see him—said, 'She's my wife, and I want her back.' And Daddy said something like, 'She's not your wife anymore. Common-law marriage isn't binding, and I married her in a proper ceremony. All legal and good.'"

"Where was Edith?" I asked.

Rose began to sob softly. "I don't know. I never saw her that night. But there's more. The other man said, 'Man, she's got a son to look after. I can't have her just go gallivanting off and leaving me with that brat. You prepared to take him too?'"

"And Dad said no," James supplied.

"Yes. Said it wasn't any of his business. He had three of his own, and that was enough for him to take care of. I guess eventually the man left, because I was so scared I crept back up to my bed. And the next morning no one acted any different, as though nothing had happened. I had a thousand questions I wanted to ask—I still do. But I didn't dare. And now it's too late."

James put his arms around her, and she collapsed into him, sobbing loudly. Finally, she mumbled, "Daddy made a mess of all our lives." She raised a tear-stained face to James, who gently stroked her hair away from her face.

David was acutely aware of the importance of what she had just said. "What do you mean, Rose? A mess of all your lives?"

She stood up and began to pace, holding a tissue to her nose. "He kept Edith from her son, though I never knew how she felt about that. Only after I was a mother, did I realize how I'd have felt. He married me off to Charles Mitchum long before I was ready to be married, let alone to that man. Dad thought it a suitable arrangement, and he saw that all the details were in place, even though he didn't live to see the elaborate wedding at the Dallas Country Club."

James looked astounded. "You didn't want to marry Charles?"

She shook her head. "At seventeen, I didn't want to marry anyone, let alone that fat, self-satisfied sonofabitch. I despised him." She hesitated, "Though I must admit I enjoyed being the belle of the ball. The year I was married I was the youngest bride, and I was treated to showers, teas, brunches, even balls. Edith was there throughout, the proper stepmother. And Charles was bursting with pride because we were the young, romantic couple. I enjoyed the parties. I hated it when we went home alone together at night."

My heart went out to her. Seventeen and caught in such a situation. It would have done no good to ask why she didn't rebel. I could see in her situation, at her age, with her upbringing, she never knew she had a choice.

Suddenly, she looked at her brother. "He ruined you too, James."

James smiled tolerantly. "I don't think so, Rosie. I'm pretty happy with who and what I am."

"But you could have been so much more. He blamed you for our mother's death. It's one reason he was hard on your about art."

James jumped, startled. "She didn't die in childbirth!" His tone was indignant.

"No, but she was never well after you were born, and when she died he blamed you. It never occurred to him to blame himself for impregnating her."

My mind whirled. The picture of Walter Aldridge that was emerging was even less pleasant than that of the man who had been a gambler and a womanizer. But who killed him? The man who claimed to be Edith's husband? I was sure we could never get her to tell us who that was. We were further ahead in this investigation, except I still didn't know which way to go. A background check on Edith seemed something obvious that we'd overlooked. But now it was time to change the subject.

"Tell me your good memories of growing up."

James and Rose hesitated a moment after I spoke, and then words began spilling out of them. They remembered hay rides around the estate, fishing in the stock tank, learning to ride the gentle horses stabled in the barn, food fights in the kitchen when only long-suffering — and then young — Lucy was present. I could tell that these reminiscences made the brother and sister happy. But I also noticed, for all the hijinks they repeated, there was no mention of Edith and little mention of Rodney.

At least the evening ended on a happy note. No one went off with specific assignments. What could we tell them to do? James did say he'd visit Edith again, and Rose said tentatively maybe she'd go with him. But she had to tend to her duties at Tremont Houses — she repeated that several times — and no one mentioned including Rodney. He was becoming the elephant in the room that no one talked about.

Rose and James exchanged a warm hug, and then Rose hugged Shelly and said she was looking forward to getting to know her well. I felt that I was watching a protective shell around Rose melt, and it gave me a good feeling about the evening. It hadn't been wrong to bring them together. I sighed as I realized the entire evening could have gone a totally different direction.

All David could say was, "Wow! Just wow! Can we talk about this in the morning?"

We put the dishes to soak. David promised to do them in the morning, after I went to the café. Both of us, worn out by the emotion of the evening, went to bed. I was never so glad to sleep wrapped in the comfort of his arms.

Gram? It's going to be all right. I promise.

No reply tonight. Not even a frown.

Chapter Eighteen

Rodney Aldridge was in the café almost as soon as we opened the next morning, before David and I even had a chance to discuss the previous night's revelations. Ignoring the possibility of other customers overhearing, he stormed up to the counter where I was rolling silverware while the sticky buns rose. I noticed he was limping rather badly.

"She shot me," he stormed. "Shot me with a shotgun. I just went to talk peaceably, and that's how she greeted me."

He looked fine to me, except for the limp. "So she missed? Must not have been close range."

"She shot at my feet, ruined my good Italian leather shoes what with birdshot and the driveway gravel it stirred up. I caught a few pellets—or some gravel—in my shin. Hurts like sin. I could be crippled."

"You ought to have that looked at. Could get infected." I offered him coffee, but that didn't seem to placate him.

"I'll go to the ER, but I wanted to come here first and let you know what kind of woman you're protecting and helping. She's crazy, that's what that old witch is. I just wanted to talk, to see if there wasn't some way out of this stalemate."

That told me something about his priorities and the pain of his injuries, if he came here first. "What time did you go visit her?"

"About eight last night." He had finally lowered his voice.

"Dusk. Maybe she mistook you for an intruder."

"She knows damn good and well who I am. She did it deliberately."

"Did you report it to the sheriff?"

He turned sulky. "Yeah. He said I was trespassing on private property. Said it served me right. What kind of law enforcement do we have in this county?"

I smothered the instinct to say it sounded like pretty sensible law enforcement to me. Instead, I asked him exactly what he wanted me to do.

"Arrange a meeting between her and me. I want to talk some sense into that old gray head."

David had come quietly up behind Rodney, and I was proud that neither my eyes nor my manner had given him away. "You mean, you want to get your way, get her to move out so you can move into that house? There's no way you could afford to maintain it. I hear you're jobless right now and in the midst of a messy divorce case."

"It'd all work out if I had that house," he muttered. "It isn't right for her to be spending every red cent my father worked so hard to get."

David chose not to mention gambling nor wasting money on a wild variety of women. "I don't believe you can contest the will thirty years later, and if you do, I'll fight you every way I know how. You need to leave your stepmother alone and get on with your own life."

"That an order?"

"A strong suggestion."

"That's just it. I haven't got a life to get on with."

"Then make one, man. That's not Edith's responsibility."

Obviously, Rodney was getting no sympathy from us, so he stalked out of the café—as much as one can stalk while limping. I noticed the limp was much more pronounced than when he had come in. I also noticed that his shoes were scratched and scuffed and his pants had a few raggedy places in them. If Edith had wanted to, she could have done serious damage with that shotgun. She apparently knew how to use it effectively.

David sat down and asked if the sticky buns were ready. I went to check, came back with a bun and poured a cup of black coffee. "I already knew about this," he said. "One reason I'm up so early. Steven Connell called me."

I nearly dropped the coffeepot. "I thought you were through with him. And how did he know?"

David shook his head. "I thought I was through too, but Edith called him last night after it happened. He says he told her to call the sheriff."

I got myself coffee and sat down. "Why would she call him?"

He shook his head again. "Blasted if I know. This isn't the first time she's turned to him, when she should have called me. I mean, sure, I put them together. He was to investigate, even protect her, but there seems to be more going on than that. I'm going to see her this morning."

"Call first, so she doesn't get out the shotgun."

"Thanks." He finished his coffee and left.

I worried more than a little about David walking into a shotgun blast, but Donna soon came in to distract me. "I don't know about that woman you foisted off on me." She was all indignation. "I had to show her how to make a bed properly, and I'm not sure she got it right even then. She doesn't know how to use a dishwasher or a washing machine. If I'm going to spend my days showing her, I might as well fire her and do it myself."

I poured some green tea with honey in it and shoved it at her. "If you fire her and kick her out, she has no place to go." *Not quite true, Kate. James and Shelly would take her in, but that might be an even bigger disaster.* "Let me see what I can do." A plan was formulating in the back of my mind. "Meet me here at eleven thirty for lunch."

Donna agreed unhappily and then flounced out.

About eleven, I made a quick trip to Tremont House, were I found Rose kind of idly swiping at surface with a feather duster which Gram would have told her in no uncertain terms was the least effective way to dust.

"Oh, good morning," she said. "I'm not good at this housekeeping business. Your sister is displeased because I don't know how to run her appliances, and I tried to vacuum but the machine just quit. Now it smells bad and whines."

I took a look, pulled out the brush, and retrieved a butter knife that had gotten caught in the brush. With trepidation, I tried the vacuum, and it hummed along beautifully. "You have to be careful what you try to pick up. It can't handle big items . . . not even wads of chewing gum." That was a lesson I'd learned the hard way.

I took Rose back to the café, where Donna sat at a corner table, drumming her fingers on the surface. I know she wanted to demand what her hired help was doing on a lunch break, but I said I thought we should all visit.

"Rose? The usual?"

She blushed. "I need to give up chicken-fried steak. I believe I'll have the tuna salad plate."

Almost in defiance, Donna ordered chicken-fried steak, a fattening dish she usually denounced. I joined Rose with the tuna, and we settled to talk, though I had to hop up from time to time to handle the register.

"Rose?" I was going to be as tactful as possible. "You apparently weren't trained in the household arts as a child."

"Lucy did all that," she said lamely, with a stolen glance at Donna.

"What things were you taught?"

"Edith taught me needlework. I mended all our clothes—mine and my brothers. And I can still sew a fine seam. And I was given art and music lessons. I play piano and guitar." She looked guilty, as though this was a frivolous admission.

"Guitar! Donna, Henry would love lessons. Rose, can you learn some contemporary songs?"

"I already know a lot of them. I never gave up my guitar."

"What do you think, Donna? Jess had always had an artistic side—some guidance would be good for her. And Ava? Would she like to play piano?"

Donna was looking at me like I was an alien from space. But slowly, her expression changed. "Could you do all that?" she asked Rose.

"I'd love to," Rose said. "My Melissa was never interested in any of what I knew."

Donna thought a minute. "In return, I could have the kids teach you about housecleaning. They do more of it than I do."

If I smiled then, it was rueful. But a deal was struck, and I felt I'd done a good day's work, all before noon. Rose would stay on at Tremont House, and I pointed out she could serve as sort of a caretaker. It was good to have someone on the property when there were no guests. And she surely knew how to function as a hostess when there were.

Donna left, as pleased as if she'd thought of the whole thing herself, and I promised to take Rose into Canton the next day for supplies—or maybe David could do that and let me run my café.

* * * *

David spent the morning with Edith, although I didn't know it until I brought ribeye steaks home for dinner that night. We didn't offer steak at the café but every once in a while I could sneak some in on our regular meat order. This was one of those times—they'd arrived today. I liked to think they were fresh, but I knew they'd been frozen. Can't be too fussy in a small town. I added baked potatoes, all the fixings, and creamed spinach, having had enough of salad. At least one good bottle of red wine waited at home, so I ducked out, leaving Sallie in charge with one other wait person and promised to be back to close up.

When I unpacked my bounty, David asked, "What's the occasion?"

"Nothing special. I just felt we needed a treat. Pour some wine?"

"Glad to."

"And cook the steaks on the grill?"

"Of course."

So David lit the grill, fortunately gas so we didn't have to wait for briquettes to turn to charcoal, and I put the spinach in an ovenproof dish and tossed a salad. Then I took my wine out to the porch to sit and visit while he grilled.

"So where were you all day?"

"Curious, are you? I spent the morning with Edith Aldridge."

The lazy evening languor vanished. I sat straight up in my chair, clutching my wine. "And?"

"She says she shot at him. Saw him coming, met him outside the front door, warned him away once. He didn't believe she'd shoot, so she did. Told me in no uncertain terms that she'd kill that—well, it wasn't a nice word—before he could kill her. I spent most of the morning trying to talk her down."

I got up and walked out into the lawn, where Huggles was comfortably chewing on a tennis ball. The smell of the grilling steaks was almost overpowering. "Why did she call Steven Connell? Does she know you fired him?"

He laughed ruefully. "Oh yeah, she knows. But she said she knows I'm a lawyer not a bodyguard, and he's more into that kind of thing. She expects he'll protect her."

"Will he?"

"If she pays him enough, yeah, he will. And he's good at it. But I'd just as soon have him gone from this case. I always trusted him, and now I've got a funny feeling about it."

I agreed. But then I remembered Edith Aldridge wasn't his entire professional life and asked about his other cases. "A couple of divorces, a really tangled estate settlement..."

"You may have another one of those someday," I said.

"I pray God not soon. Anyway, that's about it except a real estate conflict about who promised to do what when. Those are bread-and-butter cases because they drag on forever."

"And Edith pays you a retainer?"

"Monthly. Definitely bread and butter. But you're supposed to be figuring out who killed Walter. Any ideas?"

I shook my head. "If you overcook my steak, I'll come after you with a meat thermometer."

He pressed a finger on it and then said, "Perfect medium rare. Just the way we both like it."

We had a comfortable dinner, without talking about Edith, though I did tell him about the arrangement I made between Donna and Rose, and he leaned over to kiss me. "You're a genius."

"Thanks." I pushed my plate away, too full to eat another bite. I'd save the rest of the steak for a late-night snack. "What are we going to do about Edith? I don't know now if I'm worried about her safety or that of those who might threaten her. I think Rose and James are safely out of the picture, at least as far as harming her is concerned, but Rodney's the ringer."

"And we may be judging him guilty when he's not. Any number of people, including Edith, could have had reason to wish Walter dead."

"But if it was Edith, why did she hire you and enlist me thirty years later?"

"She hired me years ago, and maybe she sent Big One and John because she wanted me out of the case." He smiled. "It would have been easier to write me a letter of dismissal, and she could have done it. And why ask you to investigate? No, I don't think she's the answer. There's someone else involved in this."

Okay, back to the computer in the morning.

I'd had just enough wine that David, clever fellow that he was, thought he should go back to the café with me to close up. I protested but not loudly. I sent Sallie on her way, gathered the charge tickets out of the cash register, locked the cash in the safe, and turned out the lights. David had already locked the front door, and we were preparing to go through the kitchen and out the back door.

Sudden, loud banging called us to the front door—or would have, except David ordered me into the kitchen. "But I may know who it is . . . ."

"And you may not. Please, for once, just do as I say. Take the phone back there and call Chester. No one needs to be banging on this door at nearly ten o'clock at night."

"Be careful," I said uselessly. My thoughts were full of glass-paned double front doors and birdshot and . . . well, I didn't want to think about that.

"Let me in," a man's harsh voice demanded. "I know something you'll want to hear."

I had called Chester, but I quickly peeked through the pass-through window to see David walk boldly to the front door.

"Not this time of night, pardner. You want to talk to us, you come back in the morning. I guarantee you a sticky bun on my tab."

The man kicked the wooden panel at the bottom of the door. "Ain't good enough. I got to talk now or never. And you'll be sorry if you don't hear what I have to say. I know stuff about Edith Aldridge nobody else does."

David spread his hands in the uniform gesture of useless apology. "See you in the morning." Then he left the outdoor lights on, turned out the indoor, and turned his back on the intruder.

David, he could shoot you in the back! I held my breath as David slowly walked toward the kitchen. Had it been me, I would have run. But David walked deliberately, taunting the man, I thought.

"Were you testing your luck by turning your back on him and walking so calmly?"

"No, but I knew showing fear would embolden him. Now we stay in the kitchen, preferably sitting on the floor."

And so we did, as we listened to Chester's siren roar up. I thought maybe Chester should have left off the siren, but I was learning better than to second-guess law enforcement. Maybe he didn't want to put us in the middle of a confrontation, armed or not.

Silence followed. David got up to look outside and even went back into the main dining room. He called back to me that Chester was walking all around the property, using his torch flashlight. The flashlight disappeared to the side of the building and then apparently around the back, only to reappear on the street side of the building. After what seemed an hour but was probably only ten minutes or so, Chester knocked on the front door, his knock a gentle contrast to the demanding boldness of our earlier visitor.

David let him in.

"He's long gone, though maybe hiding in the field back behind. But I didn't see hide nor hair. Can you describe him?"

David, releasing tension, laughed, "Neither hide nor hair. No, no really. The light was on so I got some look— he was unshaven and had longish hair, untrimmed. I'd say he tried to look menacing but couldn't pull it off. One reason I was so 'brave,' but don't tell Kate."

I hugged him and went to put on a pot of coffee.

We talked until nearly midnight. My main question was what that man could have told us about Edith, but I sensed it wasn't good.

"We'll have to see if he comes back in the morning," David said.

"I'll be here first light," Chester said, "but I'll come out of uniform and in Carolyn's car so I don't scare him off if he does intend to come back for that sticky bun. Uh, Kate, save one for me too, will you?"

I assured him I would.

"Okay, you two, you may resent it but you lock this place up and I'm driving you around to the back of your house and going in with you to check it's okay. Can't take no chances."

My heart lurched. It was really that serious. And then I thought about Huggles. He was outside, and yet I hadn't heard him bark. Or had I just not listened. What if that man, whoever he was, harmed my dog? I clenched a fist in anger at the thought. "Let's go. Everything's locked up. I just have to turn out a couple of lights and lock the back door. That's the way we were going home."

"Turn off the coffeepot, too," David reminded me.

I stuck my tongue out at him, because I knew I wouldn't have remembered that.

We drove that tiny, short distance in Chester's car, with the siren going and lights flashing. Good thing I didn't have neighbors. The minute the car stopped I ran for the gate at the end of the driveway, where Huggles greeted me, unharmed, his whole back end wagging in happiness. I opened the gate and fell to my knees, burying my head in his soft coat as he licked my face. *He knows we were in danger tonight.* I wasn't sharing that thought with David or Chester.

"Come on," Chester ordered. "I got to check your house, and I can't leave you outside. Carolyn will be having a wall-eyed fit about why I'm gone so long so late at night."

We waited in the kitchen, Huggles with us, while Chester satisfied himself the house was secure. He finally stomped back in from the living room. "All okay. You all lock yourselves in and turn on that security system. I'll see you in the morning, first thing. And, Kate, don't you forget that sticky bun."

I promised, hugging and thanking him and asking him to tell Carolyn I was sorry for keeping him so long at night.

"Aw, her bark is worse than her bite. That woman just likes to worry." And he was gone.

We settled Huggles and Wynona for the night and gratefully crawled into bed ourselves. If that mysterious stranger came back, it would have taken some mighty barking from Huggles to alarm me. I was safe and happy in David's warmth.

Chapter Nineteen

Chester was as good as his word. When I crossed the grassy slope between my house and the café, I saw him and Tom Bryson, my brother-in-law, prowling the field behind the café. Tom, as mayor, had been deputized when Wheeler was briefly without a police chief, and now he occasionally helped Chester when needed. The two worked well together.

They each took a section and walked it methodically, looking for who knows what. It hadn't rained lately, so I doubted they'd find footprints. I wasn't versed enough in law enforcement practices to know what else they could be looking for.

I let myself into the darkened café, switched on the lights, and began to think about the day. I always enjoyed these few minutes alone in the empty café before everyone else arrived. It was then that the place seemed most to belong to me, and I could carry on conversations with Gram. This morning, though, I waited in vain for words of wisdom from her, except she said, "Don't let my great-grandchildren come to the café today." *Wow, thanks Gram! That sounds ominous, as though I haven't had enough scares in the last few days.*

Sticky buns were rising, coffeepot was on, and I was getting out eggs, bacon, sausages, frozen fried potatoes—a convenience I hated but couldn't bypass—when Tom used his key to let himself and Chester in the front door.

Tom wasted no words. "We found your visitor from last night. Least we think we did. In the field yonder."

"Well, where is he? I have things to ask him, like what he knows about Edith."

Chester harrumphed. "Afraid he's not talkin', Kate. He's dead. I called Doc Mason and the county coroner's crew. Can't do nothin' till they examine him. So we came for coffee."

"You just left him lying out there in that field, dead?"

"He ain't going nowhere."

I looked at Tom, but he just shrugged. "Chester's in charge. We'll go back out when Doc Mason gets here, but you know he isn't always in a rush. Meantime, coffee and a sticky bun would be good."

I frowned at both of them. "Sticky buns aren't even in the oven yet, but I'll get you coffee." And I did.

They sipped silently, and I found I didn't have much to say. I went about opening chores and was relieved when both Marj and Jesse, the daytime cook, arrived.

Tom sat where he could watch out the window, and finally he said, "Come on, Chester. Doc's here. We'll get the buns when we get back."

They trooped out, and morbid curiosity led me to the windows on that far side of the restaurant. As I watched, they appeared to be scouring the field again, and this time Chester and Tom were arguing, while Doc Mason stood scratching his head. Finally, all three trooped back to the front of the restaurant, so I went to the front door.

The ambulance crew, which doubled as a suspicious-death crew, hung around their vehicle, waiting for directions. Doc Mason waved them away with a short explanation, and I watched as they look astonished and then grumbled, unhappy, I suspected, at being called out so early for no cause. A glance at the clock told me it was seven thirty.

The three men — Doc, Tom, and Chester — came inside. Chester tried hard to put a bright spin on things. "Those buns ready yet, girl?"

"Yes, but what happened?"

He looked down at his shoes, while Tom blurted out, "Body's gone. Disappeared. Kaput."

I stared in amazement. "Are you sure he was dead?"

Chester got a tad indignant, something he almost never did with me. "I know a dead man when I see him. No pulse, not breathing, eyes rolled back. Yeah, I'm sure. And I don't want to talk about it."

I served them all three coffee and sticky buns and left them at a corner table, where they huddled together, obviously talking about what they didn't want to talk about. As I walked away, I heard Tom say, "I sat right here watching. No way someone could come by, get that body, and go out again. Didn't happen."

A driver could reach the field behind the café by the dirt road that passed the café parking lot — our building actually sat sideways on the lot, so when we told people it was on the highway that was a bit misleading. It didn't face the highway. But beyond that field, the dirt road petered out in a tangle of East Texas scrub trees and brush that had never, to my knowledge, been cleared. Someone would have a hard time dragging a body through there, and I doubted even a four-wheel drive vehicle would make it. Gram used to claim there was a pretty if small lake back beyond the tangle where Gypsies used to camp, but I always figured that was her way to keep us from going exploring. In my childhood, Gypsies were a thing to be feared, for they snatched up young girls.

None of that train of thought helped with the present dilemma. I refilled coffee cups at that table from time to time, but the men fell silent when I came by. On the other hand, they showed no inclination to leave. It may have been forty-five minutes later when Sheriff Halstead literally stormed into the café, with no thought for other patrons who might have been listening.

"How in the hell did you three dunderheads lose a body? Were you sitting in here drinking coffee and leaving that body unattended out there in that field?"

"Only one way in and out, Sheriff, and I was watching the whole time." Tom was deferential but also a bit defensive.

"You never leave a body. Ever!" He was shouting.

"I'm not law enforcement," Tom reminded him. "Just a volunteer. And Chester reports to the city of Wheeler, not you."

"I should have stayed out there," Chester muttered, not helping his case at all.

"Damn right, you should have! Okay you knuckleheads, let's go walk that field. Maybe the body has magically come back." He slammed through the doors, with the other three following him.

Apparently, after almost an hour — and the day was getting more hot than just warm — Halstead went back to Canton, Tom went to his hardware store, Chester to his office.

While they were out there, David came dragging into the café, and I told him the whole story.

"Got a beer? Just joking, but I need some help understanding. That's some story. Gives me the creeps. They didn't find anything at all?"

"No, from what they told me, not even a depression in the field grass where the body originally was. No signs of a vehicle, no indication that a body was dragged off into the woods. Besides, there's one house back there. Halstead questioned the lady—sort of a late-age hippie—and she swore she had no idea what he was talking about. Made him so mad he threatened her, but she just slammed the door in his face."

"This body wouldn't be Halstead's case. It's Chester's—in the city limits. No connection to anything else that's happened. He needs to butt out."

I was a bit indignant. "You tell him that. I'm not about to. His argument is that it's definitely related to the whole business swirling around Edith Aldridge, because I told him, in detail, about the man who tried to get in here last night and the fact that he mentioned Edith. Gave him the best description of that man I could, even volunteered to describe him for a sketch artist."

David's look was grim. "I have a feeling he headed straight to Edith's mansion, so I think I better follow and calm him down, if that's possible. See you at supper. Be careful, and if I'm late, I'll call you. I'll be at the house by five or so. But bring us supper. I want a nice, relaxing dinner for two."

In the afternoon lull, I rushed home and made a pasta sauce of tomatoes and anchovies that I'd been wanting to try—so grateful the Lord blessed me with a man who likes anchovies as much as I do. I set the table for two, put out a candleholder, wine glasses, an unopened bottle of nice red wine, and then went back to the café. I'd leave again about seven, have supper with David, and then head back to close up. A neat tidy plan.

* * * *

At supper, David didn't have much to report about his visit with Edith. "She's a cool customer. Said she had no idea who the man was, doubted it had anything to do with her or "the children," as she persists in calling them. She was indignant at Halstead, who had apparently been the same bull in a china shop he was at the café.

"Says she told him whoever that man was, he had nothing to do with her. But he told her the man mentioned her. She was upset that you'd done that." David grew a bit indignant. "I'm her lawyer, but I'm not going to twist the truth for her sake. In fact, that's against my principles . . . and job description, I guess. I felt a bit chastised, and it made me angry. I think she knows good and well who the man is . . . uh, was."

We were taking a last sip of wine after our supper—the pasta was delicious and just perfect with the light salad I tossed, and we were relaxed if puzzled about Edith. Suddenly, Huggles erupted in the most frantic barking I'd ever heard from him. We'd left him outside to enjoy the spring evening, since he'd been in the house all day.

David literally sprang from his chair, knocking over his wine glass, which fortunately had little left in it. He rushed out the door yelling, "Huggles! Come!"

Huggles ignored him, intent at barking at something at the far corner of the yard, apparently something just beyond his reach on the other side of the fence.

"Kate! Bring a flashlight!" David stumbled across the yard, and Huggles now ran to greet him, whining and leading him back to whatever.

I crossed the yard with my high-beam flashlight and handed it to David. Huggles came to stand by me, but his entire body was quivering, and he kept whining, though I reassured him as gently as I could.

David shone the flashlight and then uttered an oath. "It's the body! It's the same man. Quick, go call Chester. Take Huggles with you and keep him inside."

Since he still had the flashlight, I stumbled across the yard, grateful that it had no potholes or the like. I had to drag Huggles, who kept pulling and turning around to go back to David. The result was that I walked bent over, dragging the dog by his collar, and my back soon began to scream at me. Once in the kitchen, I hunted for my phone, found it in my apron pocket, now hanging on a cabinet knob, and dialed Chester, who must be worn out with our evening calls. Huggles was now at the door, whining, and Wynona strolled into the kitchen, stretching and glaring indignantly, as if to ask what the fuss was all about.

I stayed inside, partly because I sensed the men wouldn't want me around and partly to quiet Huggles, who was uncharacteristically beside himself. He went from me to the door and back again, whining. I was sure he'd wear a groove in the floor. He also pawed at me, and I feared I'd have claw marks. I gave him water, extra treats, but nothing calmed him.

Chester's headlights drove in the driveway. He opened the gate—my Huggles barricade—and drove across the backyard. I'd have been indignant, but I knew the medical team would have to drive back there. In the end, they didn't but approached the site from the pasture. Doc Mason parked in the driveway and used his own big flashlight to cross the yard.

I sat inside, absently petting Huggles and watching. Soon floodlights lit up the scene, and I could see cameras flashing and figures in ghostly white outfits moving about—the hazmat outfits the coroner's team usually wore. I poured myself wine, probably a time or two too many, and watched, almost desperate to find out what was going on. Huggles finally succumbed and lay at my feet whenever I sat still. Mostly I paced, and he followed me.

I did remember to call the café and asked Sallie to close up and put the receipts and cash in the safe.

"I don't know the combination."

I rattled it off almost automatically, without stopping to think if that was a wise move or not.

It was nearing eleven when Chester drove back across the yard—I'd worry about the trenches his tires left tomorrow—and the men came trooping in. The ambulance had taken away the remains.

Doc, with the familiarity that comes from knowing me all his life, sat down at the table and asked, "You got any bourbon?"

I got up to pour three fingers, neat.

"Guy's been dead at least twenty-four hours and all that moving him about didn't improve the corpse any. It'll take an autopsy, of course, but I suspect he suffered blunt trauma to the skull. Back of his head is all bashed in. Hard to tell under these circumstances."

Chester was clearly dejected. "I let it happen on my watch."

"It wasn't your fault, Chester. We all missed whoever moved the body." David was trying to be reassuring. "Question is, who was it?"

"And now I've got to call Halstead and bring him up to date," Chester continued. "I don't look forward to that."

"Give me his number. I'll call him," David volunteered.

We could only hear David's side of the conversation, of course, but it didn't seem cordial. Whatever Halstead was saying, he said it in a loud voice. David never raised his voice, said "Yes, sir," and "No, sir" but finally, "Of course we don't have any idea who dumped the body. Come daylight we'll search the area. And Doc Mason will do an autopsy." Long pause while Halstead's voice roared through the phone. "No, sir, I'm not going to ask him to do that tonight. Tomorrow will be soon enough." Another explosion on the other side of the line, and David said mildly, "No, I'm not a law enforcement officer. Chief Grimes is in charge. You want to talk to him?"

Apparently, Halstead slammed down the phone with a loud, "No."

Chester pulled out an old-fashioned cowboy kerchief and wiped his brow. "Thank goodness. That man bullies me."

David fixed him with a stern look. "Only because you let him. Chester, you're the chief of police, it's your case. Take charge. You don't report to him, and he can't bully you if you don't let him."

Chester sat a little straighter in his chair, and Huggles nestled his face in Chester's lap. The police chief absently petted the dog, his thoughts obviously elsewhere.

They sat a while longer, David and Chester sipping beers and Doc nursing his bourbon. Their speculation on who the man was amounted to nothing—just speculation. He had no wallet, no ID of any kind, no wedding ring or wristwatch. Seemed that someone had stripped the body, though nobody could tell if it was just after he was killed or just before he was dumped by my fence.

"Question is," David said, "why dump him by the café and then up here. Someone wanted us to find him. Maybe specifically wanted Kate to find him." He turned to me, "Kate, did you go back and close up the café tonight?"

I shook my head. "No way I was leaving here and going down there alone. I asked Sallie to put the receipts and charge slips in the safe."

"Give me the keys. I'm going to check."

Did he suspect Sallie of collusion or did he think someone had come in after her and stolen the money? Privately, I thought he'd find it all where it ought to be and would be bringing it back with him.

Not so. After David had been gone maybe five minutes, Chester's phone rang.

"What? Okay. Be right there. I'll call the ambulance." He ended the call and said, "Come on, Doc. That little girl was conked on the head and the safe's empty."

"Is she okay?"

"David says yes, dazed but okay. You stay here and lock yourself in, Kate."

"No way," I said as I followed them out the door, telling Huggles to stay. Out of the corner of my eye I saw Wynona stroll into the kitchen again, yowling as though we'd disturbed her rest.

Sallie was sitting slumped in a chair, holding a cold cloth to her head and crying fit to beat the band. When she saw me, she bawled even louder. "I'm so sorry, Kate. You trusted me, and I let you down."

I said soothing words to her, assuring her I didn't blame her, and her sobs subsided into occasional gulps.

Doc did a cursory exam — getting her to track his finger with her eyes, feeling her head — and finding a large goose-egg on the back. "My conclusion is she got hit on the head from behind and is lucky not to have a concussion. You live alone, young lady?"

"No. I'm married."

"Good. Tell him not to let you fall asleep for four to six hours."

"Oh, but I'm so sleepy," she wailed, tears threatening to start again.

"I know, but it's for your own good. You feel anything unusual, like nausea, you have him call me immediately. Got that?"

"Yes, sir. I need to call my husband and tell him why I'm so late. He'll be worried."

I gave her the phone and she called. Meantime, Chester said, "Kate, can you open late tomorrow? I need to get a team out here to dust for prints, check the place out. I can tell you what I think happened. It was an opportunistic crime, not related to anything else. After he dumped the body, and maybe watched us for a while, he came back by the café. Looked in, saw her opening the safe, and saw a chance to grab some cash. But I need to check."

"Chester, morning's my busiest time!" Now I felt like wailing.

"I know, sweetie, but I can't drag that crew out here again tonight. I'll have them here at five thirty. You can open by seven."

I agreed. I felt like Sallie. All I wanted to do was go to sleep.

Chapter Twenty

I didn't get to go to sleep, badly as I wanted to. It was almost midnight by the time David and I came back to the kitchen. Chester had roped off the entire pasture behind the café, given me strict orders about the café, and finally, finally left for home. It was a good thing David was out of his splint, because I leaned on him heavily as we skirted the field between the café and the house and walked down the driveway. From inside, Huggles barked and whined.

David opened the door and let Huggles out. The dog made a beeline for the spot where the body had been, but he contented himself with sniffing. Apparently, there was no need for frantic barking any more.

"Let's let him stay out a while," David suggested. "Sit, and I'll bring wine."

I was sure wine would put me right to sleep, but somehow it perked me up. When David sat in the rocker next to mine, I looked at him and said, "Rodney."

"Pardon me?" He said it in the tone he would have used for a perfect stranger.

"Rodney Aldridge. He's bound to be the one behind this. James wouldn't kill somebody, and neither would Rose. I suppose we should call and tell them what happened."

David looked at me with astonishment. "Not at this time of night. Particularly when we don't know that this has anything to do with them."

Maybe the wine was talking, but I said, "I have it all figured out. This guy was some relation to Big One and John, maybe Jimmy Baldwin"—that made me shudder—"and they worked for Rodney. He found out something he shouldn't have, or maybe talked to someone he shouldn't have, and Rodney killed him. After all, Rodney's the one who lies about his relationship with Edith and who really wants her money and her house."

David took a slow sip of his wine. "Have you shared all this with Sheriff Halstead?"

"No, but I think I'll call him in the morning."

"Better hold off," said the voice of experience. "But maybe you should call Rose and James . . . just not when you get to the café. Wait a while." He called to Huggles, who came running.

"But it's the only explanation that makes sense," I said, as he took my hand and pulled me out of my chair.

"There's always more than one explanation . . . and I'm still wondering why John and Big One—what's his name anyway?—aren't talking. But we won't figure it out tonight. Come on, let's lock up and go to bed."

I guess he locked up. I remember nothing but next morning I realized I'd slept in my underwear (had David taken off my clothes? They were on the floor on my side of the bed). I hadn't removed my makeup or brushed my teeth. There were mascara stains on my pillowcase, and my mouth tasted dry and awful. And when I woke up, it was eight thirty and David was gone. My head hurt.

I reached for my phone and called the café. Marj answered, way too cheerful. "Jesse showed David how to make sticky buns. They've been at it a while, and I tasted one—buns are pretty good. Chester cleared us to open at eight, so it hasn't been much of a problem. You take your time, sweetie. I know all this has been hard on you."

"Has anybody checked on Sallie?" I asked.

"David asked me to call her husband. He said she's fine, nearly divorced him when he kept waking her up every hour to see how she was. Doc says he needs to do that all day today. So glad it wasn't you, Kate."

"Yeah, but I feel awful about Sallie. I'll dress and be there as soon as I can."

"Take your time, Kate. We're doin' fine. 'Course everyone in town and the surrounding area has heard about that body disappearin' and reappearin' and so they're all here for breakfast. But we're managing. Don't you worry."

Well, of course I worried. My café was crowded with curiosity seekers, and I wasn't there. I scrubbed yesterday's makeup off my face, brushed my teeth until I thought they'd pop out of my head, threw on khaki pants and a white woven shirt with a collar. Then I grabbed a clean apron from the pile on the dryer, fed Wynona, let Huggles out, and sprinted to the café, cursing the roped-off field, thinking it wasn't easy to get away from my house quickly in the morning.

As I came in the back door, David greeted me. "Hi, sunshine. Want to try the best sticky roll ever? I'm pretty proud of myself."

A sticky bun was the last thing I wanted. Neither food nor coffee appealed to me, but I knew his feelings would be hurt. So I took the bun, took a huge bite and, in spite of myself, I grinned. "It's really good." I could feel my stomach quieting down with food in it.

"Don't sound so surprised. I have talents you've never dreamed of," he boasted.

"I knew you can cook, but I never thought you'd make sticky buns."

"I had a good teacher." He laughed, nodding at Jesse, who bowed his head shyly.

I checked the house and found almost every table full, so with a cup of green tea, seasoned with honey, I took up my station by the cash register. People wondered about the body as they paid their bills, but I simply smiled and said I wished I knew. When we found out, I'd post an announcement on the café's web page—a new invention of mine.

Too soon Sheriff Halstead barged through the double doors, demanding loudly, "What the hell went on here last night?"

My answer was as calm as I could make it. "That's what we'd all like to know. Have you checked with Chief Grimes and Doc Mason? They'd know more than I do."

He gave me a withering look, and without as much as a please, said, "Coffee. Black."

Marj served him without comment. He drank his coffee and left, no check, no tip. I took a dollar out of the cash register and handed it to her. "Chalk it up to lessons learned."

She pushed it back at me and said, "I don't need to be tipped for bein' so dumb. But, thanks, Kate."

Presumably, Halstead was off to check with Chester and Doc Mason. I wasn't about to share my conviction about Rodney with him. If he couldn't figure that out himself, he wasn't much of a sheriff. But then, I'd suspected that all along.

What I didn't need was a surprise visit from Donna about nine in the morning. "You're out and about early," I said by way of greeting.

"Why wouldn't I be? Whole town's talking about what went on last night at my sister's house and the café." She could never bring herself to call it my café, even though I'd bought her out. She still felt proprietary about it, which translated into entitlement to free meals.

"I don't know what to tell you that isn't already all over town. There was a body in the field yesterday morning. Then it disappeared, only to reappear outside my fence last night. And while everyone was busy investigating that, someone conked my waitress on the head and stole yesterday's cash." Long story short.

Donna leaned across the counter, as though to talk confidentially. "You must know more than that. Tell me. Who's the body? Who did it?"

I spread my hands helplessly. "None of us recognized the victim. He came to the door earlier the evening before, wanted in to talk about Edith Aldridge" — oops! Shouldn't have disclosed that much — "and we said we were closing. Come back in the morning. I feel pretty guilty. If we'd let him in, he might still be alive. But we'll never know."

"Well, I don't appreciate having Tom called out in the middle of the night. He's not a deputy anymore."

"No, but he's the mayor, and he's doing a great job of keeping tabs on what happens in his town."

She stared into space, sipping her coffee. "So it all has to do with that crazy Aldridge woman who lives in that mansion."

"Apparently so."

"How did you get mixed up in that business? I think you should cut all ties to whatever's going on and walk away, while you and David are safe. My children are forbidden to stay overnight until this is all settled."

I didn't point out she hadn't let them stay in a while anyway, but I wondered if they'd been asking.

She got up to leave — another one with no check, no tip, but at least I'd served her so it didn't matter. "Let me know when you find out who the body is . . . er, was."

"I'm sure it will be all over town instantly," I said, my way of saying that I wasn't going out of my way to keep her informed.

"I better check on that Rose Middleton or Mitchum or whatever she calls herself. I hope she hasn't stripped the Tremont House and robbed me blind as thanks for my hospitality." She left in a huff.

Grudging hospitality at best. Not offered kindly but with a lot of strings attached.

One thing David had accomplished rather quickly in those long hours while I was at the café and wondered if he was really working was to help Charles Mitchum find another lawyer and then quickly demand a weekly allowance for Rose. It wasn't much—Mitchum was a real close man with a penny, according to David—but it gave Rose a sense of self-confidence. And she was working as hard as she could at the B&B, which had no guests for the past two weeks, as far as I could figure. Rose was the caretaker of an empty house, but she cleaned, polished the bit of silver Donna had, even washed windows. Still, Donna found fault with everything. Rose occasionally came to the café for solace and company, and I fed her those heavy meals she should never have.

The day dragged on, the excitement of the evening before having subsided. By midafternoon, I snuck home for a break and was dismayed—envious? Upset?—to find David sound asleep. No, I wasn't tactful.

"How can you sleep with so much going on?" I demanded.

He looked at me groggily. "What exactly would you have me do? I know, why don't you join me here instead of worrying about what I'm not doing?"

"David, I have to go back to work. I just came to put my feet up and relax for a few minutes."

"You don't want to relax on the bed with me?"

"No, I don't. Yes, I do, but I can't. When will they identify the body?"

He swung to a seated position but stayed on the bed and patted it next to him, an invitation to join him. I sat down gingerly, a distance separating us.

"If I could predict that, I'd be a lot better lawyer than I am. Depends on DNA, fingerprints, all that stuff. I doubt anybody put a rush on it. After all, he was, as far as we know, a homeless man with no ID on him. No one else is in danger because he's dead."

"You don't know that for sure."

"Nope. It's an educated guess."

"Well, I guess I'm going back to the café," I said, deliberately mimicking his use of the word "guess."

"Nice to have had this little visit with you, sweetheart." And he flopped back down on the bed.

Who could resist? I bent over to kiss him and found myself entangled in a passionate embrace. Half tempted, half indignant, I let my conscience get the better of my instincts and pulled away. "Tonight," I promised.

I swear he was asleep again before I left, and I spent the rest of the afternoon wondering when Doc or Chester or whoever would identify those remains. Patience is not one of my virtues. David came in for supper—looking well rested, darn him! He always managed to come right at the height of the dinner hour, so my meals with him were interrupted by frequent calls to the cash register. Marj had gone home, and Sallie was taking more and more evening responsibility. She had apparently completely recovered from her blow to the head.

After we finished—pot roast for David and a chef salad for me—he rose, stretched, and said he wanted to call Brian. Tomorrow they were going to the site to look at progress—apparently the framing was up, and Brian wanted to check a few details. Guilt came over me again that I hadn't kept up with this project that was so important to David.

As he walked out the door, Gram spoke to me. "Get rid of the guilt, child. You can only do so much. You have your plate overloaded right now, and you're handling it well."

"Thanks, Gram." I said it aloud.

Sallie happened to be walking by and said, "Pardon me?"

"Sorry. I was just talking to myself."

By the time I called David to say I was headed home it was almost ten. We sat in companionable silence on the back porch in Gram's old rockers. When his phone rang, David checked caller ID and, seeing it was Chester, put it on speakerphone, warning Chester he'd done that and I was sitting close by.

"We got lucky," Chester said. "Least I think so. Victim's name is Ambrose Connell."

While I squeaked "Ambrose?" wondering who would name someone that, David turned suddenly stiff and serious. "Connell? Are you sure?"

"Yeah, I'm sure. Drifter, grafter, string of small arrests, nothing big. Can't trace him to any permanent place. Can't find any next of kin."

David answered slowly. "It's an unusual last name. I think I know his son. I'll get back to you ASAP." He stood up and headed inside. "Sorry, I've got serious work to do."

"Steven Connell's father?"

"Who else could it be? And what's his connection to Edith? I've got to track Steven down, at least let him know his father's dead."

"Maybe he already knows," I muttered.

David gave me a long look and headed inside.

I finally went to bed only to wake about three and find David was still at his computer, still making occasional phone calls. The only people he could possibly bother at this time of night were Chester or Halstead . . . or maybe law enforcement people he knew in Dallas. He talked so softly I couldn't make out what he said, and I soon drifted off again in spite of my curiosity. I didn't even know what time he came to bed, but I left him sleeping when I went to the café in the morning.

He came in about ten — late for him — looking tired and upset. The sparkle that had finally returned to his eyes was gone.

I poured his coffee, black as usual, and watched in astonishment as he put cream and sugar in it. "Needs softening this morning. One egg over easy and a piece of wheat toast, please."

"You okay?"

"No. I also need five minutes of privacy with you after I eat my breakfast."

I brought his egg and kept myself busy with other chores, principally at the computer working on payroll. But I kept one eye on David, and when he pushed his plate away, took a last swig of coffee and put the cup on the plate, I walked over to this table.

"Want me to clear that?"

"No. I want you to come outside with me for five minutes."

We sat on the bench on the porch. On busy days, like Sundays after church, the porch was crowded with people waiting for a table. In the middle of a weekday morning, there wasn't a soul around.

"Steven Connell has disappeared," David said without preamble. "Phone's no longer in service — cell and office. Landlord said he moved out a week ago — he was living in his office, always said it was temporary. I checked with a few other people, and no one's seen him."

"What does this have to do with Edith? I mean how do we find out?"

"Not we. Me. I'm going to pay her a visit right now."

"Did you call? You know she doesn't like drop-in visitors. Besides, it might be dangerous. Who knows who's lurking in those bushes?"

"Stop being melodramatic, Kate. No, I didn't call. I don't want to give her time to concoct a story. I have a feeling Edith hasn't been telling us the truth all along. And no one's waiting to ambush me."

"If she's hiding something, why ask me to look into it? And what could it have to do with burning down your cabin?"

David got a stricken look on his face, said, "Oh, shit," and pulled out his cell phone. "Brian? David here. Look, this is an emergency. I may be sending you on a fool's errand but get someone out to the site right away and leave a guard there, an armed guard—one of your guys who knows how to shoot a handgun." Pause, during which Brian must have said simply that he'd do it, and David responded. "Thanks. I'll check in with you later."

Then he turned to me. "If this is about money—stealing it, swindling it, whatever—nobody will touch the new cabin. If it's about revenge, somebody, even Steven, could torch it. And it may be about both."

"I'm coming with you."

"No, you're not. You've been in enough danger so far. No more." He knew me too well. "And, Kate, don't wait five minutes and then follow me. You know what you always say, you have a café to run. I'll call as soon as I know something."

He kissed me quickly and jumped in his car, which he'd parked outside the café instead of walking over.

Serious preplanning.

It was an endless morning, even with lunch only an hour away. That hour stretched and stretched for me. I'd look at the clock every three to five minutes, amazed it had moved no further than it had. I made two major mistakes in calculating social security withholdings and had to go back and do my work over. Marj eyed me nervously but left me alone.

The café phone rang, and I jumped to answer it. "Do you have meatloaf today?"

"Yes, ma'am, we certainly do." I know my voice fell from the high pitch with which I'd answered to almost a monotone. My patience was running out, and I wanted to jump in my car and hightail it to the mansion. I even went so far as to open the kitchen door and listen for Huggles, but he seemed in no distress, not the way he was when the cabin burned. I concluded illogically that meant David was safe.

He called, of course, at twelve fifteen, just as the first wave of customers was checking out. I called Marj to take over the register and added the counter to the newest wait staff's three tables. If she couldn't handle that much she wouldn't last long. Then I took my phone out the kitchen door and sat on the stump where Gus the dishwasher sat to smoke his cigarettes.

"You sitting down?"

"Yes." I didn't mention where my seat was nor how uncomfortable.

"Rodney is dead. Murdered."

I came close to dropping the phone, and then I was silent so long that David demanded, "Kate? Are you there?"

"Yes. He can't be dead. He's the one who wanted the money, the one that set this whole thing in motion. How can he be dead?" My mind wouldn't wrap around this new development.

David's tone was almost ironic and yet serious. "Shot with a bow and arrow. Body left outside the front door."

"Like the peacocks," I breathed. "But he was the one who knew how to shoot a bow and arrow. That's how Edith knew he'd killed her peacocks."

"Apparently, he wasn't the only one. Sheriff's people are here dusting for fingerprints—don't imagine they'll find any."

"Is Edith upset?"

"I have no idea. She's gone. Nothing in the house is disturbed, but she's just gone. Halstead is going on the theory she was kidnapped, but there's no sign of a struggle."

"Is Lucy there?"

"No, and this is what I think is puzzling. Halstead called Lucy. She says she reported for work as she does every morning at seven, but Edith told her she wouldn't be needing her today. Sent her home."

"I'm coming up there."

"That's the last thing I want you to do. I need you to call Rose and James, tell them what's happened, and tell them I'm worried about their safety. And, Kate, I'm worried about yours too. Trying to think of a safe place for all three of you. I'll be back as soon as Halstead's through with me, but I think maybe we all need to go to my place in Dallas."

"Dallas? I can't just up and leave the café."

"You can if it means your life. Also call Tom and Chester. I want them with you."

"But—"

He ended the call with a quick, "Got to go."

Chapter Twenty-One

I made the phone calls. Rose was predictably frightened and said she was coming to the café immediately. I wasn't sure it was a good idea to have us all in one place at the same time, but I knew she didn't want to be at Tremont House alone. James was just as predictable.

"Rodney's dead? Without getting his inheritance? He must be royally pissed." Then his voice sobered. "I wasn't fond of him, but he was my brother. Guess I'll have to make the arrangements. I still have his wife's phone number so I can get in touch with the kids. Even though the parents are estranged, the kids need to know."

"James, you're missing a major point here. David thinks you're in danger — you, Rose, and me."

He dismissed that. "Fuss about nothing. Edith probably went to Dallas or something — that's why she didn't need Lucy. Probably left before poor Rodney was put at her doorstep. Guess it will be a few days before the coroner releases Rodney's body, but I'll start phoning around now. May have to go to Dallas."

"David thinks we should all go to Dallas, get out of here. We could go to his apartment."

"Kate, if somebody's looking for us, they'd find us there. He's as much a part of this as you and I are. The attack and fire at his house sort of started this whole mess."

He was so right. I wondered if David didn't see this logic. "James, be careful. Do you have a gun?"

"Nope. Don't believe in them. Take care, Kate. Keep me up to date."

Both Tom and Chester said they'd be right over to the café, and they arrived about the same time Rose did. Her face was red, and she was breathing heavily, obviously upset.

"I'm scared," she gulped. "If Rodney's dead, am I next? I suspect our wicked stepmother is behind this. Rodney pushed her too hard. He wanted that house so badly. He just couldn't be content with what he had, thought the world owed him more. Or Edith did." She pulled out a handkerchief and dabbed at her eyes.

Tom and Chester were little help. They apparently didn't know what to do with a hysterical, sobbing woman.

"I wish it was five years ago. If we could turn the clock back, none of this would happen, Charles wouldn't be trying to divorce me, Melissa would be a sweet angel and not the hoyden she's turned into."

I stifled the thought that hers was certainly a self-centered approach to the problem. At least James had some words of regret for Rodney.

Chester finally put a gnarled hand on her arm. "Wishing the present away isn't going to do any good, Ms. Rose. We got to deal with what's on our plate now. And the most important things is keeping you and Kate safe."

"And James," she said.

"James doesn't feel threatened," I said. "He's sorry about Rodney and said he'll make arrangements, but he didn't seem particularly upset."

"Arrangements!" she sputtered. "There's no one left to mourn for any of us, except maybe that girlfriend of James'."

I thought it was time to move this group to my house. Rose was making a spectacle of herself, and I could see curiosity written on the faces of several customers. None of us seemed in a mood for food, and I could try to give Rose a stiff short of bourbon. My suggestion met with acceptance, and we all trudged across the field to the house. Since the weather was getting warm in the daytime, I'd left Huggles in the house, and it turned out I was very glad I had.

As we approached the back door, Chester said, "Y'all wait right here."

I followed his line of sight and saw it—an arrow stuck into the middle of my back door, pinning a note to the door. Rose saw it too and fainted dead away. Tom knelt by her and loosened her belt and collar, took her pulse, pinched her cheeks, and fanned her with a piece of paper he found gosh knows where—perhaps in his own pocket or in Rose's purse.

Chester was on the phone calling for an evidence squad—they had to come from Canton so it would take a while. We could go around to the front door, but I'd left my keys at the café. Huggles whined and pleaded with us to come in. All I could think was that if Huggles had been out, he might have been the target of the arrow. A sense of dread filled me, but I knew I couldn't let Rose see that.

Chester helped Tom get Rose, who was coming around, into one of the rocking chairs on the porch. Then he went after my keys, but first he said, "Call David and Halstead. They need to know about this. And, yes, call that James fellow again."

Neither David nor Halstead answered, which I thought was strange, and so did Chester when he returned with the keys. Tom went around to open the door and came straight through the house to let us in where it was cool. I got down the bourbon and poured one finger for Rose, who sniffed it and asked, "Should I really drink this?"

Chester's phone went off and he said swiftly, "Grimes here." There was a brief pause and then he uttered an oath, completely unlike Chester. He listened a minute more and then said, "I'll be right there." Then he turned to us and said, "David's new house has been vandalized." He took a deep breath and added, "The framing was burnt to the ground. He and Halstead are out there now."

Chester left, telling us the evidence team from Canton should be there within the hour, and, no, we were not to touch the note, the arrow, the door.

My fingers itched to get at that note, but I knew Tom wouldn't let me.

To my credit, my first thought was not selfish. It was for David. He was so excited about his new lake house, so full of plans for us, and I'd been less enthusiastic than he wanted. My second thought was one of guilt. But with the third, came a need for action. "I'm going out there." I needed to figure out who set the second fire, with John and Dan'l in jail. Johnny Baldwin leapt to my mind, and I was somehow convinced that if I could be out there, I'd find something the men missed.

Tom Bryson fixed me with a look that I'd never seen from him before. "Kate, you are doing no such thing. If I have to knock you out and hog-tie you, you're staying right here with Rose. So am I. Three men can handle a fire scene. Besides, if it's out, there's not much to handle."

I started to rebel, but the seriousness on Tom's face stopped me, and I sank into a chair.

Tom handed me a glass of cold water with an order to drink it. Then he turned to Rose, who was still pale but seemed to be mostly all right.

"Could I lie down somewhere?" she asked. "With a cold rag on my forehead?"

"Of course." I showed her to Donna's old room and fetched a washrag, wrung out in the coldest water I could coax out of the tap. "Let me know if you need anything else," I said.

"Peace, safety, and quiet," she muttered.

I looked in not ten minutes later, and she was sound asleep. I covered her with a light summer blanket and pulled the door gently shut.

Tom and I sat in uncomfortable silence. There didn't seem to be much to say. We couldn't begin to figure out who was where and why in this tangled mess, but none of it gave me a good feeling. Huggles lay coiled around my feet with what I interpreted as a sense of protectiveness. I thought about David, out there in the woods where any skilled rifleman—or bow-and-arrow expert—could use him as a target. I drummed my fingers on the table, fidgeted, glanced at the back door frequently.

"Kate, stop it!" Tom's voice was a command. "You're not doing yourself or any of us any good."

"I'll be all right when David Clinkscales walks in here," I said.

"We can't wait for that. We have to make some concrete plans. First one is that finding Edith Aldridge is not our responsibility, not any of us except Sheriff Halstead. Our responsibility is to keep everyone safe—you, David, Rose, James."

"Donna and the children?"

"They're not involved in this, and heaven help me if Donna gets wind of it."

"She was in the café yesterday morning, where Ambrose Connell's body was the talk of everyone. Of course, then we didn't know who he was. I promised to put his identity on the café web page, but I haven't done it."

"Good. And don't do it."

"Just where will we be safe?" I asked.

"Right here," he said. "We've pulled the shades, you have a good alarm system, the security is good. I can't think of any place you all can hide that's better. Chester's nearby, and I'm going to be here until this is solved. Or until Steven Connell is found—because I think he's the one behind all this, without a doubt."

"I do too," I admitted. "But you can't stay here. Donna will have a fit and complain about being left unprotected. Besides, I may end up with a houseful, if James and Shelly finally see that they're in danger."

As if on cue, the phone rang. James exploded on the other end, "Holy shit! Someone shot my dog with an arrow."

I reached down for Huggles reflexively and then asked, dumbly, "Is he okay?"

"Yeah, missed anything vital. Appears to be a flesh wound, but I'll have to take him to the vet to get the arrow removed. Shelly's keeping him quiet. But you're right—someone seriously demented is after us."

"Come here," I said. "I'll call the Wheeler vet and ask him to meet you. Bring some clothes so you both can stay . . . and an air mattress if you have it."

They were at the house within a half hour. And that's how I ended up with five assorted adults, two dogs, and a sulky cat under my protection. Actually, I called Doc Mason, who came quickly and knew better than to ask too many questions. I also knew he'd ask Chester for details. But he was gentle with Maynard Malcolm, a sweet dog of uncertain ancestry but probably a lot of lab. Doc cut the shaft of the arrow with bolt cutters and then shot some topical anesthetic into the skin so he could make a small cut, just big enough to push the arrowhead through. A few stitches, and he was done. Shelly and James both held the dog and crooned to him, and he submitted peacefully to the procedure, as though he knew people were helping him.

Doc wore gloves the whole time and when he was through he asked for a baggie. Then he bagged the arrow. "Never can tell where they'll find evidence," he said.

After Doc left, carrying his bagged arrow, we sat and looked at each other. Rose was still sleeping, and James and Shelly were on the floor, crooning to Malcom Maynard. Huggles thought this was most interesting, but I managed to rein in his curiosity. None of us spoke. I suspect we were each contemplating our version of the future.

That is, none of us spoke until Chester and David arrived, just as dusk settled over us. I had worried that David would be the same beaten-down man that survived the first attack on his house and his life. But I needn't have worried. The David who came in my back door was blazing mad.

"They burned it down. My house. To the ground. Brian's guys didn't get there in time except to help stomp out the flames so they didn't destroy every tree on the property. We'll have to start all over again, including scraping the land clean. I'll get them, those sons-of—" He looked at me and stopped, though I knew full well what he was about to say.

"Who?"

"Steven Connell, for starters. He's the only one left standing, with Rodney dead, and James here." He looked down at James and Shelly on the floor with their dog. "What happened?"

"Dog was shot with an arrow," James said. "Doc Mason took it out. He'll be okay."

"There's one big clue—who besides Rodney was skilled at archery?" Then he paused midthought and turned to me. "Rose?"

"Asleep in Donna's old room. She's terrified."

"So everyone's here and accounted for except Steven and Edith."

"Looks that way." I turned to Chester. "Any word on what the note on my door said?"

"Oh, yeah. I wrote it down." He pulled a small pad of paper out of his pocket, thumbed through a couple of pages, and read, "James and Rose must sign a quit-claim to any property or money owned by Edith Aldridge within twenty-four hours. Document must be drawn up by David Clinkscales and notarized. Delivery instructions will follow. Edith is safe."

Conversation stopped again. What could we possibly say?

Rose had wandered in just in time to hear Chester read his notes. "I'll sign," she said. "Just give it to me. I want this whole mess to be over with. I want my life back again."

James got up and put a comforting arm around her. "Rose, we're all trying to figure out what's best to do. Just wait a bit, can you? You're safe here."

She clutched his arm. "Are you sure?"

"Nothing's going to happen—we've got twenty-four hours."

She trembled. "Will you be here, James?"

"I will, and I'll take care of you."

I wondered how the pacifist in the midst of all of us planned to do that, but he seemed to calm Rose down, and I was grateful. It was past time to think about feeding this edgy, hungry group of people, and I knew I didn't have enough in my kitchen to do it. Then I thought about eggs—I had two dozen, fresh from the farm. I combed through the vegetable drawer and my frozen vegetables and came up with a respectable frittata—scallions, chopped spinach, frozen peas, and a bit of dried basil. I thought about putting cherry tomatoes into it but saved them for garnish. Fortunately, I had a good supply of white wine.

Chester said he had to go home to Carolyn and would keep us posted on anything he heard. The rest of us ate my hearty one-dish meal, sipping wine, sitting wherever — Shelly and James were still on the floor with their dog. I fed Huggles, so he wouldn't try to beg from them. Wynona wandered in, looked with disdain, and went back to her special place in my bedroom. She had plenty of food in there, and a frittata didn't interest her much.

I broke the silence. "Is Edith part of this? And if so, why did she want me to find out who shot Walter Aldridge?"

Silence again, until David said, "No idea. Unless somehow Ambrose Connell was part of this. Steven would have been a young child at the time, so why would he be involved now? She's apparently the mother who left him with a ne'er-do-well father."

"Maybe Ambrose Connell holds the clue to the mystery," I said, putting my plate in the sink. "I'm going to get my computer."

Before I could settle at my computer, household details had to be taken care of. James and Shelly fixed themselves a bedroom with the air mattress in the living room; Rose was set in Donna's room and went willingly back to bed. David and I said nothing about our sleeping arrangements, but we turned out all the lights and then I hesitantly let an impatient Huggles outside. While he did his business, I crouched on the porch steps, listening for any sound and letting my imagination run away with me at the slightest sound from the woods that bordered the far side of the yard.

Huggles sensed my fear and came running back to me as soon as he'd taken care of his needs. That was one time I wasn't going to pooper-scoop the yard right away. We went into the house, and I turned on a few lights, including outside lamps on the porch.

David did dishes, while I sat at my computer. Searching for Ambrose Connell on Google didn't bring up much — no surprise—but it did bring up a brief news item in *The Dallas Morning News.* Beyond the usual information—he was found dead of unknown cause in Wheeler, it contained a gem of information. He was born in 1940, married in 1959 to Ellie Mae Tipton. Ambrose Connell was survived by his son, Steven. Eureka! Ellie Mae had to be Edith, but how to confirm that? And that meant she was probably Steven's mother. *Oh, what a tangled web . . . .*

David had loaded the dishwasher and come to sit by me. "You still have access to Dallas County records? You could look up a birth record for Ellie Mae Tipton and then maybe a marriage license."

I did have those databases on my computer still, from days as working as David's paralegal in Dallas. "How old do you think she is?"

"Sixty to sixty-five," he said. "I'll check marriage records for late 1950s."

He got the easier chore, but I began checking Dallas County birth certificates from 1935 to 1950. At first, it seemed an endless task. I went through countless records without a nibble, and believe me, there were a lot of births in Dallas County in those years. Besides, we didn't know positively that's where she was born. But then, in records for June 18, 1942, I found her—Ellie Mae Tipton, born to Charles and Marie Tipton. A home address on Worth Street. I had no idea where that was. "She's only sixty. Married young, divorced young, widowed at thirty-eight and a recluse ever since."

"Strange life," he replied.

I scribbled down the address and showed it to him. "East side of town. Used to be a fine neighborhood. Now it's sort of blue collar, both the neighborhood and a lot of houses show signs of neglect. Parents are probably long dead."

"I don't want to look through endless obituaries."

"They have a search function in the newspaper morgue. Now that you know the names, it should be pretty easy."

So I typed in Charles Tipton and learned that he died in 1984. Ellie Mae by then was Edith and safely married to the wealthy Walter Aldridge. I wondered how cordial the relationship was between father and son-in-law. What mattered was that he was survived by his daughter, listed as Ellie Mae Tipton Aldridge (must have frosted Walter) and two sons—Edgar and Charles Jr. If they still lived in Dallas, we were on our way.

David, meanwhile, had found the record of Ellie Mae's first marriage—to Ambrose Connell—at the courthouse.

I could picture a drab affair, with the bride wearing a tacky white organza dress, carrying a bouquet of chrysanthemums, and the nervous groom in a shiny blue suit, with his Adam's apple bobbing above his red necktie. What a sad beginning, and maybe no wonder it didn't last. Then again, the notice, unlike society wedding announcements, said nothing about where the couple would live or what they would do with their lives. Maybe neither was employed, and they would go home to the Tipton house.

Chapter Twenty-Two

I began searching Dallas phone records for Charles or Edgar Tipton. Charles didn't show up, but Edgar did—living in the Tipton family home in East Dallas.

"We're going to Dallas tomorrow," I announced. "Maybe during the day isn't best—Edgar might be working. But we could go about six, at suppertime, probably catch him at home. Come to deliver sad news and our condolences."

"And what are you going to do with Rose and James and Shelly?" David asked.

I hadn't thought about that, though I knew this venture was dangerous for the two of us. "I'll call Chester in the morning."

It was already morning—three o'clock to be exact—and we turned in. David slept immediately, but I tossed and turned and played out all kinds of scenarios in my mind.

I rolled out of bed about seven, face puffy, eyes red, a mess. First thing I did was to call the café, ask Jesse to make the sticky buns though it was already late to set them to rising, and ask Marj to handle the day. "We've had a little trouble here . . . no, no, everything's fine . . . but the general opinion, including Chester's, is that it isn't smart for me to be at the café. For my sake and the café's . . . . No, I don't think it will last long." I wished the latter were true. And I never mentioned a trip to Dallas.

Chester immediately blew his stack. "You'll do no such thing! I'll notify Dallas police and they'll go deliver the news. You will not leave your house."

"Chester, come over for sticky buns and coffee. We have to talk."

"You are not bribing me, Missy, but I'll come listen."

And so he did. By the time Chester got to the house, Gus had delivered sticky buns, with a serious warning, "You take care, Miss Kate. Danger is too near."

Everyone else was awake and crowded into the kitchen. I had let Huggles out with some trepidation, but nothing happened. I wasn't sure why I thought now Steven Connell would shoot my dog. He'd made his presence and his demands known. But still I worried and fussed so much over the dog when he came in that he backed away from me in alarm.

James, less intimidated than I, let Malcolm Maynard out and sat on the porch steps while the dog explored and did his business. I finally, due to barking demands, let Huggles back out again, and the two dogs had a fine time running and chasing each other. Good to tire them out.

Chester came in loaded for a fight. "Why do you think a personal visit will get any more information than the police?"

"Because we'll come as concerned friends, in sympathy. Police immediately arouse defensiveness, even the best of them."

He harrumphed a little at that, so I hastened to add, "Present company not included."

"You better say that." But he hugged me.

"What if that's exactly where Connell and Edith went? They could be waiting for you, and you could walk into an ambush."

"I doubt it," David said. "I know their cars and can be cautious, but who knows what kind of relationship Edith does or doesn't have with her brothers? And it's too logical for them to go there—they must know law enforcement wants to at least talk to them. We just want to talk to the brother."

"Sheriff Halsted put out a BOLO for them, but no results so far. Meantime, how am I going to keep these folks safe?" Chester asked, his sweeping gesture taking in a shivering Rose and the much calmer James and Shelly. Chester himself came up with a plan. He'd put Rose, Shelly, James, and Malcolm Maynard in his jail. Carolyn would bring them exquisite meals. And they'd come back to my house when we got back from Dallas.

"Jail?" Rose echoed in horror.

"Safest place to be," Chester said. "I don't like letting these two go off on a wild-goose chase, but knowing them I don't have much choice. I'll deputize Bryson again, and one of us will be with you at all times."

"What will I do all day in jail?" Rose whined.

"I've probably got some books you could read," I volunteered, while Chester said he had a small TV he could put in her cell.

James and Shelly were more complacent. "I think this is all a bunch of foolishness, but I won't put Shelly in danger because of my crazy family. We each brought books, and some togetherness time wouldn't hurt us. Besides, sounds like Carolyn is a good cook."

"She is that," Chester said, rubbing his belly. "She'll probably fix you something fattening that she won't let me eat."

So it was settled. David and I would leave for Dallas about two, giving us time to go by his office for him to check in and then his apartment where, among other things, he'd pick up the shotgun he'd left behind. He had his pistol with him, but if we were attacked from a distance—which I didn't really think we would be—the pistol wouldn't do much good.

"I scouted around 'fore I came in just now," Chester said. "No sign of anybody having been here. 'Course we haven't had rain in a few days, and the ground is dry—easy to prowl without leaving a track."

Suddenly, the absurdity of it all came over me, and I began to giggle. Everyone stared at me, and I opened my mouth to explain, but every time I tried to speak, the giggles beat me. Finally, I was able to squeeze out words. "Can you imagine Edith Aldridge lurking in the bushes, scouting out my house?" And then I was off in laughter again.

David slapped me. Not hard. Just enough to sober me. "No, but I can sure see Steven Connell doing it."

Chester left, promising to call Tom, and we faced a long morning. David was at his computer, alternately sending emails and then muttering into his cell phone. James and Shelly drifted back into the living room, but Rose remained glued to the morning shows on the kitchen TV, which I found a huge annoyance.

"I called Melissa just to let her know I'm all right," she said.

David came out of his business trance long enough to say, "I wish you hadn't done that. Please don't call anyone else until this is all solved."

"But that could be an eternity," Rose wailed.

I wished I could call Donna to come get her charity case.

The good that came out of that long morning was that David quietly told me he'd hired another PI to investigate Steven Connell's background.

"How can you trust this one?" I demanded.

He shrugged. "He's somebody I've worked with longer than Steven, and when I mentioned Steven's name, he groaned. I think there's something there." He took a deep breath. "Kate, we have a long and difficult day ahead. Please don't make it any worse by second-guessing."

For lunch, we had tuna salad sandwiches and chips from the café, delivered again by Gus.

Shortly before two, Chester and Tom came for their charges. I noticed that Tom wore his handgun on his hip — a sure sign that he'd been deputized again. I thought I should call Donna, and then realized she might not know anything about what was going on.

Amid farewells that hid a lot of anxiety, David and I left for Dallas. Tom in particular hugged me extra tight and muttered, "You take care of yourself," while Chester just said, "You two be safe and call if you have any trouble."

* * * *

David had no trouble finding 4321 Worth Street, a modest brick bungalow once probably quite trim. Now everything needed paint — the trim on the house, the picket fence, even the bedraggled trellis that might once have boasted glorious roses. Spotty grass filled the small lawn area, most of it green weeds, and the flower beds — or spaces where they had once been — were overgrown. Along a side fence, Johnson grass flourished, and I saw a stand of bamboo at the back of the property. Good for privacy, but it would sure take over in a hurry. If Edgar didn't do something he'd have it growing up through his kitchen floor.

One car, a Ford, probably 1990s model, now with rusted places and peeling paint, stood in the driveway. David circled the block from two directions, a couple of times, but saw nothing to alarm him.

"You going to take your shotgun?"

He snorted. "I know it's legal to carry long guns in Texas, but how would you feel if you opened your front door to some guy with a shotgun? I've got my revolver—and my license. Now, look, Kate. Let me do the talking. But when we walk up there, don't be timid. Don't pull a Rose on me and act scared."

I resisted the urge to say, "Yes, sir!" and climbed out of the car, beating him to the front door, where I leaned on the doorbell.

A woman answered, wearing a splattered apron over loose-fitting knit pants and a T-shirt, wiping her hair off her forehead. She looked worn down by life. Probably not more than mid-fifties but the air of tiredness she exuded made her seem twenty years older.

"Mrs. Tipton? Is Mr. Tipton at home? We're here on a matter about his sister."

She called shrilly, "Edgar! Some people want to see you about your sister."

A disgruntled voice from the back of the house moved closer to us as he grumbled, "What's happened now? She's like a bad penny. Only shows up when there's trouble, like the time she shot that rich husband of hers." He was older than his wife but looked younger, perhaps because a job kept him in touch with the world daily. He wore stained coveralls and smelled of hard physical work done that day and not yet washed off.

David held out his hand. "Edgar Tipton, I'm David Clinkscales. I'm your sister Edith's lawyer, but I'm afraid she's disappeared."

"Got no sister named Edith. Her name's Ellie Mae . . . or was until she took on airs. Come on in, and have a seat."

We settled on chintz-covered couch and matching chairs with plastic covers protecting them. Mrs. Tipton made a vague mention of "the cats, you know" and then disappeared with, "I'd better check on the stew. There's plenty if you'll join us."

As we politely declined, saying we were on a tight time schedule, Edgar glared at her. He clearly didn't want to put up with us any longer than possible.

"Your sister disappeared yesterday morning, we think in the company of a man named Steven Connell. Does that ring a bell?"

He laughed aloud. "No, it sounds a great big gong. Steven's that son of hers, not someone I would trust from here across the street."

So much for David's choice of a PI.

"I've represented her for quite a few years now and never heard that she had a son."

"She didn't talk about him much because she wanted him out of her new life. Left him with that no-good father of his . . . forget his first name."

"Ambrose," I supplied. That name was forever emblazoned on my mind.

"Yeah, Ambrose. Strange name. Sounds like a rich man's butler, but believe me he isn't that. He's a bum. Raised that kid from pillar to post and probably taught him every trick in the book. That's why Steven made a good private investigator, even if he didn't always walk on the right side of the law. I kept in touch with Ambrose, felt sorry for him, but not sorry enough to invite him here."

Boldly I interrupted. "Tell us about Ellie Mae."

His eyes misted over. "Older than me, but as good a big sister as you could wish for when I was a toddler. Near raised me when our mother's health failed. But along about high school, she got notions that she was cut out for some life grander than ours. 'Course back then, this was a good neighborhood, and Mama had the prettiest flower garden on this block — roses, azaleas, petunias, you name a flowering plant, and Mama had it. When she died, place went to pot—I can't do it 'cause of my bad back."

"Ellie Mae?" I prodded.

"Overnight, seems like, she turned mean. Always full of schemes that would benefit Ellie Mae, and she didn't care who she hurt. She broke some high school boys' hearts, one bad enough he tried to kill himself, but she didn't care. Waved a hand and said how stupid it was of him.

"And then she run off with that Connell fellow—think he promised her the moon and more, but she was sure starry-eyed. No more than seventeen years old. Young as I was I didn't think it was smart. Didn't think she was gonna get everything he promised her. But Ma was relieved to see her go, I think. By then I was old enough to do the chores, and I suspect Ma was tired of Ellie Mae complaining and scheming—and sometimes stealing what little money Ma had so she could buy herself something fancy. Ma used to boil bones to make us a cheap broth. I tell you, I was hungry a lot of the time."

The picture of Ellie Mae sure didn't fit the Edith Aldridge I knew. "When did you last see her?"

"When Ma died, maybe twenty-some years ago. She was married to that Walter fellow by then and had become a grand lady, 'cept she didn't offer to pay for the funeral or anything. Good thing Ma had insurance. I asked her 'bout Ambrose and the kid I heard she had, but she said they were out of her life. Exact words were 'Good riddance.' Ambrose told me later they'd never divorced, so she wasn't really married to that rich fellow. Not that I cared. Told her not to ever come back here again."

That put a whole new light on things. If she wasn't legally married to Walter Aldridge, she didn't stand to inherit and shouldn't have the mansion. "So you haven't seen her in the last couple of days?"

"No, sirree. She knows I'd take a shotgun after her. Why?"

"There's been some trouble, and Steven has also disappeared. We didn't even know they were related until the last couple of days, but now we think they're together. Several people's lives are in danger. Ambrose was murdered."

"You don't say! Damn shame. He was no shakes as a man, but I hate to hear somebody's been murdered." He rubbed his chin, and called to his wife. "Susie? I got a powerful thirst for a beer. Bet these folks do too."

I declined but David gratefully accepted a Miller Lite, a brand he usually scorned. We talked a while longer, but two things were clear: Edgar enjoyed having an audience for his storytelling, and he had not one clue where his errant sister was.

As we rose to leave, David said, "Mr. Tipton, you keep that shotgun handy. I don't think Edith will come here, but you never know."

"She wouldn't dare," he replied with more bravado than I expect he felt.

We thanked him for his hospitality and time, asked him to thank his wife, and fled. Once in the car, David let out a long, "Whew! What a story. I don't know how to begin to sort it out.

"Nor to know how much is truth, how much resentment, how much just having an audience. I want to get home and check divorce and marriage licenses. How ironic if Edith isn't legitimately heir to all she's protecting so fiercely. Besides, I suspect Rose and James and Shelly would like to be rescued from jail."

"Wheeler it is, nonstop."

But we weren't out of Dallas before David announced, "We've picked up a tail. Don't turn to look but check your makeup in the rearview mirror or something. There's a tan

Camry pretty close on our tail—just one car back so as not to be obvious. What kind of car does Edith drive?"

"Not a tan Camry," I assured him.

"No telling what Steven's driving. He seems to have a different car every time I see him. No sense trying to dodge them. It's obvious where we're going—except he may be surprised when we go to the jail. Call Chester, would you please, and tell him we're on our way."

I did, told him we thought we were being followed, and spent the next bit of the drive in anxious tension, afraid to look back, afraid not to look back. At Seagoville, the Camry made a U-turn and left us. I breathed a sigh of relief but David was even more puzzled.

"I hope they're not going to Edgar's house. I guess following us to Wheeler was too big a risk."

"You don't even know it was them!"

"Instinct, Kate, instinct."

If I'd said that, he'd have jumped all over me. "Maybe they just wanted to be sure we weren't going to do anything else in Dallas."

"Or maybe they're going over to take I-20 to the Mansion, after being sure that's not where we're headed."

"I don't want to worry about it. I just want to collect our charges, go home, and get on the computer. I'll call the café and order chicken-fried steak for everyone. That will delight Rose."

We pulled up to the police office to find ourselves met by what almost amounted to an armed militia—Chester, Tom, and Doc, each with weapons at easy reach. Even James stood by, although unarmed except for a cell phone in his hand. Rose and Shelly were cowering together in one, unlocked cell.

When we walked in peacefully, Chester said, "We didn't know what to expect. A shootout maybe."

Sheepishly, I admitted the car had turned off at Seagoville. "Besides, we didn't know for sure it was Edith and Steven."

"I knew," David said firmly.

"I am so sorry. Dinner at the café is my treat. Surely there's safety is this many numbers."

"And this many armed men. But we promise not to shoot up the café," Chester said. "All right if we call Carolyn to join us? She's feeling a bit neglected these days."

Carolyn Grimes was one of my favorite people, and I urged Chester to go get her. The rest of us trooped over to the café. I had forgotten, of course, to place an order, so everyone ordered what they wanted. Carolyn hugged me warmly and whispered, "I am so worried about you."

"Don't be," I whispered back. "Look what good protection I have." I introduced her to Rose, and the two were soon deep in conversation that I doubted had anything to do with Edith Aldridge and her son.

I was pretty clever about arranging the seating, if I do say so. Having settled Rose and Carolyn at one end of the table, I put David and James in the middle, Chester at the end, and then seated myself between James and Chester. I had things on my mind, but I didn't want to appear to be telling Chester what to do. "What's next?" I asked, trying hard to be casual. "We can't keep these people cooped up at my house much longer. You think Edith and Steven went back to the mansion?"

Chester looked at me. "You got the vision, Kate? That's exactly what I think. Told Halstead so, and he went to court today to get a search warrant. He and his guys will go in soon as they get it. Me? I'm glad I'm out of it. I'm too old for that kind of foolishness."

"Foolishness?"

"Yeah. I think Edith and Steven are in cahoots, and they'll be there, holed up and ready to stand off an assault. It could get dicey. Carolyn'd never forgive me if I got hurt again."

Chester had been pretty badly injured in an accident which involved me, and I'd been both guilty and grateful ever since. Now I shuddered at the violence that might end this whole tangled mess—and I still couldn't understand what started it.

In spite of the circumstances, it was a pretty jolly supper party. David and James were talking animatedly about David's plans for rebuilding yet again. "It may have been a blessing in disguise. Brian and I have been emailing about some changes in the plans, and Sheriff Halstead has provided enough arson evidence for my insurance to cover the bulk of it."

"You think Edith or Steven is responsible?"

"I can't think of anyone else, and all I can think is that Edith has a secret she's hiding and is afraid I'll uncover it." He nodded toward me. "Or Kate will. Hope she doesn't have the nerve to try to torch the café."

The very thought sent a chill through me, and I wanted to change the subject as quickly as I could. "James, I have an odd question. Was Rodney an expert with a bow and arrow?"

He almost laughed. "Where'd you get that idea? I doubt he ever picked up a bow in his life. Now Dad and Edith, they used to hunt deer on the property with bow and arrow. Dad quit, because Edith got better at it than he was. We ate a lot of venison for a while there."

"Really?" I tried to make it sound like that was just an incidental fact, nothing more, and James turned back to his discussion with David, while I sat in utter confusion. Thinking Steven was skilled with a bow and arrow too was almost too much coincidence, but would Edith shoot her own peacocks? And then her stepson. What kind of hard-hearted woman hid behind that gentrified façade? I was suddenly more frightened than ever.

Chapter Twenty-Three

No one knew that Edith had told me Rodney was an archery expert, and I told no one at that table. But I figured it was conclusive evidence that she was lying — about a lot of things. The suspicion that crossed my mind was not comforting — she had asked me to look into Walter's murder because she thought I was inept and would give the appearance of looking into it while accomplishing nothing. That made me angry, and I knew I had to prove that she herself had killed Walter Aldridge. Talk about Jekyll and Hyde personality!

When the house had settled down for the night and I had David's ear, I told him about the archery lie.

"I was about to call Halstead and see what their search turned up . . . and who. I'll share that with him, if that's okay with you? I don't want to steal your thunder."

"No, go ahead. I'm getting online to review Walter Aldridge's murder one more time." I accessed Van Zandt County court records and studied the transcript of the trial; I read the obituary again; I reviewed my notes on the murder. Only David's voice interrupted me.

"Halstead said there was no one at the mansion. Lucy the housekeeper gave them the key. She's worried about Edith. Halstead said they searched the house. Thoroughly. Came up with nothing. Zip."

"No bow and arrows."

"No, but he thought that was an interesting piece of information."

"Where could they be?"

David shook his head. "Mexico?"

"And leave the house and inheritance behind? I doubt that."

"Halstead's pulling bank records in the morning—his and hers. You know, if I didn't know they were mother and son, I'd think this was a case of lovers leaving everything behind. But I can't imagine Edith doing that."

"Neither can I." I shook my head. There was some key, some clue we were missing. "We don't know how much money is involved."

"I do to a certain point, although it's privileged information. Let's just say she gets a healthy check deposited directly into her local account every month. And I mean healthy."

I knew he would not be more specific, but he frustrated me. "How do we know she doesn't have accounts in Dallas? And what about Steven?"

"I doubt Steven has any assets. He always seemed to live from pillar to post. He's in this for the money."

"And why is she in it? She was going along smoothly, with her 'healthy' income. Why stir things up?"

"Because Rodney made her feel threatened. I think she thought you'd pin the murder on Rodney and it would all be over."

That didn't help my ego any more than my own idea that she thought I was inept.

"But now she's—well, to use a trite phrase, she's burned her bridges behind her. Effectively given up her income and her inheritance."

"Only if she's proven to have murdered Ambrose or Rodney. And to avoid that, I have no doubt she'd—okay, another of your trite phrases—throw Steven under the bus. But the first thing is to find them. If they have an ounce of sense, they won't come busting in here."

"But is she motivated by greed or revenge?"

David shook his head. "Let's go to bed. Maybe by morning, we'll have some better ideas."

* * * *

By morning, all that was clear was that the inmates in my house were getting testy. Rose was harping on James' funeral arrangements for Rodney, saying they'd all be in danger.

"Would you let him go in the ground without a proper blessing?" James asked mildly.

"Yes. To save my skin," she replied tartly and flounced out of the kitchen.

Shelly was distant from James because she wanted to go home, had things that needed to be done like laundry and food that would spoil, and she was, she confided to me, bored and tired of the company.

David wanted to be out at his building site, but although Brian was allowed to go out there, David was not. Both Halstead and Chester were emphatic about that.

I fed everybody as best I could. I was going to have to send Chester to the local market if this kept up, and a trip to Canton was out of the question. I simply wanted to get back to the computer. I had figured out that Edith killed her husband but had to have an accomplice—at least someone to break down that French door. Or did she?

I called the Canton Chamber of Commerce and asked for a list of carpenters and builders in business thirty years ago. Predictably, it was a slim list. The first couple of calls were discouraging but I hit pay dirt—an independent contractor named Ralph Jones said he remembered fixing the doors.

"Damn near busted beyond repair," he said. "Somebody was in a fury. I always thought they couldn't have snuck up on that guy 'cause they'd have necessarily made so much noise busting that door."

"Big question," I said. "Was the door broken from the outside or the inside?"

He thought about it a long time. I waited. Finally, he said, "You know, come to recollect, it was broken from the inside."

In my mind, that clinched it: Edith had murdered Walter, shot him in the chest, and then busted up the door. Now what did I do with that information? Halstead would think I'd been meddling in what was most definitely not my business. But to me, that solved Walter's murder—but shed no light on what happened to Rodney (though I suspected Edith) and Ambrose (surely Steven wouldn't kill his own father—or would he?).

Sheriff Halsted, with Chester in tow, broke the monotony of everyone else's morning by striding in the back door, without knocking, and seating himself at the table, while Chester leaned against the counter.

"Well," the sheriff drawled, "I guess you all can go home now. Steven Connell was apprehended down in Zavala County, headed for Mexico, no doubt about it."

We waited expectantly, and the sheriff expanded his chest with self-importance. "There's been a BOLO out on him and Edith for over twenty-four hours, and some alert Texas Ranger spotted him in a roadside convenience store. Apparently took him down with no violence or bloodshed."

"What about my client?" David asked.

Halstead squinted his eyes at him. "You sure you still want her as a client? Anyway, no sign of her. All Connell said was that his mother was 'bat-shit crazy.' Forgive my language, ladies. I'm quoting."

"We can really leave?" Shelly asked, her voice breaking.

"Yeah, I don't think Mrs. Aldridge is going to come after any of you now. Wish I knew where she was, though. We'll check the house again today, let you know if we find anything."

James and Shelly were off to gather their belongings, David was out the door to the building site with a hasty kiss and a promise to see me for supper, but Rose hung back.

"I don't want to go back to Tremont House. Frankly, it scares me to stay there alone."

I wanted to shake some spine into her. "You can stay here, but you'll still be alone, except for Huggles. He's good protection. But I have a café to run, and I've been neglecting it."

She chose to stay, said she'd come to the café for lunch. I let Huggles out for a good run and then brought him in, locked the doors and showed Rose the alarm system—did I believe for a minute she understood what I was saying?—and left for the café.

Between Marj and Sallie, things were going smoothly, though by lunchtime I was greeted with a lot of "Where you been, girl?" and "We missed you," and "Glad to see you back here. Brightens my day."

Rose came in for lunch about the same time Chester called to say the alarm had gone off at my house. "I'm sure it was Rose. I'll go turn it off."

"Let me go," he said, "if you don't mind telling me the code."

The code was so simple—the house address—that he snorted and said he'd take care of it and maybe let Huggles out again.

Rose, all innocence, ordered chicken-fried steak, and hung around the café long after she finished her meal. She clearly wanted company, but I had too much to do.

I spent the afternoon mostly inventorying supplies and figuring out menus and orders. I also had to think about dinner tonight, so I went into the kitchen and started a small batch of spaghetti sauce, knowing I had fettucine in the cupboard. I'd scoop up salad makings and some Texas toast for garlic bread—three pieces. And then it dawned on me that I really wanted dinner alone with David, and I was resenting Rose more every day. She finally went back to the house about three, saying she was afraid to set the alarm, which I thought showed a rare bit of common sense. I truly considered serving David dinner at the café and taking Rose her portion, but I couldn't bring myself to be that rude.

When David came in to the café, he reported that Halstead had called, said he checked the mansion again. No sign of Edith, though Lucy was there and seemed unusually nervous. "He said he'd keep checking," David added. "I can't bring myself to worry too much about Edith Aldridge. She's a survivor. But I don't think she's my client any more. My decision, not hers."

Halstead apparently revealed something else most interesting. He told John and Big One that Steven Connell had been arrested and they all of a sudden couldn't talk enough. Steven had recruited them, given them specific orders—which included murder, if necessary—and threatened their families if they talked. Apparently, Steven wanted David out of the way—and out of Edith's affairs.

Big One had turned into a whining mess, saying he had three babies at home and he didn't want them hurt. All he had wanted was a little extra cash, which they never got.

John apparently looked at him scornfully but said nothing. Still Halstead said, "Little John had a wife and baby to worry about."

The whole sad story was unraveling, and it wasn't pretty. It was a story of greed on many levels and indifference to human or animal life. The missing piece was Edith Aldridge.

* * * *

For two long days, I worried over the whereabouts — and fate — of Edith Aldridge. Was she trapped someplace and unable to call for help? Had Steven killed her? I refused to believe that after Rodney's death and Steven's arrest, either James or Rose harmed her. They were innocents in this mess; Rodney and Steven were the evil ones. Then I'd pull myself up short and remember that Edith was no innocent either. I didn't know what I wanted, but I didn't want her to come to some sad, inglorious end.

Sheriff Halstead continued to check the house and report the same thing: no sign of Edith, but Lucy was there and seemed nervous.

David was no comfort. "We may never know, Kate. Connell could have dumped her body in a lake or even a well shaft where we'd never find it unless he talks . . . and I doubt that."

"She's alive," I said vehemently.

"Instinct?"

"Yes, strong instinct."

He really tried to comfort me, but I was anxious, antsy, and impatient. Edith was a strong woman, and I just couldn't believe that she'd let someone, even her own son, trick her into a dangerous situation. Besides, I didn't think she had many maternal feeling about that son. In fact, I wasn't sure who she had feelings for, if anyone.

I went about running the café, but always in a sort of haze, my thoughts elsewhere. I burned the sticky buns one morning, and Marj just caught me in time from putting salt in the sugar dispensers. I forgot to order steak for the chicken-fried and ordered double chicken. Without thinking, I put pepper in the chicken salad . . . and then put it in again. The result was inedible. Marj's suggestion that I go home and rest fell on deaf ears. If I were home, I'd just pace and worry.

Rose had reluctantly gone back to Tremont House, because Donna had guests—a couple from Dallas, and she was expecting another guest over the weekend, so she'd have a fairly full house. Once there were other people in the B&B, Rose didn't mind, even seemed glad to resume her duties. At least I had my home back, and David and I had privacy at night. He comforted me every way he knew how.

* * * *

On the third day after Steven Connell's arrest, Edith Aldridge came into the café about ten in the morning. I stiffened and dropped the plate of eggs and bacon I was about to serve, splattering food all over the place. My heart was pounding, my hands clammy, and my whole body shaky. *Why, when everyone was looking high and low for her, did she appear at my café?* The only thought that went through my brain was that she intended to kill me; I looked again—at least she had no bow and arrows that I could see. All right, logic wasn't my strong point in the face of downright fear.

Marj picked up the portable phone and handed it to me. In the safety of the kitchen, I dialed Chester, whispered that Edith was here and I'd leave the phone on speaker if he promised to be very quiet. He promised.

Suddenly, Gram, who hadn't spoken to me in weeks, said, "Child? Have you forgotten your manners? Go greet that poor woman. Her problems are a lot worse than yours."

"Yes, ma'am," I muttered.

Edith, meanwhile, was staring at me, as I started slowly toward her, trying to plaster a smile on my face. "Kate, is something the matter? You look pale."

"Oh, no, ma'am. I'm just embarrassed to have dropped that plate of eggs." I turned to look and saw Gus cleaning up the mess I'd made. Then I turned back to—what? My fate?

Edith looked different. It took me a minute to realize it was her eyes. Usually distant and slightly at half mast, today they were wide-open, staring directly. Edith was a person who seldom looked straight at you but had a tendency to fix her gaze on something slightly to either side of you. And today while expressing concern, the emotion didn't reach her eyes. They remained unchanged.

Bad sign, I told myself.

"May I have some tea? English breakfast, if you have it, please?"

I didn't trust my shaky hands, so I excused myself and asked Marj to prepare the tea. As I turned to go back to Edith, Marj said, "Chester's on his way."

That was some relief. I went back to try to start a normal conversation with Edith, but my phone was still on. "I'm so glad to see you. I've been worried about you."

She was completely astonished. "Worried about me? No reason, dear child."

"But the sheriff came looking for you, and you weren't at home."

"Such a bothersome man. I have a safe room in my house—nobody can find it—and I hid there when I saw him coming. Made Lucy nervous." Now she was staring off into space and not looking at me at all.

I sympathized with Lucy. This woman was making me nervous too. But she went on.

"I came to thank you for solving Walter's murder."

I held my breath. I wasn't about to tell her how I'd solved it in my mind.

"It's clear that Ambrose Connell, my ex-husband, murdered my dear Walter, and I wanted to thank you for proving it. I'll be glad to pay you whatever fee you deem appropriate."

"I, uh, don't think I did that much. I don't want you to pay me. If I helped, I was glad to do it."

I prayed for Chester to walk through the door. The café remained empty in its midmorning lull. *How far away could Chester have been when he said he'd be right here?*

"What happened to Ambrose?" I asked, wishing my heart would stop trying to beat its way out of my chest. *Kate, why did you even ask that?*

"Oh, I killed him. Had to, you know. He was there that night. He knew all about it, even helped break down the French door. And then when those bumbling idiots found his body, I had to move it. I waited all night in the trees and then, before dawn, I moved it up to your fence. Seemed like a good way to confuse that stupid sheriff."

"So you and Ambrose cooperated in murdering Walter?"

"Not really. He was angry at Walter for stealing me" — she gave a coquettish giggle—"and I just wanted Walter out of the way. It worked just fine. May I have that cup of tea?"

I wanted to shake my head to clear my brain. Had I heard right? I motioned to Marj to bring tea, all the while wondering what I'd do if Edith turned violent. From now on, I was carrying something protective in my apron pocket, even if only a wooden cooking spoon. "Where did you kill Ambrose?"

"In the pasture behind this café, close to your house. Hit him in the head with a shovel I found there. Made a really satisfactory smack. He thought we were going to talk about bribery money, but that man had been bribing me for twenty years. I wanted no more of it."

"Mrs. Aldridge, why are you telling me this?"

Her expression was guileless. "Because you're my friend. I think you should know."

"Thank you," I said humbly, realizing now that I was in the presence of a crazed woman. Steven hadn't been far off the mark with what he told the officers who arrested him. *Do I dare push her farther about Rodney . . . and the peacocks?*

Trying to make my change of subjects casual, I said, "I hear you're an archery expert."

"Oh my, yes. Walter and I hunted with bow and arrow. I got quite good, and it made him jealous, so after that we never hunted again. But I practiced with targets. And then I shot those peacocks. Nasty birds, made loud noises all day and night, would as soon fight as look at you, and left droppings all over. It was time for them to go. But I dragged them to the front door so it would look suspicious. Clever, don't you think?" Now she was staring directly at me again, with those wide-open eyes. But she had something of a self-satisfied smirk in her expression.

Stymied, I waited until she went on, "Rodney was like a peacock, you know. All noise, strutting, angry, and ready to fight. I never liked him, though I have a soft spot in my heart for James. Rose? She's a nuisance but not worth bothering about."

And there I had it—a full confession caught on my phone, and a rundown on the family and the whole sorry business. But what did I do, sitting here next to this crazed woman? I feared the next thing I said could set her off and she'd go from thinking I was her friend to labeling me as her enemy.

Chester walked in, barely glancing our way, tipping his hat and saying, "Mornin', ladies." Then he sat on a stool at the counter and said, "Coffee, please, Marj."

Marj gave him a funny look and poured his black coffee. He sat and sipped, while I prayed for him to come to our table. Finally, casually, he ambled over. "You ladies mind if I join you?" Turning to Edith, he said, "I don't think I've had the pleasure, ma'am. I'm Chester Grimes."

Thank heaven he didn't add, "Chief of police here in Wheeler."

Edith turned a gracious smile in his direction and held out her hand. But those eyes wandered all over the place, looking any place but at Chester or me.

Chester launched into a mundane discussion of the weather, wishing we'd get more rain, bemoaning the dryness of this particular spring. "Why, my Carolyn claims nothing much is blooming, and she's a gardener to beat all, let me tell you. By now, we usually have a vase of daffodils or iris on the table, but not this year. Damn shame. I suppose the critters are suffering too."

David wandered innocently in, brightened with false surprise when he saw Edith, and came right over to us. "Edith, what a pleasant surprise. Do we have any business to discuss this morning? Save me a trip to Peacock Mansion."

"No, no thank you," she said, and for a minute, those eyes darted wildly. "Now that everything's settled, I don't think I'll be needing your services any more, David."

He was smooth. "Of course. I'll return all records to you, although the Sheriff has copies."

"He does? Why?"

"Fire, attempted murder, and murder — all occurred within his jurisdiction. If you need a good defense lawyer, I can give you names."

I was beginning to feel safe surrounded by two of the men I trusted to protect me. Edith, however, began to look agitated, eyes darting from one man to the other. She never acknowledged David's offer of a defense attorney.

"I must be going. So nice to see all of you." She rose and reached into her purse.

I froze, and Chester's right hand went to the gun on his hip, but her hand came out with car keys only. *Guns aren't her style, I told myself.*

Chester rose gallantly. "May I escort you out?"

Now she was in a hurry to get away. "Oh, that won't be necessary." Without so much as a good-bye to me, she hurried through the doors, Chester right behind her.

As I sat stunned, wondering if they were going to let her just walk away, David said softly, "Halstead is outside waiting."

We heard loud screams of protest, and deep but determined male voices. For once, I was glad the café was almost empty.

And then it was over. I walked into David's open arms and began to sob. I wasn't sure what I was crying for except all the waste of lives and anger and all the greed. Finally, I looked up and said, "In a way it all started in this café when she asked me to find out who killed Walter, and now it ends here. It's like it's come full circle."

Outside a siren bleeped, and I heard cars peel out of the dusty parking lot.

Recipes

Kate uses commercial equipment and commercial pans. The recipes are here cut down for home use. Also, Kate learned from Gram to turn some traditional dishes into casseroles for easier preparation.

Sticky Buns

Sticky buns are a part of Kate's daily life. She puts the dough to rise first thing every morning. Here's the basic dough:

- 2 pkg. granular yeast
- ½ c. warm water
- Pinch of sugar
- 1 12-oz. can evaporated milk, plus enough water to make 4 cups (nowadays I use "light" milk)
- 1 scant c. vegetable oil
- 1 c. sugar

Dissolve yeast in water (add just a pinch of sugar to help the yeast work) and let it rise about five minutes. Mix milk and water, oil, and sugar. Add dissolved yeast. Stir in enough flour to make a thin batter, the consistency of cake batter. Let this rise in a warm place until bubbles appear on the surface (probably 1 hour — check it at 30 minutes).

Separately, mix

- 1 c. flour
- 1 tsp. salt (or less)
- 1 heaping tsp. baking powder
- 1 level tsp. baking soda

Sift seasoned flour into first mixture. Keep adding flour until it is too stiff to stir with a spoon. Knead well. Don't let the dough get stiff with too much flour, or your coffee cakes will be heavy. This dough will keep a week or so in the refrigerator.

To bake buns:

Roll the dough out to a flat rectangle. Sprinkle with cinnamon and brown sugar and dab with butter. Roll up into a tube and slice into pieces of about 2 inches. Grease the bottom of an 8x8 pan thoroughly and then cover it with Karo white syrup and pecan halves. Place rounds of dough, cut side down, on the Karo/pecan mixture. Bake these at 350° until brown and center rolls appear cooked. Be sure to turn out of the pan immediately, while still warm. Cold cooked syrup turns to concrete. Rinse the pan immediately with very hot water. Serve while hot if you can.

American Lasagna

Café customers sometimes request lasagna, but making the real thing is time-consuming, and Kate refuses to buy frozen products. So she makes what she calls an American version.

First layer:

- 1 lb. ground beef
- 1 14-oz. can diced tomatoes
- 1 8-oz. can tomato sauce
- 2 cloves garlic, crushed in garlic press

- 2 tsp each sugar and salt (I cut back on those, but sugar is important in tomato-based sauces; Gram taught Kate sugar rounds off a tomato-based sauce.)
- Pepper to taste

Brown ground beef in skillet. Drain grease and return meat to skillet. Add tomatoes and tomato sauce, garlic, sugar, salt, and pepper. Simmer 20 minutes until it thickens a little.

Spread in a 9x13 pan.

For noodle layer:

- 5 oz. egg noodles (approximately — they don't come in this size pkg.)
- 3 oz. pkg. cream cheese (or half an 8 oz.)
- 1 c. sour cream
- 6 green onions chopped, with some of the tops included
- Topping:
- 1½ c. grated cheddar

Cook egg noodles and drain. While the noodles are hot, stir in cream cheese, sour cream, and green onions. Spread over meat mixture. Top with grated cheddar, bake 35 minutes at 350° or until bubbly and cheese is slightly browned. Supposed to serve eight, but you'll be lucky if you can feed six with it. Freezes well.

Layered Enchilada Casserole

If guests begin to ask for Mexican, or Tex-Mex, flavors, Kate whips up this casserole.

Ingredients:

- 2 c. cooked, shredded chicken — your choice. Buy a rotisserie chicken, toss a few frozen breast in the crockpot; poach the old fashioned way.
- 1 can 15 oz. diced tomatoes, drained

- 1 15 oz. can black beans, drained and rinsed
- 1 tub Santa Fe Blend Philadelphia Cooking Crème (if you can't find, use cream cheese mixed with a bit of chicken broth to soften and a bit of Taco seasoning)
- 2 c. shredded cheese — cheddar and Pepper Jack
- 3 flour tortillas

Thoroughly combine chicken, tomatoes, beans, and cooking crème in bowl. Put ⅓ c. on bottom of pie plate or 8x8 freezer pan. Top with 1 flour tortilla;

Top tortilla with chicken mixture and cheese. Repeat layers, ending with chicken and last of the cheese.

Bake 30 minutes at 350 until casserole is bubbly.

Shepherd's Pie

Shepherd's pie is an overlooked dish, scorned by food snobs these days. But Kate's customers like this hearty casserole.

Ingredients:

- Mashed potatoes, made of about 1⅓ lbs. red potatoes. (Even Gram didn't skin them to mash.) A good trick: put some garlic cloves in the water when you boil the potatoes. Another good one: as you add butter, salt, and pepper, substitute sour cream or cream cheese for the milk.
- ½ c. shredded sharp cheddar — stir into hot, freshly mashed potatoes and set aside
- 1 lb. lean ground beef
- 2 Tbsp. flour
- 4 c. frozen mixed vegetables (I prefer corn, green beans, carrots, and sweet peas.)
- ¾ c. beef broth
- 2 Tbsp. ketchup
- ¼ c. shredded sharp cheddar

Heat oven to 375°.

Brown meat in nonstick skillet (an iron skillet is always best). Stir in flour and cook briefly. Add remaining ingredients and cook, stirring, for five minutes.

Spoon into 8 in. square baking dish. Cover with mashed potatoes. Bake 20 minutes. Sprinkle remaining cheddar over the top and bake another 3-4 minutes, until cheese melts and casserole is bubbly. Serve six, but only if they're not hearty eaters.

Vegetable Soup

Kate won't use frozen prepared foods but she does use frozen vegetables, especially when she makes soup.

Ingredients:

- 2 large cans diced tomatoes with juice
- 1 box broth — use vegetable, beef or chicken according to your taste. Fresh boxed broths are better than canned.
- Diced potatoes — Kate prefers to use canned white potatoes, because they keep their shape better when diced; you can also use frozen diced potatoes. (Sometimes Kate omits potatoes and stirs in egg noodles or cooked rice after the soup has simmered a good while.)
- Frozen vegetables to taste — see suggestions in Shepherd's Pie recipe. Use what strikes your fancy.
- Optional: a bunch of fresh spinach.

At this point you could add diced, leftover chicken or beef if you want.

Season to taste: salt and pepper; a bit of sugar to round off the tomato taste; fresh or dried herbs at you want.

Will simmer on the stove all day; leftovers freeze well.

Cheeseburger Soup

This one is hearty and always popular with café customers during winter months.

Ingredients:

- 2 carrots, grated
- 1 onion, chopped
- 2 stalks celery, chopped
- 8 cups diced potatoes, partially boiled
- 1 box chicken broth, low sodium
- ¼ c. flour
- ½-1 lb. hamburger meat
- ½ c. milk
- ¼ c. sour cream
- ½ lb. Velveeta
- Salt and pepper to taste

Brown the meat and drain. Melt ¼ c. butter in large pot and sauté onion, and celery until clear. Add cooked hamburger meat, potatoes, carrots and broth. Simmer until potatoes are fully tender. Separately, melt ¼ c. butter and add flour; stir until thick. Add to soup to thicken. Add cheese, cut in chunks, and milk to the main pot. Stir until cheese melts. Simmer as long as you want. Just before serving, remove from heat and add sour cream.

You can play with the amounts of cheese and meat to make a heartier soup if you want.

Chocolate Chip Brownies

With great reluctance, Kate buys pies from a supplier, who makes her own homemade pies. Kate doesn't have time to do that but here's a brownie recipe she makes in-house.

Ingredients:

- 4½ c. flour
- 2 tsp. soda

- 2 tsp. salt
- 4 sticks butter, softened
- 1½ c. sugar
- 1½ c. brown sugar, packed
- 4 eggs
- 2 tsp vanilla
- 2 (12 oz.) pkg. chocolate chips, semisweet
- 2 cups chopped nuts (optional — Kate doesn't like finding nuts in unexpected places like salads and brownies)

You'll note that these have all the ingredients of chocolate chip cookies. They go together the same way. Mix dry ingredients and set aside. Cream butter and sugars until fluffy, then add eggs one at a time. Add vanilla and mix in well. Add flour mixture in bits, stirring in thoroughly with each bit. Stir in chips and nuts, if using.

Spread in two, pre-greased 9x13 pans and bake in preheated 350º oven for 30 minutes or until toothpick comes out clean.

About the Author

An award-winning novelist, Judy Alter is the author of six books in the Kelly O'Connell Mysteries series: *Skeleton in a Dead Space, No Neighborhood for Old Women, Trouble in a Big Box, Danger Comes Home, Deception in Strange Places,* and *Desperate for Death.* She also writes the Blue Plate Café Mysteries — *Murder at the Blue Plate Café, Murder at the Tremont House* and the current *Murder at Peacock Mansion.* Finally, with the 2014 *The Perfect Coed,* she introduced the Oak Grove Mysteries.

Her work has been recognized with awards from the Western Writers of America, the Texas Institute of Letters, and the National Cowboy Museum and Hall of Fame. She has been honored with the Owen Wister Award for Lifetime Achievement by WWA and inducted into the Texas Literary Hall of Fame and the WWA Hall of Fame.

Judy is retired as director of TCU Press, the mother of four grown children and the grandmother of seven. She and her dog, Sophie, live in Fort Worth, Texas.

Read more about Judy at http://www.judyalter.com

www.ingramcontent.com/pod-product-compliance
Lightning Source LLC
Chambersburg PA
CBHW020400210626
46816CB00006BB/2050